BLADON'S REVENGE

BLADON'S REVENGE

JOHN PARKIN

Bladon's Revenge

Copyright © 2014 by John Parkin.

First paperback edition printed 2014 in the United Kingdom.

No part of this book shall be reproduced or transmitted in any form or by any means, electronic or mechanical, including photocopying, recording, or by any information retrieval system without written permission from the publisher.

DISCLAIMER
All the characters in this book are fictitious, and any resemblance to actual persons living or dead is coincidental.

ISBN 978-1503355583

Acknowledgements

Grateful thanks to Stephen who was so helpful with information on flying and for making the narrative come alive; also to Saul for the stunning book cover, and to the support and editing of my wonderful team of Margaret, Rachel, Sue, Mark and John. Thanks also go to Jason Carter of Kingdom Writing Solutions for his help.

Prologue

It was to be the deadliest shot ever in footballing history.

The Prime Minister, Johnny Hanbury, threw back the covers, instantly awake as his alarm clanged out its strident demand to rise. He realised with delight that it was Cup Final Day and he was going to present the trophy to the winning team. What an honour. As a keen football supporter he was thrilled to be asked.

His chauffeur whisked him away from Chequers, a country house at the foot of the Chiltern Hills, and the official country residence of British Prime Ministers since 1917, when the impressive old house was given to the nation as a country retreat for succeeding Prime Ministers.

He arrived at Wembley Stadium, enjoyed a good lunch, and then just before three, he stepped onto the hallowed turf to meet the two managers and their teams of young millionaires, one from the red side of the great Northern City of Manchester and the other from the blue side.

Firstly he was introduced to the Manchester United manager, winner of numerous trophies, and then to his captain, who introduced the PM to his teammates, all highly talented athletes. The PM then strode over to the Manchester City manager, shook hands, and started down the line of his multinational players, in the famous sky blue strip. Halfway along the line, he was just about to shake hands with Santa Barbara, their new expensive Brazilian signing, when embarrassingly he stumbled on a TV cable and fell to his knees. He looked up, and in freeze frame, he saw Santa

Barbara slump to the floor, covered in blood. The Prime Minister's bodyguards surrounded him quickly, escorted him off the pitch into his bullet proof Jaguar XJ, and away to the safety of Chequers.

It WAS the deadliest shot ever in footballing history.

Back at Chequers, a glass of malt went some way to restoring the Prime Minister's equilibrium, and so he decided it was time he spoke to the one person in the world he could really trust, his old friend Bladon.

Bladon and Lexi, good friends of the PM, were enjoying a few days break in the Derbyshire Peak District at the Devonshire Hotel, on the edge of the Chatsworth Estate, and owned by the Duke of Devonshire. Bladon, who was ex SAS, and his beautiful new wife Lexi, had found it very hard to settle down to normal life after the excitement and stress of their epic struggle against their deadly protagonist, codenamed Dreadnought, who had sought to take over the country, and had so very nearly succeeded. With the help of some friends, thirteen all told, and Johnny Hanbury before he was appointed PM, they had saved the country from a new dark age. Bladon and Lexi had then set up a consultancy operation, which did a lot of work for the PM. They specialised in conflict resolution and in particular advice on security aspects of top level Government visits. Bladon had spent a lot of time over the arrangements for the P.M.'s visit to Wembley for the FA Cup Final, but a pompous senior Metropolitan Police officer had blocked and opposed him at every step of the planning and implementation stage, and finally in utter frustration three days before the event, Bladon had given up, phoned the Prime Minister, and taken Lexi away to the Devonshire Hotel.

"Bladon, I'm sorry to disturb your retreat in the Peak District," said the PM. "How's it going?"

"Wonderful thanks Johnny. Lexi and I are really enjoying the peace and the luxury here. It's near Chatsworth. Sorry I wasn't at the match but that Commander Jenkinson from the Met was an unbelievably difficult man to work with. I just couldn't stand it in the end. Sorry. Did you enjoy the match?

Don't tell me the result; I'm going to watch the highlights later."

"I'm sorry about Jenkinson, Bladon, but it's politics, you know. But haven't you heard the news"?

"No, Johnny, we've been walking on Beeley Moor all day. What news"?

The PM explained about the assassination of Santa Barbara and how an unintentional trip had saved his life. It had cost the life of a forty million pound footballer, but Bladon's friend and the leader of the country was still alive.

"Why would anyone want to kill him, Johnny? He was a South American. Do you think it was a drug cartel?"

"No, he's Brazilian not Columbian, and anyway he's never been involved in drugs as far as we know. Hold on Bladon, footage is just coming in from Sky. Wait a minute."

He watched in horror as he saw pictures of himself walking up to Santa Barbara, stumbling, and a bullet hitting Santa Barbara in the temple.

His senior staff watched the replay once more until, almost in unison, they realised the awful truth, which should have been obvious in the first place. It was the PM! The target had been the PM. Only his fortuitous fall had saved his life.

"Any chance you can come down Bladon?" the PM asked. "I think we may need your help."

One

Whilst at the Devonshire Hotel, Bladon and Lexi were looking for a new home, and after the horrors of their previous adventures in the Peak District of Derbyshire, which were still fresh in their memories, you'd have thought that it would be the last place that Bladon and Lexi would wish to return to. Bladon's first wife, Sarah, had been drawn into great danger, through a chance meeting in London with an old school friend. It led to that friend, who was Minister of Defence, being murdered at Snape Maltings, in East Anglia, and then Sarah herself was also murdered because she had seen the face of the killer. A distraught and grieving Bladon hunted the killers, initially in Cornwall, where he met Lexi for the first time; they then quickly realised that they had stumbled upon a conspiracy to destabilise and destroy the very fabric of British life. Together, they faced overwhelming odds in Scotland, Jersey, Switzerland, Italy, Majorca, and finally the Peak District, where they came face to face with their seemingly all-powerful enemy, code-named Dreadnought.

So Derbyshire had a lot of recent bad memories for them, but they still loved it there. When they sought a place to live what they hoped would be a quieter life, they searched for their rural idyll in that county. They thought that they might have found it, not in the wild, raw, beauty of the Dark Peak in the north of the county, nor even in the less savage, but no less stunning White Peak at the Southern end of the National Park; but they found it in South Derbyshire in the gentle rolling hills of the Kedleston estate.

An old friend of John's, Paul Clancy, a Derby Estate Agent,

had recommended a property in the extensive grounds of Kedleston Hall and had arranged a viewing for them. On a bright day they set out in the late afternoon sun to look at the property; but first Bladon wanted to show Lexi, what in his opinion was a rather undervalued gem in a beautiful setting, namely Kedleston Hall, home of the Curzon family for generations, but now owned by the National Trust. It lay within ten minutes of the major city of Derby, well known for Rolls Royce, the Railway industry, and more recently, Toyota. Derby was a fine city, not as large as the other two East Midland behemoths Nottingham and Leicester, but so much more pleasant to live in. It was so close to beautiful countryside and historic houses, yet its shopping experience had been significantly enhanced by a very large new development linked to an expanding and growing Cathedral Quarter.

They had re-established friendships with many of those who had helped them overcome Dreadnought, and particularly with John and Margaret Parkin, who lived in the north of the city.

Kedleston was set in a wonderful parkland setting of hundreds of acres to the north west of Derby, about three miles from the busy Derby to Ashbourne road, and was just six miles from the city itself. This was what Bladon and Lexi loved about Derbyshire; within two miles of the city you could be in the most delightful, secluded, rural landscapes.

The estate was accessed by two entrances, one to the north, and another to the west. The north gatehouse included a small dwelling, and entry was through a narrow arch under a bedroom, down a stunning, winding lane between trees, and sheep grazed pastures, with the prestigious Kedleston Park Golf Club on the left. At the bottom of the lane a quaint old bridge crossed the narrow neck of a small lake and the vista opened out to a verdant sward of rolling pastureland, winding round eventually to the impressive house standing in all its glory above the lake. The west entrance, over a cattle grid, was again guarded, sentinel like, by a larger house, and was locked after public viewings were over. The single-track road cut through pastures and uplands, peopled by Canada Geese and sheep—with an occasional walker disturbing them—until it too opened out to the same incredible view of the house and grounds.

They approached from Derby through the northern entrance, meandered down the tree-lined lane, over the little bridge, and the cattle grid, and parked in the car park close to Kedleston Hall.

"Shall we get a feel of the Hall and the grounds, before looking at the house that Paul has found for us?" asked Bladon.

"Yes that would be very interesting," Lexi replied.

They showed their membership cards at the National Trust office for the House and grounds, although it was the grounds that they were particularly interested in. They spotted a cafe quaintly set up in the original old kitchen, a huge stone and wooden building with a massive fireplace containing a well-used spit, and a wonderful collection of brass and copper cooking pots, sparkling in the carefully placed spot lights, and sat at one of the old pine tables and ordered a cream tea.

Lexi said, "I do like this place darling. It has such a feel of grandeur and history, but at the same time has a very homely feel too. Look, they are doing guided tours of the House. Shall we tag along for a while and then try the grounds?"

"What a good idea," said Bladon. "Then after the tour I thought we could go on a short walk through the woodland."

They left the cafe and ascended the impressive stairs to the entrance to the Hall itself and found the tour party just starting to wend its way through the impressive marble pillared, ballroom, setting for the smash hit film, "The Duchess."

"Kedleston Hall was the brainchild of Sir Nathaniel Curzon, 1st Lord Scarsdale," the tour guide intoned. "He wanted a grand house for entertaining so he knocked down the existing house in 1758 and started again. He met the architect Robert Adam and a golden partnership was forged. When he met Sir Nathaniel Curzon, Robert Adam was 30 years old, recently returned from Italy and full of enthusiasm for the monuments of classical antiquity. Building a new mansion for Kedleston was Adam's first major commission."

"What do you think?" whispered Bladon to Lexi. "This boring monotone is sending me to sleep. Can we cut straight to the walk?"

"Well, it's not very riveting, I'll give you that, but let's give it a bit longer."

So they loitered at the back of the tour group as the guide took them down some impressive stairs to a collection of dresses from the film.

"Fashionable Kedleston soon proved to be expensive. Money ran out before the two planned southern wings could be built. Despite this, Kedleston Hall remains one of the masterpieces of 18th-century English architecture. These are typical of the dresses of that period and have been painstakingly reproduced by experts working from original patterns...."

"Sorry, Lexi," said Bladon. "I've had enough. Let's get walking."

They tiptoed away from the back of the group, walked quickly through the gift shop and back to the car park. From here a woodland path took them through the farthest part of the less formal grounds of the House, and then on to a delicately worked wrought iron gate decorated with the arms of the Curzon family. They walked through the gateway and onto a delightful little path that wound uphill between the car park on their right, and the rolling meadows on their left where sheep and pheasants grazed contentedly together. It meandered underneath the rich foliage of ancient trees and they walked, as if on air, on the springy turf and leaves, until they came to a little dell where the path turned uphill and the vegetation became sparser and more rugged. After ten minutes of hard walking they came to a narrow plateau with very sparse vegetation at the highest point of the Kedleston estate. They walked to the edge and sat on a wooden seat between two large beech trees, looking at a wondrous panorama stretched out below them.

They sat transfixed by the pastoral scene set out in front of them like a great Constable masterpiece for several minutes.

Finally Bladon broke the silence.

"What a perfect place to sit and dream. That ha-ha gives a completely unobstructed view for miles in a one hundred and eighty degree arc. Look, you can see down to Kedleston village, and right over to Weston Underwood and as far as the village of Mugginton. Rolling, green fields, little copses of trees, and winding little roads, seeming to go nowhere."

"Yes, it's wonderful. So restful and yet at the same time alive. But Bladon, what's a ha-ha?"

"A ha-ha," said Bladon. "Why it dates back to the 17th and 18th centuries when they were built on the estates of the landed gentry. They are walls that are constructed so that they're invisible from the House, ensuring a clear view across the estate. They are sunken walls where the top is level with the garden, with a deep ditch on the far side. It's a really effective barrier to livestock as well.

But look, straight down that slope, there at the bottom. Do you see the road? That's the road from the House to the west entrance, and you see where it meets the road, well I think the house we are looking for is around there somewhere."

"Darling, do you think it could possibly be that beautiful house we can see with the old wall around it? Oh I do hope so. I've always wanted an old walled garden."

"Well, let's get back to the car, and see shall we?"

They approached the west entrance from the House car park, and they found a little cart track which turned off to the left, just fifty metres from the gatehouse. They took the track, drove through the rough pasture land between the trees for about a hundred metres, until it reached a wrought iron double gate, standing open, and set in the middle of an ancient stone and brick wall, rising three metres tall, and in a remarkably good state of repair. They followed the track through the gates, and were stunned to see the most wonderful house, set in mature gardens of about an acre. The plaque above the imposing front door bore the legend "1932", and the mellow red bricks at the front of the house seemed to Lexi to glow in the setting sun, and give her a real sense of well being.

"I've not even seen the inside yet Bladon, but I love it, I really do. Come on let's see inside."

"OK darling. No rush. It is rather special though isn't it?"

He swept the car onto the circular gravel drive in front of the house, and they stepped through the jet black, highly polished door into a small inner hall, through a glazed white door into the main hall, and Bladon introduced Lexi to Paul, the local Estate Agent, who was waiting for them. Paul's welcome and warmth confirmed their positive feelings of security and homeliness.

"John said you were a very likeable couple, who had been through a lot, and needed an escape from everything, but also somewhere warm and comfortable and homely. I think this will really fit the bill. It's just got so much going for it. The house is large, without being rambling, and it's well lit with beautiful Georgian casement windows all through. No poky little cottage windows here. The garden is walled except where it meets the Estate grounds and at the back there is a special surprise for you both. But I'm getting too excited. Just look around and make up your own minds."

Without further ado Paul turned and showed them first the wide, almost regal stairs which rose majestically from the hall to the upper stories to the right, and then he turned to his left into the lounge and study areas. They followed him, and were almost lost for words at the stunning lounge. It was a comfortable size, with one large window looking out to the drive, but on the opposite side of the room was a magnificent sliding double glass door looking out directly onto the patio. It had breathtaking views of the garden and the amazing vista that opened up beyond the small back wall, up and up, over green and pleasant lands, to the far ridge, where stately oaks rustled in the evening breeze.

In the slowly dying light, they saw to their delight a rare Red Kite quartering the periphery of the woodlands, in an earnest search for supper, and then Lexi spotted far to the west, a lone Buzzard floating on an air current, whilst three or four crows tried to mob it from below. Bladon's attention meanwhile, was arrested by a tiny, jerky, little red shape, moving from their walled garden, up the slopes towards the line of trees.

"Lexi, look at that. Isn't it a red squirrel? I thought they were extinct in this area."

"No, that's a stoat," said Paul. "The Kedleston estate is famous for them. Another walled garden a mile or so away had a BBC film crew there a while ago, and captured some amazing footage. Apparently they can kill rabbits ten times their size, and are known to almost hypnotise their prey."

Reluctantly they pulled themselves away from the windows, and concentrated on the room itself.

"All of the furnishings are available for purchase as well if you would like them, but it's your choice! "

The room had high ceilings, and warm, rich, bronze coloured oak floors, and a red and gold, silk Persian rug in the centre of the room. From the large stone fireplace, an inviting log fire burned hungrily in the hearth. The Artistic Upholstery leather suite was stunning. It was in a dark red, almost maroon shade of soft leather, and it seemed to just welcome and draw you into the room and invite, no implore you, to rest awhile. The paintings were by Rex and Mark Preston, father and son artists, widely respected and valued for their evocative, and moving landscapes of the Derbyshire hills and Cornish beaches. Next to the lounge was a small study with a desk and bright red leather art deco chair, all furnished with a Napoleonic theme. They moved into a large formal dining room, and on to the stunning kitchen. It had recently been completely refitted, but at the same time the older cupboards had been retained in the living part at the south end of the kitchen, and they merged seamlessly with the modern kitchen and preparation area. Lexi drooled over the black granite tops, the Quooker giving instant boiling hot water, the Neff double cooker and warming drawer, and built-in Meile dishwasher, and of course the stunning white Aga. There was even a large pantry.

Paul then led them back to another inner hall, and with a beaming smile on his face, opened a part glazed door onto a huge purpose built conservatory, with an indoor pool looking out onto the garden with views up to the ridge of oak trees, that had so entranced them earlier. Bladon and Lexi were uncharacteristically speechless. What a place. The house was sold at that very moment. They had to go through the formalities of inspecting the four, first floor bedrooms, and three bathrooms, and the two loft rooms, but their minds were made up.

They agreed a price within two days and in the space of three weeks had taken possession of their dream home. They had good solicitors!

Two

Bladon and Lexi met the P.M. at a secret location near London, and found him still very traumatised by the assassination attempt.

"We have no idea who we are dealing with Bladon," said the P.M. "It is very worrying. MI5 don't think it's terrorist related, either al-Qaida or ISIL or splinter IRA groups. But the way they got into the stadium with a sniper rifle and then just disappeared afterwards suggests a high level of expertise. It could be isolated remnants from Dreadnought's defeated forces but as you know, he was killed in that helicopter crash as he was trying to escape, and we rounded up all his men as far as we are aware. All we have picked up is some information about strange happenings in South Cornwall, in an area you and Lexi know well, and I was wondering if you could go down and investigate for us. Be careful though. It could be dangerous."

"Well Johnny, it so happens that we are planning a holiday in that area whilst our new house is refurbished. We could combine the two."

"Yes that would be very helpful, but again, be careful."

The next day they travelled down to South Cornwall to one of their favourite hotels, "Tregarnon". After sampling the delights of stunning hotels in exotic locations all over the world, they always returned to this idyllic spot, set amidst a golf course and acres of woods. Stunning walks led down from the hotel between wooded slopes, by a tinkling brook filling a series of deep-water pools, until it emptied into the creek on the foreshore.

This was the Helford Passage, which fed into The Helford estuary, and the whole surrounding area of hills, woods, rivers and creeks had been brought to life by Daphne Dumarier in her famous novels. It was so delightful on reaching the foreshore to find the luxury summerhouse, which had been built just above the pebble beach. Even on dull days it was really relaxing to just read, or snooze, with a vista of bobbing yachts straining against their anchors on the rising tide.

They had been approached on their last visit by Mave, the charismatic Restaurant Manager, who organised dinner with such precision and fun, who had concerns about happenings further round the coast by the Ferryman's Inn, a delightful pub, set adjacent to the ferry over to the little village of Helford on the other side of the estuary. The three of them had discussed Bladon and Lexi's recent adventures in the battle against Dreadnought, as Mave knew Wally, the maitre d' at Tregerest Hotel, the sister hotel to Tregarnon, and he had been of great help to Bladon and Lexi at that time.

There had been reports of comings and goings late at night from a yacht anchored in the middle of the estuary, and of some very unsavoury characters hanging around the pub, and when they telephoned Mave to bring their holiday forward by a few days she confirmed that the yacht had been particularly busy in the last few days, bringing in strange bulky supplies, and more and more men.

They arrived at the hotel mid afternoon, and after unpacking, walked down through the conservatory to the dining room, where they were immediately tempted by a selection of scrumptious cream teas, almost pleading to be tasted. They succumbed easily, without a fight, and tried again the freshly made scones, with jam and Cornish cream. They walked down to the creek and sat in the sun for a while, before returning for a swim in the hotel pool before dinner.

They went down for dinner at eight o'clock, and in the middle of their main course, a delicious Dover sole on the bone, Mave came over to them and whispered, "Meet me at the summer house after breakfast."

The following day Bladon and Lexi finished their coffee, and walked down to the creek. Mave had identified the yacht moored opposite the Ferryman's Inn and the ferry, some two miles away by sea, as a possible hideout of the enemy, and had arranged to meet them on the foreshore where the hotel grounds met the sea, with some appropriate mode of transport.

They walked down by the side of the ninth hole of the adjacent golf course in the pleasant spring weather, and down the woodland footpath, by the side of the little brook, populated with strange prehistoric plants, and then down by three small, interconnected pools to the foreshore.

The whole area was deserted, but Bladon noticed a movement in the large summerhouse by the creek in his peripheral vision, and turning, saw Mave motioning to them.

She said, "I don't think we are being observed, but you never know. I've got a small dinghy tied up by the steps so let's go cautiously around the back of that little grass bank, where we can get on board, without being noticed."

All three made their way carefully along the slippery path between two tall hedges of azalea plants, descended the steps, and jumped into the small dinghy.

Mave started the powerful outboard motor, and they cruised effortlessly out into the broad middle channel of the Helford Passage, and headed north towards the Helford Estuary.

They passed some very impressive properties on their left, or as Mave corrected them, on their port side, including one built on a shingle beach, with a large catamaran birthed next to it; then a large traditional house sheltered in the lee of the deeply wooded hillside.

They soon reached the Helford Ferry, which was waiting for passengers by the Fisherman's Creek Pub, and Mave pointed to a sleek, modern yacht swinging slowly on its mooring rope in the middle of the estuary.

"There it is. I'll drop you off," said Mave. "I'll come back for you in thirty minutes so that we don't draw too much attention to ourselves. Will half an hour be enough for you?"

"Yes, that will be fine, thanks Mave."

They drew alongside the boat, named rather incongruously "Ratty's Abode", and then they both clambered aboard by the rope ladder. They stood on the deck aft of the boat, and Bladon touched Lexi's arm urgently. Mave had moved away from them, and was halfway between the harbour of the little hamlet of Helford, and their boat.

"I don't like it," said Bladon. "It's too quiet, and there's an air of neglect about the boat—almost staged neglect. Do you know what I mean? We must be very careful. I have the strange feeling that we are expected."

They searched the deck fore and aft, but found nothing. "We must get into the cabin," said Bladon. "What we're looking for must be inside, but let's be very careful."

Bladon approached the cabin door. There was no bolt on it, so very carefully Bladon pulled up the latch and pushed the door open just an inch. There was a metallic ping and Bladon jerked backwards in surprise.

"What," said Lexi, but Bladon had already processed the sound, and his instincts were roaring danger in his ears.

He turned to Lexi. "Jump, now", he shouted, and as they both launched themselves into the cold water, Bladon saw obliquely from his right, a flash of orange, and a strange projectile smashed its way towards them. Bladon just had enough time to shout to Lexi to dive, and as they both disappeared under the steely grey waters something smashed into the yacht, which disintegrated in a wall of flame.

It wasn't a missile. It was difficult to describe. It was somehow like thousands and thousands of bullets all compressed into a narrow arc of fire, and obliterating everything in its path. Impossible!

Bladon broke the surface just as a burning lifebelt flew past him, only to be swallowed by the now turbulent water. Lexi surfaced just a metre away, and they saw a desperate

Mave, racing towards them in the dinghy. She threw a long knotted rope into the sea beside them.

"It's too dangerous to get you into the boat, so grab this rope and hang on for dear life." She turned back to the outboard, opened up the throttle and powered off towards Helford village, on the opposite side of the Helford Passage to the ferry.

Bladon and Lexi grabbed the rope, and as the slack tightened, they shot through the water like championship water skiers, but their life depended on keeping hold of the rope. Bladon stole a look back, just in time to see the yacht sink below the surface of the water, and as he watched he saw a second projectile thud into the turbulent waters at the very place they had vacated five seconds earlier.

They finally came into the safety of Helford's little harbour after a few more near misses. Mave's boat ploughed straight onto the shingle beach, and then Bladon and Lexi joined it two seconds later.

Mave signalled to a house above them, and then ran back to Bladon and Lexi, who were picking themselves up and standing there shocked, cold and sodden, by the dinghy. Mave draped two blankets from the boat around them.

"Here, wrap yourselves up well. We are not out of danger yet. Follow me."

A car approached from nowhere, the doors opened and two men ushered Bladon, Lexi, and Mave into the back, and roared away. They were friends of Mave's who had been on standby for just this eventuality. The car careered down the lane, over a little bridge across the tidal river, up the narrow road the other side, and on round a hairpin bend.

"If they have prepared well, they will have helicopter back up," said Mave. "I estimate that we have about two minutes to get to sanctuary before it arrives. Bladon, what an earth was that explosion! It didn't look like a missile. It was frightening. I've never heard anything like that before."

"Mave," Bladon replied. "I'm afraid I've no idea. I've never seen anything like it before either. It's frightening isn't it? We have you to thank for saving us."

The car took a sharp left turn, and stopped by a converted chapel, that now doubled as a little Cafe and restaurant.

"Out, out, quickly," said Mave, and chivvied them into the chapel, while the car skidded its wheels in a racing turn, and prepared to head back the way it had come.

Mave entered the chapel, and introduced Bladon and Lexi to her friends; then she ran back to the car, returned to the harbour, crossed over on the ferry, and returned to the hotel.

Mave's friends led them to a flat upstairs, returned to the cafe, and quickly pushed a large Welsh dresser in front of the door to hide it. Bladon and Lexi showered quickly and dressed in the dry clothes kindly provided by Mave's friends.

After an hour, when the excitement had died down, they discussed how they were going to get back to the safety of the Hotel.

By mid afternoon a plan had been formulated, and put into action. They must split up. Five ladies from the hotel, who Lexi and Bladon had met before dinner the previous night, had taken the ferry over to Helford, and after lunch in the cafe, Lexi had agreed to go back with them on the ferry to Fisherman's Creek Pub, there to await Bladon. Meanwhile, he made his way to the adjacent yacht club, and over lunch made the acquaintance of three local fishermen, who agreed to row him to the other side of the estuary, where he planned to meet up with Lexi again at the Fisherman's Creek Pub.

But what dangers lay ahead?

Three

As dusk approached, Bladon and Lexi set out together along the little road by the side of the estuary, past the ferry, and eventually it petered out by a boat shed. They walked down the slipway along the shingle beach until they came to a small sign, marked 'footpath'.

It rose up the side of the hill rather precipitously, and was heavily bordered on both sides, by hedges and trees. They started to ascend, and after about 200 yards the path began to widen until it reached a private road with large expensive houses on either side.

Bladon whispered to Lexi to stay in the cover of the hedge, and he crept up to the end of the path. As he raised his head, to look round the corner he felt, rather than heard, the presence of three men. He turned to Lexi to warn her, and pressed deeper into the hedge, until he still had a view of the road, but could not be seen from it.

Bladon tentatively looked out towards the road again, and to his horror saw that one man was walking along the road to his right, directly towards the path from the beach where they were both hiding; another was walking along the road from the left; and the third man was walking along a little pathway from the golf course to meet the others.

Lexi felt a sneeze coming, and desperately grabbing a hankie from her coat, pressed it over her face in an attempt to dull the noise. Not once, but twice, she sneezed, and Bladon, full of concern, looked back and motioned to her to try and stop it. He raised his head slightly, and saw to his horror that the three men had met about ten metres from where he and

Lexi were hiding and stopped.

"Have we been discovered?" Bladon worried and waited.

The nearest man spoke, "Shall we go down this path to the beach, or do you think we ought to give it up and come back tomorrow morning."

"I think that little path is a perfect place for them to hide," said the tallest, most aggressive of the three, and almost cowed the other two into carrying on in the rapidly approaching darkness. The other two were still reluctant to go down the dark and treacherous path, and thought it too dangerous in the gathering darkness, a perfect ambush site.

They argued, and for a moment Bladon feared that the tall aggressive one would prevail, but then they saw the lights of an approaching car, and they gave it up, and walked quickly away towards the main road, three hundred metres to the right.

Bladon crawled back to where Lexi was hiding, and they waited a further ten more minutes, before making any move. Finally, they crept to the road, but Lexi's hankie fell to the floor in the middle of the dark track unnoticed. They saw figures round the car, and carefully keeping to the shadows, they hurried down the little pathway to the hotel golf course. They opened the gate and ran to their left, alongside the seventh fairway. As they reached the seventh green, they walked by it, through the little wooden gate, and out onto the highest point of the hotel's wooded grounds. A path to the right, used frequently by the hotel's dog owners, meandered gently downhill, with woodland on the left and the golf course on the right. Instead they hurried down the left hand path, a steep but short distance to the foreshore of the Helford Passage. At the bottom, a path wound slowly uphill to the hotel, with interlinked pools on their left, and steeply wooded slopes, joining the other path, on their right. Bladon thought this path better than the more direct one, as it seemed to be more protected from their pursuers than the higher path.

In the meantime, when the three men reached the car, a tall, bearded, brute of a man, opened the door and jumped out.

"Have you found them yet, you incompetents," he yelled at the three.

"No sir, there's no sign of them."

"Have you searched down that narrow path on the left? It goes steeply down to a pebble beach, which accesses the road to the ferry. It's an obvious place to hide. Then they can slip through to the golf course, and up through the hotel, to the road to Mawnan Smith village and on to Truro."

"Well sir, we searched all along this road, and down the track to the golf course."

"What about the track to the sea? Are you so stupid you didn't try there?"

"Well," said the tallest of the three, lying to the intimidating leader, "we did try to search the top part of the path but it looked too dangerous, and seemed a perfect place for an ambush."

"So, they could have slipped through then?"

"No sir, definitely not."

"Why don't I believe you?" he said, opening the back door of his 4x4, to let two huge German shepherd dogs out. He restrained them, but they viciously pulled on their leads, trying to get at the other three men.

"You do well to cringe. They are trained killers; but don't worry it's only at my command."

All four hastened to the place where the road branched to the left down to the sea, and to the right over to the golf course, and he released the two dogs, down the narrow dark path, to the pebble beach below.

"Now you three idiots, take your flashlights and follow them, and look for any signs of disturbance."

Three strong strobes of light flashed up and down the track to the beach, and then after a minute, an excited cry from the bigger man brought the leader over to him.

"Here sir. I've found a handkerchief. A woman's."

"Great. Recall the dogs. We have Bladon and his woman now, as long as we're not too late."

The dogs were given the scent of Lexi from the hankie, and immediately they were off down to the golf course in hot pursuit, the four men running to keep up, but ever falling further behind, with their weapons on safety.

Bladon and Lexi reached the halfway point in their climb up the path, and were beginning to feel safe again, when they heard with dismay, the baying, blood curdling cries of attack dogs on the higher path.

"Oh no," said Bladon. "Dogs. I hadn't thought of that."

As they looked around for any means of defence, they heard the ominous sounds of the two dogs leaving the path and starting down through the wooded slope.

Bladon looked at Lexi, and saw a terrible change in her, at the mention of the dogs.

"What's wrong darling," said Bladon.

"I have an almost pathological fear of attack dogs, since I was badly mauled when I was a child. Oh Bladon, I am so afraid." She seemed to have visibly shrunk in stature, and wilted in front of his very eyes. This vibrant, strong, woman who had been so steadfast at his side on so many occasions in the past, was a quivering wreck.

"Don't worry," said Bladon, as he saw for the first time the headlong rush of the attack dogs down the slope towards them both.

Bladon frantically searched for a weapon, anything to defend themselves, but there was nothing. He looked up again and saw that whilst they were both big brutes, and perfect killing machines, one of the dogs was much bigger and menacing, and he had outpaced the other and was only ten metres away from impact.

Bladon searched again desperately, and then with his peripheral vision saw a fallen branch, about two metres in length, from a partly rotten, and lichen-covered birch tree. He picked it up quickly, and as he straightened up, realised the first dog was on him. Its vicious jaws were peeled back in a killing rictus, and its black staring eyes seemed to transmit unutterable malevolence, but as it launched itself into its killing leap, with hardly any back lift Bladon hit it full in the mouth and neck, with all his pent up frustration and anger, and the hateful creature dropped dead at his feet.

"There Lexi. Don't be afraid," he said, but as he turned to Lexi, he saw from her eyes focussed just above him, that he had forgotten in the exhilaration of the kill all about the other dog.

As he turned back, it hit him full on the right arm and shoulder, with the velocity of a runaway train, and lifted him bodily, throwing him into the deep pool beside the path. Down he went, into the dark, murky, and muddy waters, but though his arm was screaming with pain, he realised that the odds had changed in his favour. The dog was not as at home in the water as he was. He surfaced and wiped the blood, and gore, and slime, from his face, and saw as he expected, the dog paddling back to the bank, to get to dry land again.

But then a horrible realisation came over him. It was going for Lexi now, who was terrified and defenceless. He swam hard for the side of the pool, but he realised he would be too late. Lexi backed away up the path as the dog's cold, purposeful eyes locked onto hers, and then it slithered and clawed its way up the bank, towards her.

Four

Bladon recalled that stomach-churning occasion over a year ago, during their hunt for Dreadnought, when Lexi was snatched from a high Swiss Alp in front of his very eyes, and he thought he had lost her. This time he really could do nothing to save her. He was a metre from the side, and the dog was now circling its prey, before going in for the kill.

Lexi's eyes were on Bladon for a moment, as he tried to clamber out of the pool, and she saw the mixture of blood and water, cascading down from his damaged arm, and in that moment a remarkable transformation came over her. She was transformed into a warrior, fighting for her wounded soul mate struggling to reach her.

Her gaze returned to the attack dog, but this time it was firm, implacable, and purposeful. But she had no weapon; she had nothing to defend herself. Surely she would die a terrible death, with her throat torn open, before he could reach her.

And then she reached into her coat pocket, and took out a long thin object, without her eyes leaving the dog for a moment. Bladon heard a loud click, and a large six-inch blade shot out from the now visible bone knife handle. She had a flick knife, or as their American cousins called it, a switch blade. The killer dog raised itself on its haunches, and with a leap and a blood-curdling howl, launched into the final killing attack. Lexi raised the knife and threw it in almost the same instant, and it flew unerringly towards the dog, hit it just under its jaw and sank in right up to the hilt, and the dog stopped with a shudder, quite dead.

For a moment, Lexi just stood there, staring at the hideous, bloodied, and motionless corpse of the dog, and then she snapped to attention, ran over to Bladon and helped him out.

"Oh my darling. Let me look at your arm. I must try to quench the bleeding."

Without further ado, she tore off the sleeves of her blouse, and bandaged him carefully, but Bladon thanking her, knew that they had very little time.

"We must get away from here. Those men could be close behind. Let's get back to the hotel. I'll call Johnny and get some medical help and back up."

They hurried up the path as quickly as they could, and when they reached the swimming pool complex in the grounds, Bladon collapsed onto a sun bed and phoned Johnny Hanbury, the PM. He had a private number at 10 Downing Street that he had given him for emergencies.

The phone was answered instantly.

"Prime Minister please?" said Bladon.

"Who are you, and what makes you think you can speak to the Prime Minister?"

"This is Bladon, and I need to speak to the Prime Minister immediately."

"Bladon. What sort of name is that? I cannot possibly burden the Prime Minister with a call from someone I've never heard of, who has no security clearance. Phone the general enquiries line and explain yourself to the clerk there."

"Listen, who ever you are, you bumptious, odious, little bureaucrat. This is Bladon. Unless you get the PM immediately you will be taken to the Tower of London; that's assuming I don't get you first."

Bladon sensed that the receiver was about to be replaced.

"Don't you dare put the phone down on me," yelled Bladon. "I'll call him on his private mobile, then you'll be in real trouble."

Four

There was a click, a silence, and then the PM came on the line.

"Thank you. Johnny. Real problems here I'm afraid. I need back up and urgent medical attention please."

He put the phone down and turned to Lexi. "Johnny is sorting out the medics. If we can make it to our room, he'll get someone there in ten minutes. Also he's scrambling an SAS squadron that he has standing by at RAF Culdrose about ten minutes away. He sent them there as soon as he knew we were coming here. He'd also been informed of some very unsavoury characters arriving in the Falmouth area, but he hasn't found their base of operations yet."

Lexi helped Bladon up and they struggled across the lawn of the hotel until they reached the little golf shop, which thankfully was still open. They checked to see if the coast was clear, took the lift up to their bedroom and waited. The hotel owner, William, arrived within two minutes.

"Bladon, Lexi, I'm so glad you've made it. I was in the dining room when I got a phone call from the Prime Minister. I've been sworn to secrecy. I've phoned Dr Arthur, who trained at King's College London with your friend Wilf. They are great friends and Wilf has phoned him too. Dr Arthur lives on the little lane at the top of the golf course and will be here very quickly. Wilf has said he'll be here himself in the early hours. John Parkin's neighbour, Steve, is flying him down to Newquay Airport, and the Police will rush them over here straight away."

"Thank you William. You are too kind. I'll be OK until Dr Arthur gets here. You get back to the guests; and William —thanks."

"You're welcome. You have always been my favourite guest. If we have thugs and murderers around my hotel and its grounds, we have to stop them."

A sharp rap on the door interrupted William. He opened the door and a distinguished looking man in his late fifties, walked in.

"Hi Bladon. Hi Lexi. I understand you've been in the wars old boy! Introductions can wait. I understand my old pal Wilf Ali is coming down here later tonight. He, and Steve the pilot can stay with me, to stop him bothering you too much!"

They liked Dr Arthur immediately, as he carefully and tenderly took off Lexi's valiant attempts at bandaging, and surveyed the bloodied arm and shoulder.

"We'll have to make do with what we've got here old chap. I'll just have to ask you to sit in that chair for a mo."

With William's help they stripped the bed, and covered it with a sterile plastic sheet, and covered the pillows too with the same material. He took some painkillers and antibiotics from his bag.

"Right old chap. Back on the bed and then I can have a proper look at you."

Lexi made them all a coffee, and as she gave William a cup, he drew her to one side and reassured her.

"Don't mind his manner Lexi. He is the top trauma and casualty Consultant at Treliske Hospital in Truro, and a visiting Lecturer at Harvard in the States. He is very eminent, but he wears his brilliance lightly, just like Bladon's old friend Wilf."

Wilf was the GP friend of John and Margaret's, and had helped Bladon enormously when he had been shot in Derbyshire by Dreadnought's men, and had sought refuge in John and Margaret's impressive home in Derby. Bladon remembered the first time he met Wilf and heard his warm friendly Yorkshire accent that greeted him and put him at ease immediately and started the slow process of healing. Wilf had then joined his small band of friends who took on the might of Dreadnought's evil organisation and ultimately defeated him.

"OK Bladon old pal", Dr Arthur continued. "If I were you I'd keep away from attack dogs in the future. It looks like a charnel house in here. I may have to admit you to my little hospital. We'll see old chap. Right oh, let the dog see the bone! Oops sorry, wrong term old boy."

Four

Dr Arthur carefully cut away the bandages that were left, and then very gently cut away Bladon's coat and shirt from his right arm. He gave him some antibiotic tablets, and then injected him with a booster tetanus jab. He cleaned the wound, administered some local anaesthetic, and sutured the biceps, before sterilising the whole area again, finally bandaging it.

"Well old chap, I think you have been extremely fortunate. The good Lord has blessed you tonight. There is no significant muscle or ligament damage, nothing broken, and no major blood loss. In summary, you'll have a headache tomorrow, and feel a bit stiff, but in a few days you'll be as good as gold. Well done old fella."

With that he packed his case and left as quickly as he had arrived.

Five

Earlier, the four hostiles chasing Bladon and Lexi, reached the gate onto the golf course boundary and rushed through, the leader a few metres ahead.

"They must have come through here," he shouted back to his men.

"One of you come with me, and we'll go down this first path straight to the creek below, and you two go down the right hand path. Keep an eye out for them. The dogs should have caught up with them by now. Be careful, it will be very messy. We'll rendezvous at the top of the path below the hotel; but keep a look out. We don't want anyone to know that we've been here."

The two men went straight down the steep path to the creek below, taking care to keep their presence hidden. They needed speed now but they still had to be circumspect. They reached the bottom and made straight for the large summerhouse, an ideal place to hide. With weapons drawn they stealthily approached the quiet building. The leader kicked in the door, but the only thing that met him was the warm, slightly stale smell, of a mixture of damp and sunshine. There were sun beds and privacy screens by the far wall and the second man kicked one of them angrily aside, but there was no one there. The room was empty. They ran down to the foreshore, checking the side of the creek down to the little anchorage and the raised bank on the other side. There was no sign of their quarry. They met by the receding water line and then they both turned and started up the main path back to the hotel.

In the meantime the other two pursuers had reached the bottom of the path down by the side of the golf course where it met the other track, and seeing no sign of Bladon in the trees on the way down, they started up the path to the hotel.

"Wait," said the bigger more aggressive man. "There's blood on the path down there. Let's go and see what's happened."

They ran warily down the path to the creek, which was covered with blood. Who's blood was it though?

All four men met by the pool where Bladon and Lexi had fought their epic battle with their ferocious foes.

"What a mess," said the leader. "This is where the dogs caught up with them. But what happened?"

They searched the area round the pool and found the larger attack dog with his head crushed and a large branch lying at its side. Then they found the other dog in a pool of blood where Lexi had stopped it in mid attack.

"Somehow they've managed to kill the two dogs. I've no idea how. But surely that blood on the path higher up can't be from the dogs? In fact look here. This dog still has some of Bladon's coat in his jaws. They must be hurt, and hurt badly, by the look of it. Quick they can't have got far. Let's go."

The four men, all armed, started up the path to the hotel in hot pursuit. When they reached the swimming pool they stopped. "Look they've been here. See the blood. We've got them. They must be round here. Either in the pool or the hotel."

They started to enter through the pool doors.

"Wait," shouted the leader. "Do you hear that? It's a helicopter. They must have called for help.

Let's go!

We'll separate.

One of you come back to the car with me, and you two go down to the creek and make your way back to base along the shore. It's difficult, but the tide's going out."

Five

The two Sea King Helicopters from Royal Navy Culdrose on the Lizard Peninsula came in low and fast, up Port Navas Creek and then straight in to the grounds of the hotel. One hovered over the hotel itself and then dropped quickly to the lawn below the hotel, and eight black clad SAS troopers jumped out and ran quickly to the swimming pool entrance where they split into two groups, one running straight down the path to the creek, and the other up the path to the golf course.

The other helicopter, taking advantage of the noise and pandemonium caused by the first, slipped away over the golf course, landing quietly in a field just above the Ferryman's Inn. Four SAS troopers jumped out and ran the short distance to Barr Road, which bordered the golf course, and the Sea King immediately took off again. The four man SAS squad headed for the car left at the end of the road by Bladon and Lexi's attackers, and while two took up observation positions, the other two fitted tracker devices to the underneath and roof of the car, undetectable to the naked eye, and then like a wisp of sea mist, they vanished from the scene.

The other combat group soon caught sight of their quarry. The two hostiles who had decided to escape along the coast were making very hard work of their attempt to evade escape. The shore of the Helford Passage looked passable but it was very difficult to negotiate. They were halfway along the shoreline of the first bay when the SAS team reached them. Two commandeered a small dinghy, and launching it, made their way to the middle channel and were soon in contact with their quarry. The other two followed along the muddy shore, and within forty paces had a full and unhindered view of the enemy. They had handguns, but the SAS were fully equipped with Heckler and Koch machine guns and sniper rifles. The two fugitives increased their pace but after a few sighting shots from the SAS they realised there was no escape. They turned and dropped their weapons and raised their hands, but as the shore based soldiers approached to within twenty metres they suddenly threw themselves onto the mud and reaching for their weapons, trained them on the approaching SAS. A fusillade of lead whipped in from the water and snuffed out the danger before they could even aim their weapons.

"What a shame we couldn't take them alive; we may have obtained some useful information from them," said the sergeant as he checked for vital signs, and then the four returned quickly to their transport waiting on the lawn.

The leader of the hostile forces and one of his men had taken the top path by the golf course. They opened the old wooden gate to the course and ran along the periphery to the path back to Barr Road, where they had left their car. As they opened the gate they risked a look back to the hotel grounds and saw their pursuers, all in black, in hot pursuit by the 7th green. They ran in a break neck rush to the car near the end of the road.

The four SAS pursuing the hostiles reached the wooden gate, rushed down the path and reached Barr Road. Their quarry had not yet got to their car, but the Major in charge of the group reminded his men of their orders.

"Don't forget. Make it look good but they must escape," and with that four weapons opened up, but except for a broken front lamp on the car, they jumped in completely unscathed, reversed down the road at speed, round the corner, and away to safety.

"Well done lads. Let's get back. Mission accomplished."

Six

Back at the hotel, when the Doc had gone, Bladon turned to Lexi.

"Thank you sweetheart. You saved my life tonight. But how come you've got a flick knife—they're illegal you know."

"Well," said Lexi, "it's all this contact with Sandy and your old SAS mates during our last adventure in the Peak District against Dreadnought. They thought I should be well prepared. The knife's from one of the lads that helped us in the final attack on Ilam Manor, and another showed me how to throw it, and then when I got a bit of time alone over the last few months, I practiced until I was reasonable."

"Reasonable! You were brilliant."

They held each other close until the tension leaked away to be replaced finally by relief.

The following day reaction had begun to settle in for Lexi, and over coffee she seemed far away.

"You seem pensive this morning Lexi. What's the matter?"

"Well I think the horror of yesterday is just starting to sink in for me, darling. I thought that after the death of Dreadnought we were done with all this constant danger and tension, but now it all seems to have started up again. Why?"

"I'm sorry but I have no answer to that," Bladon replied, "but a few friends from Derby are coming down here to join us for lunch, so we might know more when they arrive."

As Bladon looked at her worried countenance his mind went back to the first time he had met Lexi.

He was lying hidden in a foxhole next to the fairway on the Trevose Head Golf Course in Cornwall, hiding from some ruthless armed men, when her golf ball landed near him with a thud. He knew he should be burrowing further into the sandy soil and not raising his head, but for a moment all fear of exposure fled, as he looked at the beautiful woman who walked casually into view. She was tall; about five foot ten inches; and her beautiful long blonde tresses fell in glorious abandon over her lovely face. She wore a red cashmere sweater, which singularly failed to hide her exciting curves. Their eyes met, and as he lowered his gaze, the three men who were chasing him burst through the brambles onto the golf course. They were arrogant and aggressive with hard cruel features and none made any attempt to hide their intimidating armoury.

One in particular was the obvious leader. He exuded an evil malevolence that was almost tangible and very frightening, but the woman fixed him with a stare, and demanded that they leave the course. After a tense standoff they left and Bladon's hideaway remained undiscovered. Bladon emerged and thanked her profusely. He asked her to dinner that night in his hotel as a thank you, and after a lovely meal they chatted in the lounge over coffee.

"Where does the name Lexi originate from?" said Bladon.

"Well," she replied, "I was christened Alexandra, but I've always been called Lexi ever since schooldays. It was my nickname."

Bladon found himself engrossed in this beautiful and self-assured young woman, and to speak so fully and openly to a stranger was completely against his nature and training, but his instincts told him that it was all right. He looked at her and she held his appraising gaze. She had stunning brown eyes and a wonderful smile that seemed to light up the room and refresh the air with warmth and exhilaration, and yet she

Six

also had a serene calm about her which was so reassuring and enabling.

"Tell me all about yourself", he said, and the words seemed to cascade from her like a fresh sparkling stream.

"I had been living near Lincoln with my parents and attending first the Prep, and then the Senior section as a day-girl at a school in the East Midlands; but I hated the way they tried to mould the girls into priggish, snobby swots and much to my parents disappointment, I insisted on leaving when I reached 13. I was then sent to a prestigious boarding school near the Cathedral City of Litchfield, where I felt treasured and happy, and enjoyed hockey, tennis, and languages. I went to the University of Kent in Canterbury and graduated with a 2.1 in French and Italian. I was headhunted by a Merchant Bank in New York and spent a hectic seven years on assignments in Paris, Milan, Geneva and London. I had all the financial rewards expected of such a position, with a Porsche, flats in London and Geneva, and a comfortable little cottage near here, between the sea and the golf course."

"Are you married?" asked Bladon and immediately wished he hadn't. What would she think? Was he being disloyal to the memory of Sarah, who he missed so much it was like a physical, deep-seated ache? However, she put him at his ease so quickly.

"Why do you want to know?" she asked. "Do you want to have a mad, passionate fling with me in the bunkers, in between dodging the thugs?"

She reassured him that she was joking and then opened her heart.

"I loved a wonderful young man in my last year at University but tragically he died after a short illness. I then found most of the men I met puerile, superficial and amoral; until today," she playfully told him.

He found himself telling her everything that had happened, including the brutal murder of his wife, Sarah, on the bleak, snow covered beach in Norfolk in the dead of winter, and of his burning desire to avenge her death. Lexi could see how raw the wounds of his tragic loss were; but as they talked it through, he found it so wonderful to be able to share his heart with someone else, and for the first time in months Bladon felt the first signs of spring birthing in his life, after such a dreadful winter.

"What about you though." asked Lexi? I know nothing about you except that your wife was viciously murdered and that your life too is in great danger."

"Well I was in the SAS for quite a while, and I loved my time in the Regiment, but it wasn't just a longing for adventure and machismo deeds, it was also the camaraderie with the other men, and of course I was intensely patriotic, and loved to take on the baddies. Maybe the key to my love of the Regiment is that I have always been an intensively competitive person, and it gave me more opportunity than anywhere else to pit myself against the elements, and against others at the very highest level. I just loved the physical and mental stretching that being in the SAS entailed. It also meant on occasion great periods of boredom and waiting, followed by intense periods of highly brutal action, but that wasn't the raison d'être for being in the Regiment; it was only a part of it."

Lexi encouraged him to talk, as she just longed to know more and more about this wonderful man who had come into her life.

"When I was in the SAS, I was a communications expert, but in the aftermath of the Iraqi invasion of Kuwait I got involved with a lot of close protection work, and eight of us were assigned to the Saudi Royal family. We were very successful and foiled a number of Iraqi-inspired coup and assassination attempts, but just when I was settling down in the Middle East we were sent back to Northern Ireland under very deep cover. After two years I was sick of it, and when the tour finished I asked to be what they call RTU'd, and I returned to the Royal Greenjackets, and then made plans to leave the army all together. So I became a civilian again, but I was immediately headhunted by a Kuwaiti Prince for protection duties, and had a very happy and rewarding three years with him. The pay was good, but the bonuses were fantastic! I personally foiled three assassination attempts in Kuwait City, London and Rome *and on each occasion my grateful employer gave me a house in London as a reward. But then I met Sarah, and we settled down, until we became drawn into the conspiracy that was to claim her life and lead me to a fortuitous meeting with you when you saved my life as I was hiding on the golf course."*

Surely those terrible days were gone forever. He hoped and prayed so.

Seven

Steve flew Wilf down to Cornwall early the next day, and they joined Bladon and Lexi at the hotel for lunch on the terrace in the warm sun. Bladon and Lexi shared a Cornish salmon salad with prosciutto on brioche, with home made chutney, and Wilf and Steve had the homemade Cornish pasties. They had a great time together, forgetting for a while the dangers here in the beautiful south west of Cornwall. Bladon brought them up to date with all that had happened so far.

"We have to find out who's behind all these murderous attempts on our lives. Presumably it's an attempt to take both of us out at the same time. Why are they, whoever they are, trying to wipe us out? Is it revenge for how we foiled that plot by Dreadnought before? If so, we must also contact the rest of The Thirteen and warn them. Surely it can't be Dreadnought though, as we saw him go down in that burning helicopter in the hills of Derbyshire. He couldn't have survived that maelstrom. But if it's not him, then who is it?

Bladon rested in the conservatory, while the other three walked down to the creek below the hotel, passing the pool where the dog had attacked, and sat in the sunshine by the creek. They returned in the late afternoon and spent an enjoyable hour together, swimming in the pool, soaking in the outdoor hot tub, baking in the sauna and resting on the sun loungers.

Wilf checked Bladon's wounds, which were healing nicely, and later all four ate together in the formal dining room, and slowly they began to relax and ready themselves for whatever the morrow might bring. Bladon and Lexi both chose goat's cheese in breadcrumbs with beetroot, followed by Dover Sole on the bone, grilled in butter with sauté potatoes and a green salad. Wilf chose sorbet, followed by guinea fowl with mash and celeriac, and Steve tried the beef with Yorkshire pudding and roast potatoes and they all finished with a wonderful rhubarb crumble served with Cornish cream custard. They tried the cheese board, and Wilf and Steve particularly enjoyed Bladon's favourite, Cornish Yarg, with fresh chutney and grapes. They shared coffee in the lounge, and left wonderfully replete at midnight before agreeing to meet after breakfast to try to track down the enemy.

The next day William, the Hotel owner, made a meeting room available for the four friends, and the SAS Major and his Sergeant arrived thirty minutes later. They brought weapons for them all, and over coffee they began to look for a clear way forward. The SAS major, known as Willie, explained that two of the attackers had been killed but they had deliberately let the other two go.

"Why," asked Bladon?

"Well," Willie replied, "we wanted to trace their base here in Cornwall, and so we bugged the car and let them get away. We've never been able to find their headquarters before; we suspected it was somewhere round the Helford Estuary, but we weren't sure; and despite a huge effort by the local Police, a whole squadron of our men, and a Special Boat Squad unit from Poole who have been patrolling the creeks and shores around here, we've had no success at all. But this time we've finally made a breakthrough. Thanks to you and Lexi they've showed themselves for the first time. We now know where they are.

"Where's that Willie? Is it near here?"

"Very near," said Willie. "It's very close to the Helford Estuary. It's at a place called Mawnan, and it's an old Manor House, named Nancenoy Towers, built in the Mid-Nineteenth Century, and set in eighty acres, about half a mile from the sea. It's stands high on a hillside sloping down to the shore, with wonderful views of the estuary and the open sea beyond. We can land on the foreshore at the bottom of the grounds, but it's very open ground up to the Towers. However, it is in heavy woodland, which keeps it very private, but actually helps our assault. We can come in from woodland at the back, or fields and woods on either side, or straight up from the sea. Or all four!"

William arranged for lunch to be brought in for the six of them. After the initial shock of the attack on Bladon and Lexi, William had grown to really appreciate being trusted with Official Secrets, and had been a little conspiratorial with Susan his wife and Alonso the Manager. They were very discreet for they must have realised that two close encounters with naval helicopters and fleeting glimpses of black clad heavily armed soldiers in their grounds presaged something even more exciting, but they remained very professional and were able to deflect any concerns or worries from the guests.

They were just finishing their lunch when Sandy, the Prime Minister's aide, phoned.

"Hi Bladon. I'm so glad to hear that you're recovering. I've had a briefing from the PM earlier today and we've had a bit of a breakthrough. Army intelligence has discovered something very disturbing. A British scientist, Professor Luis Lane, who has invented a new gun with devastating firepower, has disappeared, presumed kidnapped. He was developing it in Italy in a secret project, backed with Italian and British finance, but he has just disappeared and we have no idea where he is. We suspect he is still in Italy. This weapon could revolutionise warfare, but could also be a terrible force for evil in the wrong hands. It has an electronic firing mechanism, and was reaching the final prototype stage, after successful testing by the military, and full production was only a few months away. Apparently it is a revolution in weaponry. Its firing mechanism is initiated electronically rather than by the traditional percussion method. It has almost no recoil and no moving parts; bullets or grenades can be fired at a rate of up to half a million per minute, either from a single weapon or multiple barrels grouped together in pods. Just to give you an idea of what this means, an Uzi machine gun, which is itself a fearsome weapon, fires at a rate of 3,000 rounds a minute. The weapons could be powered by long-lasting battery packs giving them much more versatility."

"Very few firearm revolutions have taken place in the last 60 or 70 years but this is one of them. If it gets into the wrong hands then it's a very worrying development. Not only has he invented an assault gun but also a multi-barrelled gun which can direct withering fire at any enemy infantry or tank advance, or even enable a warship to fend off a missile attack. Experts at the MOD tell us that you can put an awful lot of lead into the air very quickly, and you could even have a pod of up to 60 barrels. You could then send out a cloud of gunfire in one or two seconds obliterating anything in the vicinity.

There are also rumours that he's perfected a multi-barrelled incendiary gun. Normally, incendiary rounds will not ignite everything, and it may take hundreds of rounds to start a good fire quickly, but this weapon does just that.

We understand that the Prof had developed a special fire control electronics device, which fires the bullets or grenades by an electronic charge. Weight had been a real problem for the Prof, particularly with the large multi-barrelled guns, but just before he went missing we learned that he had made a real breakthrough by using a special lighter carbon fibre moulding compound to make some of the parts. However the large multi-barrelled weapons were still quite heavy and not very portable, and still needed to be lifted into position. The Prof had been developing a lightweight pulley system to give them more portability.

The MOD knows that other countries are trying to develop a similar weapon but there is nothing on the lethal scale of the Prof's gun anywhere in the world. If a terrorist organisation or a hostile country were to get hold of the gun it would be disastrous. That is why we are so worried that the Professor has just disappeared."

"Perhaps he has been kidnapped in Italy. If so that's

terrible. I do hope he's alright," said Bladon. "We've got some good news this end though. We've tracked down the enemy's base here in Cornwall, and we're putting together a plan to attack in the early hours of this morning. The weapon they used to attack me and Lexi on the yacht in the Helford Estuary could be part of the Prof's experimental work in Italy. If we could only capture one of the enemies guns, it would be a huge leap forward for us."

"Why not fly down and join us. Besides Lexi and me, there's Wilf and Steve, and of course Willie and his sergeant? I don't know whether or not you've heard about Steve, but besides running a very successful engineering business in Derby, Steve still keeps his hand in on the flying side. Have you heard about 'Seal Team 6', the elite US Special Forces outfit that killed Bin Laden, and rescued those hostages from Somalia? Well Steve was seconded to their unit for six months to liaise on air support, and he had to endure the same intensive training as the Seals do. He came through with flying colours, and I'm sure he's going to be a great help to us."

Sandy, Willie and Bladon worked on the plan for the attack on Nancenoy Towers, and finally in the late afternoon Lexi, Steve, Wilf, and representatives from the armed forces assisting them, joined the meeting. Bladon explained that the attack would be a three pronged one from the north, east and west, also with a feint from the seaward side to the south.

Bladon, Steve and Wilf and eight SAS troopers would attack from the east of Nancenoy Towers, initially from the car park of Mawnan church, through a stile into the next field and then across to a small wood on the perimeter of the house, to reach the outbuildings and cottages adjoining the house. It was very important to take control of these buildings before any of the formidable weapons could be deployed.

Sandy himself would attack from the west with another eight troopers and make straight for the conservatory and leisure complex before trying to access the lounge and dining areas.

Willie would command the bulk of the force, ten SAS

troopers, and eight Special Boat Squadron combatants, and try to force entry through the main entrance from the woods bordering the drive and front parking area.

Lexi had insisted she wanted to take part, and she was included in a force of Royal Marines from Culdrose, who would mount a direct attack from the sea across the fields in front of the house. This was to be a diversionary attack only, as this was the most dangerous approach, in view of the unknown number of any new weapons, which Bladon had nicknamed 'super-guns'. In such an open environment a full attack here could lead to devastating casualties, so they were very carefully tasked as to their tactics, in particular not to leave cover and not under any circumstances to launch an all out attack on the house.

They planned the assault for 3 o'clock in the morning.

Eight

Those coming by road arrived at their specified positions by stealth at 2 o'clock. The Royal Marines coming in from the South side up the Helford Passage arrived initially by helicopter, and then transferred to fast assault boats, to get them close to the perimeter of the grounds nearest to the sea.

Lexi met up with the Royal Marines by a circuitous route from the Gardens of Glendurgan, a busy tourist attraction during the day, abutting the coastal footpath; but it was agreed that she take a safe position in the rear with the communications team of the attack group, led by Major John Steerforth.

Meanwhile Bladon, Steve and Wilf with eight men from the SAS arrived in the car park of Mawnan church. It was a very secluded place and as they left their cars, the eerie call of a hunting owl screeched overhead. Bladon shuddered almost involuntarily, but continued along to the small stile exiting the car park, and on into the first field.

He spoke in whispered tones to Wilf, and the leader of the SAS group.

"This is the most dangerous part, as we have to cross this open field as quickly as possible and reach that small copse by 2.45am. Our intelligence shows that there is only a short distance of about 100 metres from those trees to the lawn at the side of the house. Very conveniently there is a ha-ha around the lawn where we can hide until the assault commences."

They hurried across the field, seemingly totally undetected, and took up positions at the edge of the lawn in the ha-ha. Bladon risked a look towards the house and confirmed that all was quiet.

Meanwhile Sandy had also made good progress with eight SAS troopers and took up his position on the west of the house ready for the attack.

Willie, however, made more difficult progress due to the dense undergrowth, and by 2.45am his force of eighteen were really struggling to keep to the timetable, and even to keep in contact with each other. Willie realised this was becoming a real problem as all the four attacks had to be initiated simultaneously, otherwise the whole attack could end in chaos or disaster. What should he do? Communication with the other three attack groups was very problematic. If he opened up comms, it may very well compromise the whole operation. They wanted to take the building and also capture the defenders alive and see if there were any of the deadly weapons or further incriminating evidence about the headquarters of the enemy. But that depended on complete surprise and coordinated action.

Willie decided not to try to contact the other teams, but redouble his efforts to get on station by 3am. The problem was that Willie's attack group was the biggest and the most heavily armed. Without it the attack would be seriously compromised.

From the south the Marines made their way cautiously up the long narrow field from the estuary to the south facing lawns. It was probably about a thousand metres from the coastal path up to the house and they started at 2.30am very cautiously. Lexi should have stayed with the communications team in the rear, but she didn't want to miss any of the action and sneaked in behind the Marines attack team.

Their remit was to be a diversionary feint from the front to draw enemy fire whilst the other three groups sprung their

Eight

trap, and for the first five hundred metres they made good progress as they reassessed their position at 2.45am. Timing was of the essence, so they resumed their careful progress up towards the house.

They reached a deep ditch and small hedge, which intersected the field from east to west and formed a small piquet line behind it and waited. Their brief was to make a lot of sound and fury but not to risk a full out attack. Major John had not noticed the smaller darkly clad figure who joined the marines on the outer perimeter of the ditch.

Bladon looked at his watch. It was 2.59 am. They were ready to go. However Willie had met such difficult conditions with dense undergrowth and deep, foul smelling, clinging bogs, that he still had not reached his rendezvous point. He was about 100 metres away with even more difficult terrain to cover. But as he urged his force on, the sound of a terrible explosion knocked him to the ground, and for a moment he found himself and his men totally disorientated.

Meanwhile Bladon, from his vantage point next to the lawn had witnessed at first hand the terrible events, which had unfolded in front of his very eyes. The defenders of Nancenoy Towers must have seen movement from the diversionary attack in the field running down to the sea. A terrible weapon had been used on the small decoy force of Marines, and as the smoke and detritus of the hedge cleared he saw the most terrible picture of devastation. How many were dead or wounded?

Major John had just given the one-minute warning to start the attack, but one young Marine was too anxious to wait the full sixty seconds and had jumped up prematurely, and wrestled his way up and over the small hedge. The Marine sergeant had tried to stop him, but could not hold on to him as a huge explosion assaulted their ears, and the air was filled with the wailing and whistling of literally thousands and thousands of bullets. The noise was like the cawing of hundreds of rooks in unison, but somehow harsher and more metallic.

Bladon was the first to react. He yelled over the comms to attack immediately, in a three-pronged pincer attack from the back and the sides, whilst the defenders attention was on the small diversionary force in front.

Bladon's group and Sandy's group hit the house at the same time with very little response from the defenders, just a desultory cry from within, but Willie was still not close enough to the front of the house to coordinate the attack.

Nancenoy Towers was laid out in a very similar way to other English country houses. The house had been used for several months as an overflow convalescent home during World War 2 and the plans that Sandy had obtained from the MOD showed a house with about thirty bedrooms and twenty bathrooms on the first floor.

Four rooms in the south annex faced south, down to the Helford estuary, and the rest were situated on the east and west sides of the property.

The ground floor comprised, in the south wing a small chapel, bar, and smaller dining room. Then a long corridor lined with dusty old oil paintings of family members of ancient lineage, and armour from the Civil War right up to the Peninsular and Napoleonic War.

Various rooms bordered the corridor until it turned right for a short distance and then straightened again. It ran for some distance before reaching the impressive oak door to the car park at the north of the house, accessed from the main entrance.

Inside the house, the incursions from the east and west and of course the south, had been belatedly spotted and the alarm klaxon was now clamouring throughout the house. Frantic activity raged through the whole building, as armed men took up position on the ground floor, some to the rooms on east and some on the west, ignoring the south, as they didn't believe anyone could have survived their counter attack. Their leader's menacing voice rang out throughout the house:

Eight

"Put down some covering fire but don't try to make a stand. Just let them think we are heavily armed and dangerous, but get out as soon as you can."

Bladon and some of his men launched their attack on the chapel in the south wing, whilst the rest attacked the butler's pantry which had a large window concealed from those above.

Sandy went straight for the wine cellar and smashing down the heavy oak door they rushed inside.

Both attack groups laid down a withering fire at the defenders in the corridors, and though fire was returned it was not the devastating firepower that had poured from the south wing. Bladon was in radio contact with Sandy and above the cacophony of sound he shouted.

"Don't risk an all out attack until we've reconnoitred the corridor area, because one blast from that gun and we're all history."

They slowly checked and secured all the rooms and moved down towards the north end of the ground floor, when they were met with a loud bang as the north door blew open to reveal Willie and his men.

"Cease fire", said Bladon, and he and Sandy ran to meet Willie.

As Willie entered the house he found to his surprise that it was empty. He saw Bladon and Sandy running towards him and he and his men lowered their weapons, but before they could speak their ears were suddenly assailed by a monstrous noise coming from close by, and running back outside and looking north to the source of the tumult, they saw rising steadily out of the trees, a huge helicopter. It dipped its nose in an almost derisory manner, and thundered off to the south west, then following the Estuary, headed east.

How had they escaped so easily? Where had they gone? They had covered the southwest and east sides, and belatedly the north, but had seen no sign of the enemy forces. How had they just vanished into thin air?

Bladon searched back along the ground floor corridor as perplexed as the rest of his disappointed men.

"I thought we had them at last and that we could capture and examine one of those terrible weapons they've been using," said Sandy.

"I know," said Bladon. "I'm as disappointed as you, but they can't just have vanished into thin air. Let's search this whole floor and look for anything unusual, but in the meantime, let's scramble two of the helicopters and see if we can catch them."

The first Sea King helicopter received instructions from Sandy and took off from the pebble seashore on the Estuary straight away, and launched into headlong pursuit. The top speed of these helicopters, which here in Cornwall were mostly used for air sea rescue work, was a maximum of 125 knots so Sandy called up a Royal Navy Merlin from RNAS Culdrose close by. The Merlin was a specialist submarine-hunting helicopter with a much greater top speed of 167 knots, and would soon catch the Sea King.

Nine

Meanwhile, back at Nancenoy Towers, they searched for several minutes, until Bladon shouted in delight.

"I think I've cracked it! Look here."

Bladon was standing where the corridor turned back to the north, and where a spiral staircase wound up to the first floor, but Bladon was intrigued by a small oil painting on the wall that didn't look quite right. It looked incongruous, hanging there in splendid isolation at the bottom of the staircase with not another painting in view on the corridor walls. Why should this be here, he mused? Then on closer inspection he noticed that it stood proud of the wall as if something was protruding from behind. He took the painting down and there on the wall behind it he saw a small partially concealed switch.

He pulled the switch up and immediately it clicked and a clever hydraulic apparatus sprang into life revealing stairs leading down to the basement level not shown on any recent maps. The bottom of the staircase had been cleverly disguised to show no stairs descending and the fitted carpet carefully disguised any signs of it. They descended the spiral staircase and found themselves in a basement not shown on the plans given to Sandy. These were the servants quarters, specifically built to usher in the below stairs staff so that none of the occupants or visitors to the house saw them! It was similar to many country houses where the paid help were neither seen nor heard. The basement ran the full length of the ground floor and replicated the same route as the corridor above, with the major difference that at the north side it continued for a further hundred yards, quite an engineering feat for the builders at that time.

They followed the corridor along to where the basement ended, and where iron stairs climbed up to ground floor level and opened out onto a natural mini amphitheatre, with the south, east and west sides covered by old brick walls and impenetrable trees and foliage.

The north side however opened out through a small gate to a large, concrete-block floor, on which had recently stood the dull green Sikorsky helicopter, camouflaged from the sky by a huge net in greens and browns, which lay discarded on the ground. Beyond that lay a large garage in which had been standing three black BMW X6's, lurking in the dark interior, mottled and dappled by errant small bursts of sunlight bursting between the tree branches, through the skylights. Now they were gone. All that was left was the smell of diesel and three sets of skid marks where the cars had left in a hurry.

In the heat of battle, Bladon had forgotten all about the devastating assault on the southern attack force. He left Sandy to coordinate the pursuit of the helicopter, but called Willie, Wilf and Steve to come with him and check for potential casualties. When they got to the ditch, they saw what looked like a war zone. Fortunately those marines in the ditch and below the hedge were unscathed except for the shock of the attack, and the damage to their ears. They were tending the marine sergeant who had tried to snatch the young marine who had made a premature rush for the house. Though badly wounded in the arms and upper body, he would recover, but the young marine would not. His body seemed to have been shredded by literally hundreds of high velocity bullets and Bladon covered him with his coat and turned to Major John.

"Bad business Major. I'm sorry you took the brunt of their firepower. That wasn't meant to happen."

"Don't worry Bladon. If it hadn't been for poor Jimmy jumping the gun our casualties would have been much greater. They didn't know our numbers and spread their fire along the whole length of the hedge, but that dissipated their firepower somewhat. If they had just concentrated on us in the middle, they would have blown us apart. That is the most monstrous and formidable weapon I've ever seen. I wish I had one!"

Bladon thanked him again, but his eye was drawn to the far end of the ditch. Under a huge clod of dirt and turf and remains of the hawthorn hedge lay a dark prone figure.

"Major, I thought all your men were in night attack fatigues. Who is that on the end? They seem dead."

Bladon ran towards the body but as he got closer he began to panic.

"Major that is no marine. The figure is too slight. It looks like a woman. Oh no! Where is Lexi? I hope she's still with the comms team down by the estuary."

As he reached the body he saw to his horror and panic that it was in fact Lexi. He clawed away the debris from around her and pulled out the seemingly lifeless body. Fearing the worst he brushed away the dirt and detritus from her beautiful face, but as he was about to try resuscitation her eyelids flickered and a gulp of air signalled that she was still alive. He sat her up, her breathing steadied, and one of the marines emptied his canteen over her head to clear her eyes and ears and mouth.

Back at base on the estuary, a doctor checked Lexi over, and miraculously she had suffered no damage whatsoever to her precious body, she had just been stunned by the weapon's ferocity. A hot bath back at the hotel and a hearty full English breakfast restored her equilibrium and positive spirit. Bladon left her to return with the Marines and ran back to Sandy to see how the pursuit was doing.

Ten men had escaped from the house in the three BMW's, under cover of the confusion caused by the helicopters departure. They had one of the two devastating weapons with them, and the other that could so nearly have caused terrible carnage to the attack from the south was with the other six men, including the leader. They had escaped in the helicopter, which was making good its escape towards Newton Abbot in

Devon. The three cars sped up the A30 making good progress in convoy, when Leo in the first car received a phone call from their leader in the helicopter.

"Where are you?"

"Just approaching Bodmin on the A30. We'll continue along here until Exeter, then we'll go up the M5 to Bristol, and on to the safe house in Derbyshire."

"We. What do you mean we? Are you all travelling together?"

"Yes, of course. We're in convoy and making very good progress too."

"You buffoon. What happens if you pass a police car? Don't you think it will look a bit suspicious with three black 4x4s one behind the other roaring up the outside lane? Here's what you do. You continue as planned past Bristol up the M5, onto the M41, then the A38 to Derby, and finally to Ashbourne.

Ivan in the second car will leave the A30 and then take the A38 to Saltash, and on to Exeter, and then he will go straight up the M5 until he reaches Stafford, cutting back east to Derby, and on to Ashbourne.

Jorge meanwhile, will get off the A30 at the first exit, make for the A39 and stop the night in Barnstaple. Tomorrow, he'll follow your route and meet you at the safe house at lunchtime. Do you think you can manage that?"

"Yes boss."

"Brilliant. Why do I always have to do your thinking for you?"

The leader clicked off his mobile and saw to his delight that the helicopter was making good progress, and felt that after all he had done well to extricate himself from the situation. But then he took a call from Italy, which soon disabused him.

"What's happening? What's all the noise?" a sinister voice demanded.

"We're in the helicopter. We didn't manage to kill Bladon and Lexi, in fact they found our headquarters and we have had to exfiltrate the whole area. We're heading for the railway station at Newton Abbot in the Sikorsky, and the others are in three cars making their way north to the safe house near Ashbourne. What are your instructions?"

"You imbeciles. Do I have to do everything myself? I can't be in England and Italy at the same time."

"Sorry sir. I thought I'd done well."

"Done well! I don't believe it. The whole of my careful, painstaking planning to set up a formidable secret base in Cornwall has now been compromised. No, not compromised. Blown away." He sighed, and a long minute's silence elapsed before he spoke again, with barely concealed anger and impatience.

"Here's what you do. You make your way to Gatwick and take a scheduled flight to Bologna, and then come to our secret headquarters here in Italy. Make sure you're not followed. Do you think you can manage that you fool? Use the special escape route I set up last week as a back up. However, I'm still not finished with my plan to wipe out "The Thirteen". Tell Giuseppe that when he gets to the safe house I want him to urgently start to take them out. Greg first, then the rest of them. I don't want them foiling my plans again. Do you think he's capable of that?"

The leader, on the helicopter, put down the mobile, and saw that his hands were shaking. What a mess. It couldn't have gone much worse. Well actually it could. They could have all been captured, together with the top-secret guns; but they had escaped and escaped easily without loss.

The Sikorsky headed east towards the town of Newton Abbot, but instead of going straight across the bay, it kept close to the coastline, hugging the cover of the villages and farms next to the sea. It passed St Mawes, Mevagissey, St Austell, Polperro and Looe, and then flew out to sea, to skirt the large promontory containing Kingsbridge and Salcombe, and then on past Brixham and Torquay, and to Newton Abbot, the rail hub for the southwest. From here trains ran north to Bristol or east to Paddington.

As they started to move out to sea, the Merlin from Culdrose, which was about a thousand metres in front of the Sea King by now, confirmed visual sighting of the Sikorsky with Sandy, back at the Towers.

"I have line of sight. Do I engage?"

"Yes," Sandy replied. "But be very careful. They may have one of the weapons with them. I doubt very much whether your conventional defences will work against it. Engage but don't get too close. "

The Merlin closed with the Sikorsky, which then changed course back inland towards Salcombe and Kingsbridge. The Sikorsky also slowed its headlong flight, almost imperceptibly, so much so that the Merlin closed to only five hundred metres before it realised what was happening. At the same time as it slowed, the Sikorsky pilot also turned 90 degrees, so that the port side was facing the Merlin.

Too late, the Navy pilot realised that the door of the copter was open, and just like the old movie clips of the Vietnam War, a man was strapped in his seat facing him and manoeuvring a strange looking multi-barrelled gun which was fixed to the helicopter, towards him.

The man fired, and before the Merlin pilot could launch his missiles, his helicopter disappeared in a hail of bullets, and noise, and flames.

The Sea King's pilot following, watched in horror as the Merlin from Culdrose burst into flames, fell out of the sky into the English Channel, and slipped beneath the slate grey waters, taking the crew to their deaths. He banked his Sea King to the port side quickly, at the same time taking counter measures, and backed off until he considered he was out of range of the horrific weapon.

Sandy came over the radio and urgently asked, "What was that explosion? What's happening? Are you ok? I've lost radio contact with the Merlin."

The pilot explained the tragic events and asked for new instructions. Sandy reacted quickly and decisively.

"Follow them, but don't get too close. I don't want to lose

them, but be very careful. You've seen what the gun can do."

The Sea King backed off until well out of range, but he could still see the helicopter visually in the distance, and also on the radar.

Ten minutes later the pilot's voice rang out over Sandy's radio.

"He's descending. I think he's going to try and land on Thurlestone Golf Course just inland."

"We'll just observe. It's too dangerous to get close in at the moment."

Ten

The Sikorsky landed on the golf course, but well away from the Club House in an isolated part of the course. The leader, Franz, hurried his men out and over to a transit van, hidden under a tarpaulin by the side of a green, delaying his own departure by thirty seconds before jumping from the helicopter grasping a small black box, and joined his men in the van.

"Right, let's go and quickly."

The van roared down the side of the course, through the car park and out into the village and on up the main road. Franz clicked a switch on the black box to activate a timing mechanism, and placed it on the seat next to him. The driver took a right turn down a narrow lane shut in by high banks and almost covered from above with overhanging branches and foliage until they reached a narrow track, signposted to Soar Mill Cove. They parked in the grounds of the Soar Mill Cove Hotel, and ran down a footpath to the Cove.

"We're here, and we're safe now," Franz reassured his men, and as they reached the sandy beach, they saw to their relief a large cruiser, bobbing in the swell, just offshore. They waded through the surf and were helped into the boat by the captain and his two-man crew. The captain of the boat and Franz from the helicopter stood together in the cockpit and waited. The boat still continued to drift with the incoming tide. There was no attempt at movement for the next five minutes. What were they waiting for?

And then, from the direction of Thurlestone, they heard

and felt the shock wave of a huge explosion, and almost simultaneously the engines started, reached full power, and moved off into the Channel at speed.

The Sea King had approached the golf course just as the small van raced off towards the Club House car park and on to the main street of Thurlestone. It didn't attempt to land, but hovered a safe distance away and radioed Sandy.

"I don't like it," said Sandy. "It looks like a trap to me. Keep your distance and I'll get a bomb disposal team down there. There might be valuable Intel in the helicopter and maybe even the gun. Just see if you can find where the van's going. We don't want those murderers to get away."

The Sea King withdrew to try to find the van, and although the roads and lanes between Thurlestone, Bantham, Bigbury-on-Sea and Hope Cove were all searched, the van had disappeared. They returned to Thurlestone just as a huge explosion ripped through the golf course, completely destroying the Sikorsky and devastating a huge area around it. The pilot of the Sea King struggled to try and control his craft in the massive shock waves that enveloped him, but finally he managed to land it. Meanwhile the motor launch with the hostiles aboard had used the confusion following the explosion, to make their way quickly out to sea.

They were safe, but in their desperate hurry to escape they had left the gun in the helicopter, which was now a burning wreck.

The cruiser continued past Salcombe, Start point, Dartmouth, Paignton, Torquay, until half way between Torquay and Teignmouth they reached the remote Blackaller's Cove. The captain slowed the engine, and cruised into a lonely landing stage by a seemingly deserted house. Franz and his men all jumped ashore and made for the house. The dilapidated garage door creaking on its rusty hinges was easily forced open, and standing there in all its glory, was a dirty, but inconspicuous mini-bus.

They all piled in and soon reached the A379, the main road between Torquay and Teignmouth, where they took the Torquay road. Just before Torquay Golf Club they turned right up Moor Lane and followed the narrow country road, which wound through idyllic little hamlets and by country pubs and ancient Norman churches, until at last it reached the Exeter road. They crossed it, and pulled into the Newton Abbot Railway Station car park, and to safety.

Meanwhile in their three black BMW 4x4's Leo, Ivan and Jorge went their separate ways.

Their hideaway had been carefully chosen and was deep in the most popular tourist area of Derbyshire's White Peak, the southern most part of the Peak District National Park and the most picturesque and beautiful walking country. Their base was called Cloud View Cottage, and it was situated in the small village of Thorpe. One of the roads through the centre of the village was Digmire Lane, and Cloud View Cottage was at the top of an unmade track about 150 metres from the lane. It was an ideal situation for the ten escapees from Nancenoy Towers; remote and yet very close to fast roads to most of the county, close to Bladon's house in Kedleston and to a lot of The Thirteen's homes as well. It had large private grounds and a small indoor pool and a well-equipped gym. There was no need for anyone to leave the house except for re-provisioning.

The building itself consisted of three large stone cottages, all knocked into one and yet retaining three bathrooms and three quite separate kitchens. There were seven bedrooms, more than enough for their purposes, and cable TV in all of the rooms. It was ironic however, that the house was only 100 metres away from The Grange, which The Thirteen used as their base for the attack on Ilam Manor in their previous struggle against Dreadnought. Dreadnought was actually a code name for the mastermind behind the plot to take over the country—Colin Morgan, the Deputy Prime Minister and Defence Minister, and one of the most powerful men in the British Government at that time.

Leo arrived first around breakfast time, Ivan next at midday, and finally Jorge around lunchtime on the following day.

The phone shrilled its urgent call.

"Are you all installed and ready to go?"

"Yes sir."

"Ok. You know what we want. Get on with it as soon as you can. We are back at base in Italia. You know how to report back? Don't let us down."

Eleven

Bladon and Lexi returned to Derbyshire from their adventures in Cornwall, and decided to spend the day looking round Haddon Hall, the location for several blockbuster films including the latest Jane Eyre classic. They dined at the Pheasant, a centuries old coaching inn, now a luxury hotel, little more than twenty minutes away from Haddon, popular with the County set and County set wannabes. The service was deplorable, the restaurant manager was abrupt and off hand, and they were left to wait expectantly for their meals for an hour.

Towards the end of the meal a phone call from Greg to the hotel, was passed through to them. Greg was one of the "Thirteen" who had helped Bladon.

"Some very important news, Bladon, I must see you today. It's urgent. I've had a message from the PM. He couldn't get you, due to the usual hopeless mobile reception in the Peak district. Can you meet me at the Black Swan at Idridgehay for two thirty and I'll bring you up to date. I can't go into too much detail on the phone, but we've found something on a burnt out computer at Nancenoy Towers. The two words Il Tredici. We couldn't recover the contents of the file, only a reference to an area of Italy called Le Marche, and the file name is Italian for The Thirteen. Interesting! I think we are all in danger—particularly me. If the P.M.'s office phone is bugged I could be in real trouble."

The food had been tolerable, but very expensive. They left the dining room quickly and with spirits lifted not at all, they made their way up the A6 in the direction of Bakewell.

After a few miles they turned left at the duel carriageway and made their way carefully up the narrow main road through Alton, towards the large village of Youlgreave.

"Are you okay?" said Lexi. "You seem a bit tense."

"Well Lexi, if you really want to know, I'm annoyed at that rip off meal we've just had, but it's more than that. I am very concerned by that message from Greg. What can it mean? I have this feeling that we are driving into danger and that we must both be very alert. You remember how dangerous the Peak District was when we were struggling against Dreadnought, well I feel the same apprehension and disquiet now."

They passed the cricket ground on the left, and as they reached the centre of Youlgreave, the road narrowed and the dark stonewalls and buildings seemed to hem them in even more.

It was almost like driving into a dark tunnel. Cars were parked up on both sides of the road and as they funnelled between them they expected at any moment to be met by a tractor or Land Rover.

The road ascended slowly up and out of the village with scarcely room for two pedestrians to pass until at last they reached the car park on the outskirts of the village and the road widened to a more conventional width.

"There, we made it. Does that feel better now Bladon."

"Well no Lexi, I still have this sense of foreboding. We must still be very careful."

They drove uphill for another hundred metres, in their White Nissan Juke Turbo, and as they turned left towards Ashbourne they entered a narrow muddy lane. As they continued down the lane, Bladon slowed to a crawl as he saw in front of him, eight or nine cars and vans parked along the road, leaving only just enough room to get through.

"I don't like it," said Bladon. "Normally you never see any cars parked here, and if we meet a car coming the other way, we are trapped and helpless. I am not happy. The sooner we get to the road to Ashbourne further ahead, the better."

Eleven

As he moved slowly along past the first four cars, he felt, rather than heard, the approach of a large vehicle. It sounded like a JCB or a tractor and was coming towards them very fast. Then he saw in his rear view mirror a black BMW X6 coming up behind him far too quickly.

"Darling we're trapped", Lexi said. "What can we do?"

Even as she spoke, Bladon yanked the steering wheel hard to the left, smashed a path between a Ford Transit and a Shogun and dropped off the road onto the steep sides of the typical Peakland valley below. The land was precipitous and very waterlogged and as he powered the Juke onwards it seemed to stop for a moment, but then easing up on the power it regained traction. They were so grateful for the security offered by the independent four-wheel drive and traction control.

Bladon levelled out the car at the bottom of the valley and they ploughed on along very rough terrain by the side of the rushing stream below. They looked back and saw to their horror that the black BMW was following them and even starting to catch them up.

"Your Juke, Lexi, is fantastic in 4x4, but that BMW is made for terrain like this, and it's much heavier and loves this rough marshy land. I must get us back to the road."

Bladon looked up to the road on the right and saw that it was now clear of parked cars, and as the elevated section to his right levelled out a little, he spotted a rickety old farmer's gate giving access back to the road. He pulled the wheel to the right and spoke calmly to Lexi.

"See that gate darling. I'm aiming for the road but I'm afraid it means I've got to smash through that old gate. If there's any more damage to your car, it will be paid for!"

Lexi was amazed that even under such stress he still had time to joke, but the smile was wiped from her face as she saw that the black pursuer had also changed direction, and was seeking to cut them off before they reached the gate. It was also gaining rapidly on the swampy ground. Would they make it?

Bladon wound down his driver's window as he raced for the gate and a nasty looking thug in the rear of the BMW did the same. They were now on a collision course with about five seconds to impact. He reached over to the centre console of the Juke to a plastic bag, withdrew the contents, and threw them back at the windscreen of the black destroyer, just as the thug poked a strange looking weapon out of the rear window. A messy brown substance filled the windscreen of the BMW, completely obliterating his vision, and as the driver fought desperately for control, he slewed off to the right, and ploughed into a huge hawthorn hedge and ground to a halt. The man in the rear reacted fastest and jumped out of the BMW, levelled his strange gun, and fired at the gate, just as the Juke swept through it and on up the road. The only effect of the weapon was to completely demolish what little was left of the gate, and to shred a mature oak tree standing next it.

Bladon put his foot down on the accelerator, and at the junction ahead, roared left towards Newhaven, and on to Ashbourne.

"Well done", said Lexi. "We made it to safety. But what an earth was that missile you threw at their car. It certainly did the trick."

"Actually Lexi it was very high tech. Do you remember that horrible dessert they served us at the Pheasant? I think it was Rum Baba, or something. Well it was so horrible I sneaked it into that plastic bag meaning to throw it away, but it served a much better purpose in the end!"

"I thought the head waiter gave you a withering look as you left the restaurant. Good on you darling!"

"I know, the pompous twit, but we are not safe yet Lexi. There's another black BMW hot on our tail. Look. They must have at least two of them. Let's see what your old bus will do. "

On the face if it, the BMW should have had far more power than Lexi's small Nissan Juke, but this was no basic, bog standard version. Few knew that in collaboration between Nissan and a specialist rallying company, they had somehow shoehorned under the bonnet the massively powerful engine from the Nissan sports car, and completely redesigned the body shell. Lexi's Juke R, had this up-rated engine and tweaked suspension, and it could reach 60 mph in less than 4 seconds. It was a phenomenal speedster.

Twelve

And so began a headlong chase, down the country roads, towards the Buxton to Ashbourne road at Newhaven.

The road they were on was undulating, but ran straight as a die for two miles, until it reached the little hamlet of Friden and on to Newhaven. Bladon knew that there was one or maybe two BMW's behind him but he had a plan to evade them. The X6 drew closer until it was only about 100 metres behind them and then Bladon reached down and switched to sports mode on the Juke. Instantly the front of the car almost rose off the ground with the surge of power. He floored the accelerator and their speed rose from 50 to 70 to 100 and on to 130 on the country road. It was very scary as small roads criss-crossed their progress regularly, but he reluctantly kept up his headlong rush down the road.

He had to put some distance between himself and the X6 for his plan to work. The distance steadily increased to 200 metres, then 400 metres until they were about 1000 metres ahead, with the BMW X6 straining and failing to keep up. Although the road was straight, when it dipped in places the X6 lost sight of them, until they came after two miles to a sharp left bend in the road, and four austere terraced dwellings on the right. This was the little hamlet of Friden, where they rushed past the houses under a bridge carrying the High Peak Trail, and immediately opposite the entrance to a huge cement factory on the right they turned a sharp left onto a Tarmac entrance road, swung left again and powered the Juke into the car park of the High Peak trail.

Bladon parked quickly at the far end of the car park, right

next to the old disused railway line, which had now been transformed into a walkers' and cyclists' paradise, cutting through the raw beauty of the wonderful upland country of the White Peak moorlands. He found a space right at the end of a cluster of five cars and tucked in so that at first glance the Juke could not be seen from the entrance.

He switched off the engine and they waited.

"I think we've lost them," said Bladon. "We'll give them about fifteen minutes and then we'll retrace our steps and approach the Black Swan from a different direction altogether. I need to check something out first though," and with that he got out of the car and mysteriously disappeared down the track to his right returning three minutes later.

Meanwhile, the "pursuer in black" came belatedly to the little hamlet, roared past the four houses, under the bridge, past the factory and the entrance to the Trail, and on to the Newhaven to Cromford A5012 road.

"We've missed them," said the driver of the X6. "Have they gone right or left. Let's see."

They moved out onto the road and turned right towards Newhaven, which was a rather grand name for a dilapidated old house and a filling station. The road split into two to join the Ashbourne to Buxton main road, and between the two prongs was a triangular green space where another identical BMW X6 stood awaiting their arrival. They were so positioned that they could see any vehicle that approached them.

"Have you seen their Juke?" asked the passenger in the pursuing BMW X6.

"No. We've been waiting here for thirty minutes and we've seen no sign of them. They've certainly not come this way."

"Well they must have hidden somewhere nearby, between here and Friden. You go down towards Cromford, in case they evade us, and block off the road at Graymile. Let's go."

The X6 returned to Friden and there on the left was the large factory complex, where cement was produced leaving an incredible scar on this beautiful countryside. They noticed a gatehouse where new entries were carefully checked in and various offices and stores dotted around the edge of the road, but the driver continued on a short distance, stopped his car and turned to the three others.

"I don't know about you, but I don't fancy drawing attention to ourselves do you?"

They murmured their assent. He looked around for a moment and he spotted the sign to the picnic area of the High Peak Trail.

"What about the car park over there? Shall we take a look? Have they gone up there? If they have, they are cornered, like a rat in a trap. Let's just check."

Bladon and Lexi decided to wait a further five minutes before leaving, when to their distress they spotted a black X6 drawing cautiously into the car park. They hadn't been spotted yet, but if they stayed where they were, they would soon be trapped.

"We're in real trouble now Bladon."

"Yes, Lexi, but we're not finished yet," and with that he switched on the engine, and slowly, so as not to draw attention to themselves, he eased the Juke out onto the Trail and turned downhill in the direction of the hamlet of Pikehall just a mile away. They would be in plain view of their pursuers for just ten seconds, but that was the critical time, until the Trail turned sharply left downhill. It was their moment of greatest danger.

Whilst Bladon freewheeled down the steepening slope, so as not to draw the attention of the BMW, Lexi craned round in her seat and watched for any reaction from the car, now in plain view. The driver and front passenger had got out of the car and were in animated conversation when a third man joined them, looked up…. and saw the Juke about to disappear down the Trail.

The chase was on.

"Oh no," said Lexi. "They're going to catch us easily along here. It's too narrow and steep to use our speed and if they have their gun with them we're helpless. "

But Bladon was oblivious to her concerns. He pushed down hard on the accelerator and roared round the corner of the trail for fifty metres through a sort of metal gate or vehicle trap, and then conducted an emergency stop.

"There is an automatic locking mechanism on this car trap, but sometimes the Peak Park Wardens leave it open if they're returning later. I checked it earlier and thankfully it was unlocked so I opened it up in case I needed a quick and safe exit. We did need it Lexi! I'm going to lock it behind us and it will stop them following us."

They drove as quickly as they dared down the Trail through glorious countryside, way up in the high moorlands, with the comforting sounds of skylarks rising in the thin air, until after about a mile of slow descent they came to a place where the Trail intersected the A5012 further down towards Cromford.

They joined the road and went through the little hamlet of Grangemill where five roads met, and continued in the direction of Cromford. They were now on a road rapidly descending through a picturesque heavily wooded valley, known as Via Gellia. The road dropped from 240 metres to sea level in under four miles and it was a cyclist's paradise—except for the traffic of course! You could actually free wheel from Pikehall at 300 metres high all the way down to Cromford, about seven miles in all. It was a wonderful experience.

He had been down this road with his first wife Sarah. She had been savagely murdered on a desolate isolated beach in Norfolk in the midst of a winter snowstorm, and although he was idyllically happy with his new wife, Lexi, he still missed Sarah and this place brought back memories of times spent together. His imagination was reliving the phone message he received under the light from the pub. It was less than two years ago, but with all that had happened since it seemed like an age.

It simply said, "Help darling. Please." He could remember running till his lungs burst with fear and anguish, but still

Twelve

he pushed on through the terrible conditions. As he turned down the little lane to the beach he remembered that across the greyness of the approaching sea there was no barrier to the assaults from Siberia except this remote and desolate coast. As he rounded the bend the full force of the storm hit him and almost knocked him backwards onto the sand. He peered across the cauldron of wind, sand, spray and snow and there against the breakwater, huddled forward against the savage assault of winter was Sarah.

He remembered as if it was yesterday, how she looked strangely vulnerable alone on that bleak stretch of beach, and yet at the same time some sixth sense warned him of danger. Why did she think they should meet here? He looked around at the lonely scene before him; it was still imprinted painfully on his mind, but what other danger than winter's serried ranks of warriors could there be in this place at midnight? Every part of him wanted to rush over to her immediately, but it could be a trap for both of them, so he dropped slowly to the sand and surveyed the scene.

The snow was now slanting in viciously from the sea, towards the dunes to his right, which were now almost obliterated by whiteness, and only visible when the wind dropped. The sand was changing hue before his eyes from sandy yellow to bright white, and the sea was becoming a cauldron, a maelstrom, of foaming power churning and breaking malevolently on the steep shore; and yet still Sarah made no move to find a more sheltered sanctuary. He realised with rising panic that something was wrong and jumping to his feet he ran towards her, heeding nothing. As he drew near, he noticed that she seemed unnaturally still and very pale in the light of the winter moon. He called, but his cry was swept away by the raging elements. He redoubled his efforts against the Siberian wind and as he drew near he looked straight into her lifeless eyes. A thin line across her neck leaked her precious lifeblood and he realised that she was dead.

The grey foaming waters threw themselves on the beach, and above that, the snow was driving harder and harder towards him, but he could see nothing. He peered though the driving snow again, but this time noticed a strange ship on the periphery of his vision, then it was gone leaving him wondering if it was real, or a figment of his imagination. It had not been long since he had left the SAS, but it was the start of the most difficult and dangerous days of his life. The fight against Dreadnought.

He remembered what his old Sarge at Hereford had taught him, time after time, particularly in his SAS training in the Brecon Beacons and the Black Mountains in South Wales. He used to say, "Try to see things differently, beyond the normal view. You are good Bladon, if not the best, but you must learn to be more instinctive and proactive." He told me to take the fight to the enemy, and his favourite dictum was, "Firepower by itself won't do it. Learn to turn your hunter into the prey."

He needed to relearn that lesson now.

Thirteen

"What's the matter darling," said Lexi. "You seem far away?"

"I'm sorry Lexi. It's just that Sarah and I used to come down here on our bikes. I'm sorry."

"No, don't be sorry darling. From all I've heard of her, Sarah was a very special lady. What do you remember?"

"Well, before we were married we used to stop at Youth Hostels nearby, and cycle or walk all over the Peak District. I remember one holiday where we spent a night or two at Hartington Hall, in the delightful little tourist trap of Hartington Village, and then cycled to Matlock Bath hostel along this very road. It was a very steep climb up from Hartington to the main Buxton to Ashbourne road, which was not as busy as it is now, and then we turned right and down to Newhaven where we got on this road. We stopped along the road at Pikehall, and found a panoramic picnic spot nearby, which was actually on the same Trail as the one we've just got off, but further south. The hostel had provided a packed lunch which we wolfed down, and then we lay in the warm sun for a while before continuing our journey."

"We went on for a mile, and then started downhill and we never had to pedal at all again until we reached the town of Cromford straddling the A6."

"They were happy carefree days Lexi, but they couldn't last. Who would have guessed that I would find such happiness again with such a wonderful lady as you."

His reminiscences were interrupted by a shout from Lexi. "There's a sign showing a right turn to Idridgehay coming up."

Bladon signalled his intention to turn up the road but as it opened out they saw yet again to their disappointment another black X6 waiting for them ahead.

He cancelled his partly completed turn, and carried on down the road, until finally he reached Cromford. They stopped the car, by the duck pond to discuss their options, being careful to keep a look out for the chasing X6.

"We can turn onto the main A6 road near here, but it's a long way round and will take us a lot of time. Or we could turn right up this big hill towards Wirksworth, and on to Idridgehay, and be there in about fifteen minutes, but we risk meeting another of those black beasts," said Bladon.

"Well I'm fed up with being pushed away every time we get close to a road to the Black Swan," said Lexi. "I can't speak for you, but I say let's go straight there from now on, and not let them push us around. There must be some reason they want to keep us away from meeting Greg, and we're already thirty minutes late, so let's get our skates on"

"That's the spirit Lexi. I agree. But let's expect the worst".

They turned right onto a B road, up the very steep hill towards Wirksworth. At the top of the climb Bladon pulled in to a car park of Black Rocks, a small outcrop of rocks on which he had once got stuck in his schoolboy days. He parked in the far corner away from the few cars near the entrance to the rocks, and got out of the Juke. He lifted the tailgate and removed the spare wheel and took out from the wheel cavity two small bundles of cloth. He rejoined Lexi, and carefully unwrapped two automatic pistols, gave one to her and put the other in his pocket, ensuring firstly that they were loaded, but on safety.

They turned back onto the road, and finally reached the market town of Wirksworth, a cross between an austere north Derbyshire mining village, and a town left behind by time, stuck in the fifties. They made good progress through the town, and passing by grey, sombre, council houses on both sides of the road, they left the town and crossed the railway bridge back into rolling countryside, peopled by sheep and cattle.

After a few miles, the road turned left over the railway line and on towards Duffield and the City of Derby. Then they turned right before a picturesque bridge over the railway line, to follow the signs to Idridgehay. As they approached their elusive destination at last, they saw the flashing blue lights of Police and Ambulance crews, and just before the Black Swan they saw a roadblock was in place.

"I do hope it's not Greg," said Lexi with some prescience.

They continued into the little village, past the Post Office and Store, until signalled to stop by a policeman, so they pulled into the side of the road and both got out.

Bladon started to walk round the roadblock obstructing the road, but the young constable stopped him.

"Sorry sir. No one is allowed through at the moment. There's been an accident."

"We have an urgent meeting with our friend at the Black Swan pub," said Bladon. "Please let us through."

"I'm sorry sir, that's not possible at the moment."

Bladon insisted, but a Police Inspector, dressed in full dress uniform, stopped them both.

"You can't come through."

"I've told him that sir, but he insists."

"Look here civilian", said the Inspector imperiously. "I am Inspector Fordingley and you are making me very angry and that is not a wise thing to do. Get in your car and take a detour, the longer the better."

"But it's most urgent that we get to the Black Swan", said Bladon. "It's a matter of life and death."

"Right. I've had enough. Unless you're gone in less than ten seconds I'm arresting you for obstruction."

Bladon finally lost his cool. He drew two cards from his wallet and pushed them under the Inspector's nose.

"Now listen very carefully you stupid, pompous, idiot. Unless you let this lady and me through immediately I am calling your Chief Constable and by tonight you will be busted down in rank to a constable on the beat. Do you understand? Move. Now."

The Inspector looked at the cards presented to him, sprang back in surprise and profuse apology, and turned a deathly shade of grey, ushering them through.

"Sandy's done well there," he remarked to Lexi.

"What were those cards?"

"One's an SAS identity card, and the other is Special Branch. Take your pick. All completely fictitious of course, but absolutely authentically fictitious!"

As they approached the pub car park they saw a terrible sight. It looked like a war zone. Somebody had wanted to silence Greg and they'd ensured his silence in the most brutal fashion. His body lay on the Tarmac of the pub car park beside his car, and the whole scenenario resembled a scene from troubled Bagdad. His body had been pulverised by hundreds of bullets, which had in turn totally destroyed his car. Greg would have had no way of escape as he arrived expecting to see his old friends Bladon and Lexi. The X6 with the gunman in, must have extricated itself from the hedge and gone straight on to Ashbourne, and then directly to Idridgehay and waited for Greg to arrive. These people were ruthless. Bladon struggled to control his anger and grief for his friend. That terrible weapon had been ruthlessly used again.

Bladon turned to Lexi, and the pain and sorrow and weariness was etched deeply in his grey face, but as she comforted him and spoke quietly and lovingly to her precious husband, the old Bladon started to reassert himself and he spoke with real conviction.

He phoned the Prime Minister, "They've killed Greg now, Johnny. We're at the scene at the moment. He gave me the gist of your message whilst we were at the Pheasant, particularly the information about Il Tredici, and Le Marche in Italy. They are obviously targeting The Thirteen—and you. We must stop these people, whoever they are. They must be tracking our mobile phones and landlines, or have a very extensive spy network. They must have some very sophisticated equipment. It's the only way they could have tracked our movements and Greg's. I'm going back home, and getting together as many of the team as I can, and I think it will mean a trip to Italy, and very soon too."

Fourteen

The next day a few friends started to arrive at Bladon and Lexi's spectacular home at Kedleston. Sandy was unable to come until later in the week, but Willie from the SAS team in Cornwall had made the journey and he arrived first. Wilf arrived about the same time, then John Parkin and Steve arrived together, and finally, Martyn and Stefan arrived ten minutes later. They all met together over welcome drinks in the lounge and when everyone was comfortable Bladon spoke.

"Welcome, welcome, dear friends. It's so good of you to come. Most of you will know about recent events in Cornwall and Derbyshire, and that another threat seems to have arisen in this country rather like the last struggle we had with Dreadnought. We're so sorry about the death of Greg. He's an old and faithful friend and a great loss to us all. He also had some important information for us, which he wasn't able to tell me in time. However he had spoken to Martyn and he's here tonight and might be able to shed some light on what was on Greg's mind. Thanks Martyn for coming and Stefan too, and once again, I'm so sorry about Greg.

Willie, the SAS Major, asked Bladon if he could share some news he had received that morning from Sandy.

"On the morning of our raid on Nancenoy Towers, a local patrol car on the A30, spotted three big black BMW 4x4's travelling in convoy northwards, and going very fast. Unfortunately the patrolmen didn't realise the significance of this and when it was finally reported, the cars had disappeared. We think that they had been given new instructions on the hoof, and afterwards travelled separately to an unknown destination. In view of the problems that you and Lexi have had in Derbyshire, we think they must have a base in the Peak District, maybe very close to here. We haven't found this safe house yet, but I have my men looking and also the local Derbyshire Constabulary are conducting a low profile search, but we estimate that there must be between nine and twelve of these very dangerous men at large in this area. We must be very careful. It does seem that there is a high likelihood that they have one of those terrible weapons with them. We would like to capture it—and the men too of course?"

To save time Lexi had ordered a Cantonese takeaway from a local restaurant, and as the front door bell rang, Lexi opened the door and took the food into the kitchen to get it ready for them all.

"I'll be about ten minutes," she shouted to Bladon. "So relax for a while and we'll talk over dinner".

Martyn and Stefan, in studied conversation, wandered out of the lounge towards the large patio doors, framing the wonderful view of Kedleston Park stretching as far as the eye could see. The grasslands stretched from the boundary of Bladon's property southwards, rising slowly towards the tree line, where the circular walk from Kedleston Hall wound its picturesque way towards Prestwood Farm, and the road. It was about two hundred metres from the pathway in Kedleston Park, where Bladon had first stopped and looked down over the ha-ha. The view down to the twinkling lights of Bladon's beautiful house, was a wonderful sight.

Three men, dressed all in black, lay completely still at the tree line. They had no interest in the beauty or tranquillity of the scene below them. Theirs was a much more sinister preoccupation with the house below. One of them was obviously the spotter, as he had high-powered binoculars dangling from his neck. The other two had sniper rifles, both equipped with night sight scopes.

Martyn and Stefan opened the patio doors and strolled

Fourteen

out into the garden, deep in conversation. Bladon saw the movement of the opening doors from the hall, and realising what was happening rushed out and into the room, but it was too late. As he looked out through the glass doors in helpless frustration, he saw, rather than heard two distinct flashes from the tree line above, and to his horror, saw Martyn slump to the floor and then Stefan too.

As he looked in panic at the prone figures, two more shots aimed this time at him, hit the patio doors with great velocity. Fortunately for Bladon, when renovating the house, he'd had the foresight to make sure that the doors were armour plated, and the only sign of the assassination attempt on Bladon, was two small cracks in the glass.

The room filled with his friends, but he had now composed himself sufficiently to warn them to stay inside. Then Willie, The SAS major took over.

"Please stay exactly where you are. We have the position under control."

And as he spoke Bladon noticed at least four muzzle flashes, from two SAS men lying concealed in the field, at the bottom of his garden.

"Two gunmen down," shouted the SAS sergeant, who had now taken up a kneeling position. "One more unarmed hostile to deal with, but we have operatives nearby. It is safe to see to our wounded now."

Bladon rushed through the open patio doors followed by Wilf.

"Let the dog see the bone", said Wilf in his broad Yorkshire tones, and proceeded to kneel at Martyn's side.

"I'm so sorry old pal," he whispered to Bladon. "Martyn has not made it. Your old friend is dead."

He turned to Stefan, who to everyone's delight, was trying to sit up. "Good news though. Stefan has been shot in the arm, but the bullet has exited. He's losing a lot of blood but he should be OK. Let's get him inside and call the ambulance."

There proceeded a headlong chase to capture the remaining

hostile who had now dispensed with his binoculars, and taken out his automatic pistol, and the two SAS men who had been hiding close by followed in hot pursuit.

"I hope for his sake he surrenders," said Bladon. "Otherwise it will be a very uneven fight."

Their quarry made for the path, climbed up between the tree line and the hedge, and hurried towards the road running from the village of Kedleston to the farm where he had left his car in the lee of a hedge. He rushed onto the road and had just reached his car when his two pursuers burst from the pathway onto the road.

"Put down your weapon, and put your hands palm down on the bonnet, where we can see them."

He turned and considered for a brief moment complying with their request, and then in one fluid move he dropped the pistol, pulled open the rear door of the car, and reached inside.

The SAS troopers didn't hesitate and opened up with a deadly barrage of firepower from their Uzi machine guns, and he flopped lifeless onto the road.

One of the men radioed Willy.

"I'm sorry sir. He wouldn't surrender and went for something on the back seat, and we couldn't take the risk that it was that terrible weapon, so we had to take him out."

Willie reported back to Bladon and his friends.

"It looks like we'll never know what Greg and Martyn were so worried about now," said Bladon. "But at least three more have been eliminated, but they have more men and they still have that gun."

They reluctantly and sadly finished the superb meal that Lexi had set out in the dining room. The food was delicious, but no one really enjoyed it. They were just going through the motions; as yet another friend and member of The Thirteen had been killed.

They were finishing their coffees in the lounge when the

Fourteen

doorbell rang. Willie was the first to react and he reassured them all as he made for the hall.

"I asked my men to let me know if they could find anything incriminating on the men or in their car," he said as he left the room. "I know it's early days but you never know."

The front door was closed again after ten minutes or so, and Willie returned with a pensive look on his face.

"We found nothing at all on the three men, but we did find this. It must have fallen out of a pocket and slipped under the rear seat."

He produced what looked like an old train or bus ticket but nothing that anyone recognised—it was definitely foreign.

Finally John Parkin spoke. "Can I have a look please Willie? Something is ringing a bell. It looks to be Italian. Do you mind if I scan it on my iPhone and send it to my son in Italy? I'm sure it's from there, and I have a feeling that it's very important."

The friends said their goodbyes and left. Martyn's body had been taken away, and Stefan's wife, Susan and their two sons, were with him at the local hospital. Bladon and Lexi took one last sad look towards the patio where Martyn and Stefan had fallen, and headed up to bed, burdened by this horrific turn of events.

Fifteen

The next day brought a phone call from Sandy.

"Bladon, it's Sandy here. I understand you've had some problems since you left us in Cornwall."

"You could say that Sandy, but how are you?"

"I'm back in London at the moment, but I can't talk now because I rather think the phone lines have been compromised. I understand that you've had similar problems up there. I'll call you in exactly thirty minutes from a public call box. It is very urgent."

He rang off, and thirty minutes later Bladon's mobile rang again.

"It's Sandy."

"Hi."

"Bladon, I'm so sorry to hear of the murder of Greg and Martyn. It's horrific news. I've picked up some chatter through Cheltenham on both murders and I must see you urgently. I know it's sad that two of your team have been killed but I suspect there's more to it than you might think. Greg had just returned from Italy where he does most of his buying from around the Bologna area, and whilst there he visited the Le Marché area, not too far away. Something had badly spooked him, because he urgently wanted to see Martyn, and then, lo and behold, both of them mysteriously die just after the meeting. Nobody else knows this, but before Greg met Martyn, he phoned me to talk it through, and although we were interrupted, I have some information for you that's dynamite. Can we meet tomorrow at midday? I'll meet you in the Peak District in the Leek area. I will phone you later with precise map coordinates. Bladon—you and Lexi must be very careful."

The following day, Bladon and Lexi travelled from home; a leisurely drive through Weston Underwood, Hulland Ward, Hulland, and on to the town of Ashbourne, known affectionately as the "Gateway to the Peak District." They slowly negotiated the twisting streets of the old town and taking the Buxton Road, climbed the very steep and narrow hill, until the vista opened onto a view of the glorious White Peak. They left the A515 after a mile, turned sharp left over the glistening River Dove, and on up a long winding road, tightly hedged in by woodland on the left, and tall hedges on the right.

They reached the outskirts of the tiny village of Thorpe, and with a stunning view of the impressive hill known as Thorpe Cloud guarding the way onwards, they descended another steep hill, turned sharp left by the Peveril of the Peak hotel, threaded their way though the little village and on down to a gated cattle grid, where the most beautiful view opened up before them. It was the entrance to Dovedale with its twin sentinels, the impressive hills of Thorpe Cloud and Bunster. Under Bunster was their refuge for the night, the Isaac Walton Hotel, named after the well-known author who had fished these waters just below the hotel.

They had decided that after all the dangers and deaths of the last few days they would have a short break here before seeing Sandy.

They had a good dinner of roast beef and roasted vegetables, Bladon being careful this time to take the meat as it came, and not insisting on it being well done. The last time he had dined in the restaurant the waiter had insisted the beef could only be served at the chef's discretion, but Bladon puncturing his supercilious bombast insisted it be presented well done. The waiter had the last laugh however, as they were made to wait for another thirty minutes, and when it came it was indeed well done—it was more like charcoal!

They woke early and after breakfast put on their walking boots and made their way towards Dovedale. They walked by the river until they reached the famous Stepping Stones and crossed the river.

"They look different since the last time I was here," said Lexi.

"Yes." said Bladon. "It's the dreaded 'elf and safety' brigade. These stones have been enjoyed by so many over countless years, but the bureaucrats decided they were dangerous, and then totally spoiled them with new mortar and new stones on top. It's scandalous."

They climbed over the stile on the far side of the river, and on up the valley. It was so peaceful and quiet at this time in the morning before the crowds arrived from the large conurbations of Derby, Nottingham, and Sheffield, and they strolled together up to Lovers Leap before retracing their steps to the bottom of Thorpe Cloud.

"Bladon," Lexi said quietly, almost apologetically. "I'm still worried that we are getting dragged into all that horror again like last year. I know Dreadnought is dead, but I still have deep foreboding about meeting up with Sandy. I've had enough danger and excitement to last me a lifetime. Do you understand?"

Bladon turned to her and seeing how upset she was, gently held her and reassured her.

"Lexi, darling, I do not intend to take you into any danger again. You are far too precious to be put into harms way. I was just concerned about the deaths of our two friends, but we'll just listen to what Sandy has to say, see if we can give him any useful information, and then get back to our lives again."

"Thank you darling, I am so pleased you said that."

Little did they know what lay ahead ....

They continued their walk up Thorpe Cloud and down into

the little village of Thorpe, not realizing how close they were to their enemies' base nearby; then they walked down the valley and back to the hotel. They were just enjoying a well-deserved coffee when Bladon's phone rang.

It was Sandy's voice. "OS OL 24056613—12 sharp".

Bladon reached for the two Peak District maps on the dining room table.

"OL means the big outdoor leisure double-sided maps. Lets have a look—oh yes number 1 is the Dark Peak and number 24 is the White Peak."

He found the reference on the map—it was a little farm called Lower Evergreen. He pointed it out to Lexi.

"Sandy must be very concerned about them tracing his call—he's only given us an hour. We'll have to rush. I want to reconnoitre the area first."

They left the hotel in their car at 11.00am, descending slowly down the hotel drive, past grazing sheep and inquisitive cattle. They then turned right onto a the narrow road which had dropped sharply from Thorpe on the left, and then wound alongside the River Manifold into the tiny hamlet of Ilam, scene of their titanic struggle with Dreadnought the previous year. At the entrance to Ilam Manor they took the right fork up towards Stanshope.

They continued as the road rose steadily with Bunster Hill rising majestically on their right. They passed evocatively named farms and tiny settlements along the way called Steeple House, Ilamtops Farm, Beechenhill, Damgate, Hopedale, and Mamtops, climbing steadily along the narrow winding road all the way to Alstonfield. Here they took the road where it forked northwest, cruising over the undulating road by lush sheep grazed pastures, down, down, until finally the road met the Warslow to Hartington road by the popular little pub on the river at Hulme End. The journey over the top from Alstonfield had been exhilarating and it seemed to Lexi that they were on the roof of the world as they sped past Galham Farm, Paddock House Farm and Alstonfield Moor Farm, before they dropped down steeply almost 100 metres to the river.

At Hulme End they took the left turn towards the village of Warslow, a dour, dark, depressing place, and then on up again to the north west and the lonely moorlands where Sandy would be waiting. The road climbed up in a straight line towards their destination rising steadily all the way, until it brought them to a long straight road to Shawfield and Little Fennyford. The road dropped down again and they looked across to the north and west to the incredible beauty of the moorland in late summer, as the deep purple flowers of the heather peatlands vied with the verdant green pastureland of the moorland.

"What a wild and yet beautiful place this is", said Lexi.

It was a haven for all kinds of wildlife and as Lexi noticed a large hare hop quickly across the road, Bladon spotted a rare Merlin, a smaller bird of prey, often found in these uplands. They pulled up at the side of the road and Bladon pointed out, next to them, a quaint little contraption for fighting fires on the moors. It was a bit like a broomstick and a bucket, but it looked fit for purpose. On either side stretched vista after vista of rolling moorlands, the delicate shades of purple shimmering in the gusting wind.

From the bottom of the road they climbed steadily up towards their ultimate destination, against a mixture of green, purple and brown. The road branched off to the right, but almost immediately an unfenced road turned off to the left and wound sharply uphill towards the bleak moorland nearly 500 metres above sea level.

"This moorland is owned and used by the Ministry of Defence as a live firing range, and a huge area between this road and the Buxton to Leek road is clearly marked on the map as a danger area," said Bladon.

He thought, but didn't voice his concerns, that those words could indeed be prophetic ones for them all before the day was done. His instincts were telling him that it was getting dangerous.

Almost at the bottom of the road was a little turn off on the left marked to Little Fleargrass, their ultimate destination, but Bladon was still fifteen minutes early and he wanted to reconnoitre the immediate area. He continued northwest until he reached another unfenced road between the hamlets of Newton and the firing range, which formed a crossroads. He took the left turn and following the road southwards just past a little row of houses named, he hoped not literally, Folly.

The road split and he took the wider road down to the isolated and dreary looking pub called The Mermaid. He had heard stories about this place as a youngster cycling in the Peak District, and he could imagine that in the dead of winter, with an icy mist surrounding it, it would be a forbidding place indeed. The pub did, however, give a wonderful vantage point for miles around, straight across the Buxton to Leek road to the west, and to the village of Upper Hulme with Tittlesworth reservoir below, and then higher up to the impressive rocky outcrop called, the Roaches. 'Hen Cloud' stood majestic at the beginning of the Roaches and he could see, even at this distance, rock climbers on the escarpment just north of Doxey pool. Just a little higher, adjacent to the road and just below Ramshaw Cottage, were the impressive Ramshaw rocks, a shark-toothed, dragon-like assortment of rocks that were featured in the H. G. Wells film version of War of the Worlds.

He studied the landscape to the west for any movement or anything suspicious or out of place. Satisfied that no danger lurked, Bladon eased the car back onto the tarmac, and rejoined the one he had left near Accringlow, cutting back in an easterly direction towards Warslow. He stopped just as the road began to plunge steeply between the heather clad moors. He had effectively circumlocuted his ultimate destination in a lozenge like shape, and had been able to check it from every direction.

He stopped, took out his binoculars and surveyed the ground to his left. Lower Evergreen was a substantial farmhouse; approximately 200 years old, built of Derbyshire stone and slate, and although the house looked weatherproof, it seemed to be unoccupied.

Fifteen

They remained perfectly still, lying low in the grass for five minutes watching the house. Nothing moved, neither animal, bird, nor human.

Bladon whispered to Lexi, "It looks clear; I think we can go?" So they drove down to the farm.

Sixteen

The farm and the outbuildings enclosed three sides of a large courtyard; on the north side stood the farmhouse itself, and on the east and west sides stood two buildings in various states of disrepair, which seemed to have been used for sheltering cattle.

They approached from the south and left their car adjacent to the west barn, after Bladon had positioned the car ready for a quick exit. They warily approached the front door of the farmhouse, a big impressive oak edifice with a small peephole near the top.

No sound, no movement at all, just a sepulchral silence. Bladon tried the door. It opened easily with a loud creak, which must have been heard across the entire valley, and then they both stepped inside to a large dark, dank, and echoey hallway. They stood perfectly still for about sixty seconds, letting the silence settle around them once more.

There was nobody there.

But then, Bladon felt, rather than saw, one of the shadows on the wall move almost imperceptibly, and Sandy stepped forward.

"I'm pleased to see that none of your skills have deserted you old friend", said Bladon, and they greeted each other again warmly.

"Come into the dining room, or what's left of it," said Sandy, and together they entered a large room with damp, peeling and faded wallpaper, trying desperately to stay in contact with the spore spotted, green walls, and failing miserably to do so. A large oak table was still set for six, but the plates and cutlery were thick with dust and decay.

Bladon dusted off a chair for Lexi and the three of them sat around the far end of the table.

"Well, what's so urgent," said Bladon.

Before replying, Sandy got up and looked out of the dirt caked windowpanes of the high set window frame. He stood silently surveying the moor for a long time until satisfied, and then he sat back down with them both again.

"As you know, I am the Prime Minister's aide now, and we have been very concerned about the attempt on his life, the terrible events in Cornwall and the deaths of Greg and Martyn. We have also been getting some confidential information from MI5 and MI6 about attempts to compromise SAS communications in Hereford, and some rather nasty characters seen again in the UK, and rather worryingly, in Italy too. If I didn't know that Dreadnought had been killed in that helicopter crash, I would say that this has his evil fingerprints all over it. It must be bad for MI5 and MI6 to volunteer any information. We are tracing the rest of The Thirteen and keeping a close eye on them, but the really sinister development is that MI6 have heard the words, 'Il Tredici', cropping up a lot in a remote area of Le Marche in Italy. That's an area between the Adriatic and the Apennine mountains.

"Il Tredici. That's what Greg referred to in his phone call to us at the Pheasant, but he was killed before we could reach him?"

"It means, as you've probably worked out, The Thirteen," said Sandy. "The number of your little band, including the bravest of them all of course, Lexi. It's those who attacked Dreadnought in that final battle at Ilam Manor. Tell me more about that Bladon. It could have a bearing on recent events."

"It's a long story Sandy. You must know some of it. Are you sure you want to go over old ground again."

"Yes. It could trigger something for all three of us."

"Well," said Bladon, "The Thirteen was a small group of

friends that I put together to try and foil the most dangerous plot against the country since the Second World War. The mastermind behind it was a shadowy figure known only as Dreadnought. His identity was a secret known only to a few in the top echelons of his mysterious nefarious organisation, but Sir Christopher, who was Minister of Defence, and an old school friend of my first wife, had found out not only his identity, but details of his Machiavellian plot to take over the country through a deadly virus he had developed. Sir Christopher had been ruthlessly killed, but had been shrewd enough to commit photos of Dreadnought, and the formulae for the virus, onto a wooden jigsaw puzzle, which he then parcelled up into small lots and left with a few friends just in case something should happen to him.

Dreadnought's men had then killed my first wife, Sarah, who had witnessed Sir Christopher's assassination, and then I met Lexi, and together we fought back. Over time, and through many dangers, we painstakingly traced separate batches of the puzzle pieces in places like Milan, London, Scotland, Cornwall, Norfolk and Switzerland, until finally we were able to put the puzzle together and identify the virus and the evil mastermind. We finally traced Dreadnought to his headquarters in Ilam Manor, not far from Thorpe, and with the help of our friends, The Thirteen, we attacked the headquarters, destroyed the virus, and as he tried to escape, Dreadnought's helicopter was shot down by a Stinger missile, fired as a last resort by Lexi, and sent to his death as the fireball fell to the earth.

"Wow," said Sandy, "I didn't realise what a close run thing it was and how brave you were. Well done. Obviously the PM knows all the details, and I believe he was himself directly involved in the endgame. We are both very concerned, particularly by the latest developments. The Prime Minister wants to see you both in London again as soon as possible. He's asked if you could come to London and stay at Claridges, at his expense, and then meet him for breakfast the next morning.

But secondly, and the PM will expand on this when he

sees you, he wants to contact the rest of The Thirteen, not only to warn them personally, but to see if they can add anything to our Intel so far, and maybe find any other hot spots where the opposition is in this country. MI6 have a watching brief in Italy and you'll be kept in the loop. I'm sorry Bladon. It doesn't look good."

Lexi spoke and voiced all their fears. "Oh dear. I thought this was all over, but it seems to be starting up again. Why? Is there a remnant of Dreadnought's organisation that we didn't eradicate last year? Are they looking for revenge? Or is it more than that? Surely they can't do that without leadership and we saw Dreadnought die in that helicopter nearby?"

Sandy replied, "I am cleared to the very top, to try and work out a strategy with you both. It's important that..."

A massive shockwave ripped through the room, and then Bladon's voice rang out clearly in the still echoing room.

"Down on the floor—now."

As the dust cleared they saw to their horror that the whole of the outside wall of the dining room had disappeared, and in its place was a pile of smouldering rubble.

"What on earth was that?" whispered Sandy to Bladon. "Was it an RPG or an anti-tank shell? It's destroyed the whole of the side of the building."

Bladon replied, "I don't think so Sandy. It looks suspiciously like the weapon we came up against in Cornwall, only this time at much closer range. It looks to me like the house has been hit by thousands of 'bullets.' I think it's happening again."

Sandy replied, "Okay, let's prepare ourselves for an imminent attack. If they are any good at all, they'll follow up with a fully synchronised assault. What weapons do we have? I have a small revolver but nothing heavy. What about you Bladon?"

"I've only got a pistol myself. I didn't expect anything like this."

"You are completely surrounded by overwhelming force,"

Sixteen

a disembodied, metallic voice, bellowed out.

"Come out slowly with your hands above your head and do exactly as I say. You will not be harmed."

Silence.

"I don't think we have any option but to do as he says," whispered Bladon.

They picked their way over the rubble, dusty, bedraggled, and forlorn, and shuffled into the middle of the courtyard, with the remains of the farmhouse behind them. In front of them they saw seven sinister figures in black combat suits covering them. Three of them stood on the west side, and three on the east side, all with assault rifles, and between them stood a tall, commanding figure, holding a strange weapon, which was presumably the cause of their precarious predicament. It looked at first sight like an ordinary assault rifle, but it was very far from ordinary. It was Leo and all of his men from Thorpe. They were trapped.

"You have all been under observation for some time. Do not make any silly moves. My men are all professionals and will not hesitate to kill you. I don't want that to happen, but be warned. I only want to talk. Tell me exactly what you were discussing in the farmhouse."

"We have a real problem here," whispered Bladon. "They're not going to let us walk away from here. Have you any ideas Sandy?"

The silence was all consuming. Behind them a kitchen curtain fluttered out of the partly demolished parlour window and a jug clattered to the floor.

Sandy let the silence settle again and then stepped forward.

"Put your weapons down. Unless you do, you have only 5 seconds to live."

The leader replied sarcastically, "You are hardly in a position to give us an ultimatum Colonel."

Sandy replied, "5—4—3—2—1".

Seventeen

The heads of all seven hostiles dissolved in a hail of bullets.

"What was that," said Bladon, as he walked over to the leader to check his vital signs.

"Well," said Sandy, smiling, "You don't think I'd come out here without backup do you old friend?"

"What do you mean?" asked Bladon, as Lexi joined him.

Sandy waved a hand towards the surrounding moorland, and to Bladon's surprise twelve camouflage-clad warriors rose from the heather and walked towards the courtyard.

"Why do you think I arranged the meet for today at 12", said Sandy?

"A company of the West Mercia is exercising on the live firing range today, so it wasn't too difficult to get a detachment of SAS to go along with them as observers. They are the same men who helped us in Cornwall, including their Major, Willie, who's in charge. I arranged for twelve of them to slip away and wait for any possible developments."

"Well done," said Lexi. "You saved our lives today Sandy."

"You're welcome Lexi. What are friends for? But I do believe they've made their first mistake and it's quite a big one. We have the gun, and we've been after one of those for ages. I'll get it up to Hereford, and the experts can take it apart and find out what secrets it's hiding."

The next day, after their ordeal, Bladon and Lexi left Derby Midland Station at 12.05 pm and at 1.40 pm pulled into the magnificently refurbished St. Pancras International Station.

Leaving the platform and walking past the impressive statue of poet John Betjeman, they quickly found a black cab, and precisely two hours after leaving Derby, they found themselves close to the famous Claridges Hotel.

"Do you know the history of Claridges," said Bladon?

"No, not really," Lexi replied.

"Well, I've been reading about it on the train whilst you had a nap. Mr. and Mrs. William Claridge bought the hotel in 1854, and six years later they received the ultimate accolade when Queen Victoria visited the hotel to see her friend Empress Eugenie of France. That was the beginning of a tradition of royal visits, which continues today. In fact it's even been called the annex to Buckingham Palace. I'm really looking forward to staying there.

It's been popular with Kings, Presidents, Prime Ministers, and millionaires the world over and it's also attracted most of the Golden names of Hollywood over the years including Yul Brynner, Audrey Hepburn, Cary Grant and Bing Crosby. In fact Spencer Tracy once remarked, not that I intend to die, but when I do, I don't want to go to heaven; I want to go to Claridges.

It will be exciting just to tread where the famous have trod before. Wait till you see the wonderful art deco foyer. It's fantastic with a black and white, chequered, highly polished marble floor, which matches the marble pillars and polished mahogany woodwork."

"I can't wait," said Lexi. "I've always wanted to stay there."

They checked in and made their way to the lift. The lift to their floor was stunning. The attendant pulled back the doors for them both and to their surprise a liveried doorman, who ushered them to a full-length velvet bench, greeted them. It was the first time they had been seated in a lift!

In their room they rested after their journey; and at seven they walked into the famous Reading Room Restaurant, and then on through to the dining room proper. Under monochrome photographs of Princess Margaret, the Duke and Duchess of Windsor and the Queen Mother, they were ushered to their table. What really impressed them about the restaurant were the large and comfortable easy chairs, but also the pillars, which were covered in rich antique red leather.

They chose their starters from the extensive menu and Lexi chose a veloute of organic fennel soup, with a lemon, thyme, beignet, and Bladon chose a ham, pea, and foie gras risotto, with truffle nage.

"To be perfectly honest, Lexi, this is a bit disappointing. The risotto is just a bit too bland for my taste, and I don't like the foie gras. It's the first time I've tasted it and it's a big disappointment. How's your soup?"

"Delicious thanks. Sorry about yours."

For the main course, they both chose Tournedos of Aberdeen Angus, with truffles, butternut squash purée, and pecorino gnocchi. This time, Bladon waxed lyrical about his main course.

"The beef was delicious; so tender and succulent, and perfectly cooked, but what was a revelation to me was the gnocchi. I don't think it would be too much of an exaggeration to say that before today, I hated gnocchi. My friend John Parkin's Italian mother in law, a wonderful cook, made it to a homemade Northern Italian recipe and it was delicious—to everybody except me, I'm afraid. I also remember vividly, the time I was dining in the best hotel in Bologna, the Baglioni, and I saw with excitement that one of the starters was potato dumplings. I ordered it and with great anticipation lifted the first forkful to my mouth. What a disappointment. It was gnocchi!"

He pulled his thoughts back to the present as he tried another forkful of gnocchi; this was so different. It was absolutely wonderful. He called the Maitre d' over, and explained the reasons for his long-standing antipathy towards gnocchi, but then explained how wonderful this was. He thanked Bladon, and then explained that it was made from semolina and then baked in the oven.

They chose their desserts. Lexi chose red berries salad,

with champagne granita, and Bladon chose roast apricot, and chocolate mousse, with Verbena ice cream, then they relaxed in the bar with a coffee.

Johnny, the Prime Minister, phoned Bladon when they returned to their room.

"Hi Bladon. Give my love to Lexi. You've really been through the wars again haven't you? Can we meet for breakfast tomorrow at the Langham Hotel, instead of Claridges? I've arranged a secure private room there. It's not far. Say eight. "

The next morning Bladon and Lexi walked from Claridges to the Langham. They walked up Regent Street, past the wonderful Nash designed church of All Souls Langham Place, and into the foyer of the Langham Hotel. The main dining room was impressive but they were ushered into a side room, and as they entered they saw that Johnny had already arrived and had started on some toast and coffee. They passed four heavily armed Met officers and greeted Johnny with a warm embrace.

Johnny spoke immediately. "I am concerned about two matters. Firstly, this gun and the problems over its possible development in Italy. Secondly the attacks on The Thirteen, resulting in close calls for you two, and the death of Martyn and Greg, and the attempted murder of Stefan. I want to hand this whole matter over to you if I may, despite opposition from the Met and Special Branch, and although personally you will have my full support, it will be a completely deniable operation, because of the problems on the Italian side. Can you live with that? It will be very like your last adventure against Dreadnought. I will put the SAS, your old unit in fact, on standby for if you need urgent back up, as you did in Cornwall, but that's a last resort. Is that understood?"

"Perfectly," replied Bladon, with a twinkle in his eye.

The P.M. continued, "I've been speaking to Cobra and the Commanding officer of the SAS and I suggest that you approach it on two fronts—both very dangerous ones. Firstly I suggest you get over to Italy yourself to try and resolve what's happening over there, but secondly we need to ascertain what the threat level is in this country. If I didn't know that Dreadnought had been killed in that helicopter crash in Derbyshire last year, I might have thought that it was him looking for revenge. But it can't be him. We need to know whether there are any enemy forces over here after their setbacks in Cornwall and Derbyshire; whether they are doing development work on the weapon over here; and also whether there is still a major threat to the other Eleven. Finally, we need to know whether Italy is their main base or whether they have relocated over here."

Bladon looked thoughtful. "I agree with your summary Johnny, and I suggest I take Lexi and Wilf and get over to Italy as soon as possible to find out what's going on. I'll book us on to the next plane from Gatwick to Bologna and then we'll hire a car to get to the Le Marche region. We'll need to do it surreptitiously though, or our cover will be blown.

Secondly, can I ask you to redouble all your efforts on the intelligence front please? We need MI5 and MI6, and also Special Branch at the airports and ports. We need to know whether any more hostiles are coming in, and also what forces they already have here, but most importantly, where they are. We have got to find them. I have a hunch that the East Midlands is an important base for them, and I also think they could even be doing development work here too, in parallel with Italy.

Thirdly, and critically, we must put all of the rest of The Thirteen on full alert, but more importantly, use them all on a search mission, to try and locate the enemies headquarters. I can't help but feel that their main base of operations will be in the Nottingham, Derby, Burton, and Chesterfield areas, especially as all their attacks so far have been around Derby and the Peak District, since we closed down their place in Cornwall.

What Lexi and I intend to do first, is go back home and brief the team. Whilst we are away in Italy I will ask Andy to head up a team to go after these people. I'm suggesting Andy, Patrick and John, with Willie from the SAS; and Phillip,

Stefan, and Sandy too if that's OK. I'll also ask John if he has any more information on some disturbing incidents that have apparently been occurring in Urbino, a city in Le Marche, where his son Riley lives."

"OK, Bladon. Keep me informed. I ..."

A frantic pushing at the partitions, and raised voices, stopped Johnny in mid sentence.

"What's going on Filby? I told you we are not to be disturbed."

"I know sir, but this man is insisting he knows you and Mr Bladon, sir."

"Who is it," grunted the P.M., rapidly losing his temper.

A face peered round the partition. It was John Parkin. "Is that anyway to talk to an old friend, Johnny."

Johnny leapt to his feet and flung his arm around the newcomer. He was one of his oldest friends, and one who had been seriously injured in the firefight the previous year when Bladon and The Thirteen had attacked Ilam Manor in order to save the country from the evil Dreadnought. He was a Chartered Accountant by day, who practised in a small Derbyshire market town, but he was one of Bladon's most stalwart companions. His son, Riley, lived in Italy, with his wife Gaia and their two thirteen-year-old twins, Leone and Arco.

"I'm so sorry to interrupt you Johnny. Bladon told me in confidence that he was meeting you in London but I tried Claridges first. Please forgive me, and you too please officer, I know you have heard of the disappearance of that Oxford Professor in Italy but I've been speaking to my son, Riley, on the phone and I'm sure it's all linked to our recent adventures, and that terrible weapon. My son Riley lives in the Le Marche region, in the capital Urbino, and he has been telling me about some strange things happening nearby. Riley's friend who lives in the same area, has a father who is a Professor, who normally lives in Oxford, but has also bought a place in Italy to be near his son. Their children go to the same school. The rumour is that the Professor is involved in very hush

hush work for the Italian Government, or possibly a foreign government, and rumours mention some sort of military application.

Anyway, the strange thing is, the Professor seems to have disappeared about three months ago. One day he was fine, and playing with his grandchildren at his house, and the next he just vanished. His son, Giacomo, asked Riley for help in finding him, with little success. However, Riley and Giacomo had obviously been getting too close for comfort, as Giacomo's children have just been threatened and my thirteen-year old twin grandsons have also just narrowly escaped kidnap themselves. They had been coming out of school when an attempt was made to snatch them, but Riley and his wife Gaia, had turned up to fetch them out from school ten minutes earlier than usual, and had been able to thwart the attempt and stopped the thugs at the school gates. Gaia had pulled them both back from the would-be kidnappers, who then attacked Gaia in turn, but Riley had been able to intervene and fight them off. It had been a close run thing though, and both Gaia and Riley were badly shaken. He wants me out there as soon as possible, but he asked if Bladon and Lexi could come too."

Bladon and Lexi and Johnny looked at each other in amazement.

Bladon took the lead. "That's very interesting John. We really seem to be getting somewhere at last. We have just been discussing this very matter. But I have the feeling that it's going to be really dangerous out there. We must be very careful. The opposition seem to know every step we take, even before we do, so let's keep this very much on a need to know, basis. You can be sure they'll know our next step is to go over to Italy, so let's confuse them. I intended to fly with Lexi and Wilf from Gatwick, but I bet they've got the airport sewn up. I know it's a big ask because he's got a business to run, but he was brilliant in Cornwall, so I wonder if you could you ask your neighbour, Steve, if he'll fly me, Lexi and Wilf, directly to Urbino, so we can get there undetected. In the meantime John, could you please fly to Ancona from Stansted, as you won't attract any suspicion just going out to see your son? We'll all meet up when you arrive. I don't want to involve your son, or his boys, or his friend, as I sense it will be very dangerous there, but you know the area too. We're going back to Derby tonight for a meeting with the rest of The Thirteen so why not come back with us and then fly straight away to Italy."

John phoned Steve on Bladon's behalf, as his train passed through Bedford, after making sure they could not be overheard. Steve was a good friend of John, and they had known each other during the Desert Storm operation in Iraq, where Steve had flown ground attack aircraft during the difficult early days. He and his delightful wife Julia had settled in Derby, in a stunning house just opposite John and Margaret, and using all his previous expertise and skill he had recently started his own hi-tech engineering business from scratch, and was doing very well indeed. He had his own plane, which he kept at a small aerodrome nearby, and jumped at the chance of excitement and adventure again. He agreed to study the best flight plan to Urbino, and promised to fly them out as soon as possible.

Eighteen

John, Bladon, and Lexi, arrived at Derby station at midday and caught a taxi to the house at Kedleston, and as a lavish Indian meal had been ordered for six thirty, started to make preparations for the important conference. Although all the ten hostiles had been killed, Bladon suspected their house was still known to the enemy, and therefore it could be dangerous to go back there. Both Bladon and Lexi though were fed up with being the quarry all the time. Precautions would be put in place but now their "little band" were on the offensive.

Meanwhile, Andy, Patrick, Phillip, Giancarlo, Jeremy and Stefan, Willie and Sandy, Steve and his wife Julia, arrived in three separate cars at different times, arriving at Bladon's house at Kedleston, in the early evening. The last part of the journey was a delight. They left Derby on the Kedleston Road, drove through Allestree, and on to the Quarndon road, before turning off to the left through farmland. They passed the Kedleston Golf Club, blessed with stunning Park views and glorious vistas up from the course to the Hall itself, but instead of continuing along the direct road to Bladon's house, they turned off into the Kedleston parkland, all owned by the National Trust. Bladon had arranged for this entrance to be unlocked just for them, and they passed under the gatehouse, then made their leisurely way down a winding lane, between established trees and stunted grasslands. They reached Cutler Brook, which had been widened just below the house into a lake, and then crossed over the lake by a delightful little bridge designed by Robert Adam. They climbed up through fields full of grazing sheep towards the House, but took the right fork taking them away from the House and up to a viewing point, before dropping down, past the babbling brook on their right to Bladon's house.

Over drinks old friendships were renewed. The caterers had set the sumptuous banquet out in the dining room and they all sat down to savour the delicious food as the log fire danced its warm images across them all.

Bladon explained their plans, and in particular about their arrangements for getting to Italy as surreptitiously as possible. He was immensely grateful to Steve for agreeing to take them in his plane, but he had a strong feeling that it was going to be fraught with problems and danger and not a routine trip. Neither was it going to be a cakewalk for those left behind, and as they discussed options together the extent of their problems became clear.

"We need to find out where the enemy base is, the extent of their resources and manpower, details of their mission, and how we can stop them. Willie and Sandy are permanently attached to us, and we have back up whenever we need it from SAS headquarters, but for the moment we want to keep it between ourselves so that we are flexible and mobile and don't draw attention to ourselves."

Sandy spoke next. "Do we wait for them to come after us, or do we go after them? Personally I favour the latter, but the problem is finding their base, or drawing them into a firefight. How do we do that, or do we think a waiting game is a better course?

Stefan, who was recovering well from his injuries, also favoured a more proactive course of action, as did most of the others; but he articulated everyone's concerns when he said, "we can't just wait and let them take us out one by one; but how do we find them; and what if they've got any more of those weapons? Even if we knew where they were hiding out, we couldn't get near them. Neither the security services nor the intelligence community have any idea where they are, or what forces they have gathered in England. What do we do?"

Eighteen

A nervous silence descended, and seemed to envelope the room, with chill foreboding.

And then Andy spoke.

"I think there is a way. It'll need careful planning but I think it could work. They always seem to know where we are and what we're doing, so why don't we use that against them. We need to draw them out of their fortress and I think we could use their impressive intelligence to trap them, and hopefully identify their main base."

"How on earth can we do that Andy?" said Sandy.

"Well", he replied, "what I have in mind is at Sawley, near the town of Long Eaton, the centre of furniture manufacturing. There is a place on the river called Trent Lock, and it's very popular with boating folk as two canals and two rivers converge at the end of a narrow road. There are two very popular pubs there, and a sailing club; but just across the river, and accessed by a large private ferry, is a small hotel and spa. It's not very large, but it's very exclusive. It can only be accessed by their own ferry, or by boat, for the short trip over the river. What I propose is very dangerous, and daring, but it could be the ideal scenario to tempt the enemy out into the open."

"Dangerous and daring. I like the sound of that," said Jeremy. "But how would your plan work?"

"Well, I want to present them with such a tempting target, that they will not be able to resist it. I plan to get together the remainder of The Thirteen, plus the Prime Minister, in one place. Of course we will not actually risk Johnny, and some of us will be in Italy, but they won't know that," said Andy mysteriously. "Johnny can come up the M1 to pay an unscheduled visit to Rolls Royce and Toyota, and then on to a Prime Ministerial visit to the new and exclusive Trent Lock Hotel and Spa, where the stunning furniture exhibition will be held. We will take him to the Trent Lock Golf Club to open their new indoor driving range, and then switch him for a look-a-like, very secretly, and drive him back to London, with his escort.

"Go on then. Tell us why you think they'll be interested in a furniture exhibition?" said Giancarlo trying to curb his impatience."

"OK. Here's what I am thinking. It needs a lot of work on the details, but here it is in outline. When Steve flies Bladon's little contingent to Italy, I will arrange a special event at the Trent Lock Hotel. We have just completed our latest range of leather furniture and it's absolutely phenomenal, although I do say so myself! We were going to launch it simultaneously next week in Milan, Paris and London, but why don't we give a select group of buyers from Harrods, and other top European houses a sneak preview at very short notice. I can ask some of my contacts to provide security, and you can bet your life the information will leak out—in fact we'll make sure it does! I propose that we have Patrick, Phillip, Giancarlo, Sandy, Jeremy, Stefan and me based at the hotel, and then Willie and a few SBS Marines will have a fast inflatable attack boat ready if needed; and hidden at the Sailing Club, a few hand-picked soldiers from the SAS will be in reserve.

If they do attack the hotel, we can try to capture them and their weapons, but if we can't do that, then as long as we can fight them off, then when they try to escape we can follow them, hopefully back to their base. It would need to be coordinated down to the last detail, but I think it can be done, and it will mean we turn from being the hunted to the hunters. What do you think?"

There was a long silence finally broken by Bladon. "Andy, I think it might just work. Don't put yourselves in unnecessary danger particularly from their super-gun, but yes, I think it might work."

Sandy agreed to contact the hotel's owners in strict secrecy and reassure them that the Government would cover any damage to the hotel.

One by one the company expressed a similar view, with very little dissension, and as the night drew around them, they all began to contribute their own thoughts and tactics until by the time their meeting ended at midnight, they had the beginnings of a good working plan.

They left it to Andy, John and Bladon to fine-tune the arrangements and Steve agreed to be on full alert for a flight to Italy.

Nineteen

Three days later, Steve was busy in his development workshop in Derby, with one of his bright young engineering graduates, finalising some details on a part for one of the top F1 teams. The part was one of the first to use a new high temperature composite compound that Steve had been developing for several months.

Suddenly he felt his mobile vibrate in his pocket, followed by a discrete audible warning. Steve retrieved his phone and the screen identified the caller as John Parkin, his friend and neighbour. Steve answered.

"Hi Steve. Thanks for agreeing to fly us out to Italy. Could it possibly be tomorrow?"

It was already late afternoon when Steve phoned his local airfield at Tatenhill and asked them to get his Piper Comanche G ATJL out of the hangar, and have it fully fuelled; he explained that he had to get away early in the morning, for a business trip to the West of England. He felt a little uncomfortable being so devious, but he guessed the flight was going to be dangerous, not only in the air, but also on the ground, as dark forces seemed to be about, so he persuaded himself that safety and secrecy were the overriding needs at this time.

He had already told John to get to the airfield for 6am, which would give them time to takeoff about half an hour before sunrise. Night flying was out of the question, as Steve intended to fly very low to try and avoid detection, and the possibility of alerting their enemies to their progress.

That night Steve sat at his computer, dialling in the flight details, as he guessed the flight from Tatenhill to Urbino would be stretching, both for him and his aircraft, taking them all to the very limit of their endurance, both physically, and perhaps more importantly, on fuel. He had flown Tornado's in the Iraq war, low level too, but then he had a state of the art fighting weapon underneath him, and a lot of people backing him up. This was completely the opposite, and in flying terms he was on his own.

Although the Alps were a bit of an obstacle, he quickly had the basic route sorted, avoiding the major areas of controlled airspace. The authorities are only really interested in the areas round airports, to make sure the public do not fly into a Jumbo jet with a small aircraft.

Modern flight planning software is brilliant, and the computer told him it was 783 nautical miles to Urbino and on the chosen route it would take 4 hours and 57 minutes. More importantly, it told him that he would need 364 litres of fuel and here lay the problem, as the tanks in the aircraft only held 340 litres. Fortunately, the programme automatically built in some contingency fuel for when things go wrong, so Steve quickly recalculated, and worked out that if everything went to plan they could just reach Urbino, without refuelling, but they would be flying on fumes at the end. If things went wrong they could land to refuel, but that would both blow their cover, with untold consequences, and leave Steve with a lot of explaining to do, as international flights had to be communicated in advance to all the national security authorities to avoid terrorist attacks. It had to be a non-stop flight if they were going to have the best chance of getting Bladon and his friends safely to their destination.

The next problem was the weather; there was a low-pressure system to the north that would give them a bit of a tail wind going east, but towards the Alps they would enter a high-pressure system, and that could mean head winds, which was the last thing they wanted. Cloud base looked to be about 1500ft for most of the way, but hopefully as they approached the Alps, the high-pressure system would lift the cloud base enough to give them a route through.

Steve punched the print key on the computer, and seven pages of flight planning details quickly appeared. Next, he connected his new Garmin 795 portable GPS to the computer and downloaded the route. The Garmin unit was amazing; besides providing a full moving map display, it also had a synthetic vision capability, something only seen on some of the most recent jet fighters. The screen could show a graphical view from behind the aircraft, with all potential obstacles in front highlighted in red. He had never used the system in anger, but it could prove useful.

Julia, Steve's wife, came up to the study to see what he was doing. She guessed there was danger involved but she trusted him completely. They had known each other since they were at school together from 5 years old and while Steve had always been totally honest and transparent, when he was doing something difficult or dangerous, he was very focused in his own world. They had flown together for years and Julia was a good pilot herself, although she had never bothered to formally get a license. She would have loved to join Steve, but all four seats were already taken, so she would have to sit this one out at home.

After a fitful night's sleep, Steve slipped out of bed, kissed Julia goodbye and hoped he would see her again. It was 4.30am, and the roads were pretty deserted as he drove to the airfield. Once there he parked the car round the back of the hanger; there was no need to hide it, as he was supposed to be going on a legitimate business trip. He pulled the Comanche out of its single hangar, now fully fuelled, and lined her up with the taxiway. It was still very dark, just a hint of light in the eastern sky. There was also a hint of mist in the air as it was still quite chilly. He loaded the safety bag and connected up all the headsets. The Comanche was a special aircraft, this one was 47 years old, and Steve had bought it the previous year as a bit of a project. It was unusual in that it could take off and land in less than 500 metres, but could cruise at 180mph; a brilliant design that even the latest plastic aircraft could not match. Following a year's TLC she was now in as new, peak condition.

Steve checked his watch; his passengers should not be far away. He had told John to bring them down to the bottom entrance of the airfield close to the hangers, as security cameras covered the top entrance. Suddenly, he saw headlights in the distance, but at the top end of the field. He was sure John would not have made a mistake; had they been discovered? The lights pulled up next to the air ambulance hangar, and he relaxed; he had forgotten they operated from sunrise to sunset.

All of a sudden Steve heard movement nearby, Bladon just seemed to appear from nowhere; Steve was impressed!

Lexi and Wilf quickly followed, to Steve's relief, as the eastern sky was starting to brighten significantly, and they needed to be on their way. Bladon joined Steve in the front while Wilf and Lexi settled into the back seats. Steve primed the engine and fired her up. Next Steve turned off the transponder that told air traffic who and where they were. They were now off the radar!

The Garmin showed five hours to destination as Steve taxied out to runway 08 and set the aircraft up for take off. The slight wind favoured a takeoff in the opposite direction, but that would have taken much longer taxiing, and the Tatenhill runway was more than long enough to get airborne with a slight tail wind.

Steve switched on the electric fuel pump, checked the compass and gyros, and smoothly pushed the throttle to full, and the Lycoming engine roared into life like an angry stallion as they started to gather pace. Steve was conscious that they were more than 150lbs over the maximum safe weight of the aircraft, but they needed maximum fuel, and there was no alternative.

They continued to gather pace, but the airspeed was only rising slowly, 40, 45, 50, they needed at least 80 to get off the ground safely. By this time they were more than half way down the runway and Steve could feel his hand tighten on the

Nineteen

controls, 55, 65, 70, it seemed to be taking an age. Maybe the tail wind was more than he expected. He had certainly never flown the aircraft so heavily overloaded; surely he had not made a mistake in his urge to get away quickly. 75 came up, at the same time as he could clearly see the end of the runway racing towards them. It was touch and go. Were they all going to end up in an inferno at the end of the runway?

Twenty

Dreadnought was alive and planning his revenge and he had a master plan to make himself a multi billionaire! He sat in the study of his three story, traditionally designed, Italian villa, tucked away at the bottom of a mile long, tree fringed drive, in the district of Le Marche in the middle of Italy, close to the mountains to the north and the azure tinted Adriatic to the east, on his 100 acre, wooded, hillside, estate. He still seethed with hatred for Bladon and Lexi, and their entire band of thirteen, and also for the man who was now the Prime Minister instead of him, and had helped them foil his plans for domination of the country.

Dreadnought was in fact a code name for Colin Morgan, who was previously an old friend and guru to the former Prime Minister, Robert Martin; and he had been given rare power by adding the Minister of Defence to his post as Deputy Prime Minister. He was disliked by many, but feared by more. Early in his political life he had callously murdered a troublesome local Party activist, and was a very dangerous man. He was at first sight a smooth media manipulator, but beneath his urbane facade, he was a truly brutal self-seeking thug. The fact that his grandfather had been an active member of the IRA in the period between the two world wars, and the leader of a hunger strike, had been carefully buried, and Dreadnought's ruthless side was for the most part skilfully hidden.

He was a man of immense power and influence; but that was not enough for him. Previously he had masterminded a secret plot, using his code name to take over the country by releasing a deadly virus on the innocent population, but had been thwarted by Bladon and his friends, known as The Thirteen. As they destroyed his headquarters and all the deadly virus in a final attack, he was shot down in his helicopter as he tried to escape.

Dreadnought remembered with a deep ache of loathing, that day under the lee of the hills of the Peak District, where he had managed against all the odds to elude his pursuers, and was making good his escape in his helicopter. That wretched woman, Lexi, (who he should have killed months earlier in Switzerland or Jersey) unleashed a deadly stinger missile to destroy all his hopes and plans. They thought he was dead; but he was very much alive because as the helicopter exploded in a ball of flame, he had been thrown clear, and bloodied, burnt, but unbroken, he had managed to slink away to fight another day.

Now he had regrouped and was stronger than ever. He had developed, or rather the kidnapped Professor from Oxford had developed, a weapon of astonishing destructive power and brutality. It was so effective that it not only destroyed everything in its path, but any observers who were unfortunate enough to witness it at first hand were left in deep shock. It was a revolution in weaponry. Bullets or grenades were fired at a rate of up to half a million per minute, time after time, either from a single weapon, or a large multi-barrelled weapon. These multi-barrelled guns could direct withering fire at any enemy infantry or tank advance, or even enable a warship to fend off a missile attack, and send out a cloud of gunfire in one or two seconds, obliterating anything in the vicinity. It was a truly fearsome weapon. But then even the handheld weapons were capable of terrible destruction. Any hostile state would love to get their hands on this weapon.

Dreadnought was motivated by three burning desires.

Firstly, a simmering hatred, and desire for revenge on "The Thirteen", and The Prime Minister.

Secondly, a desire to sell his guns and the blueprints to

China for billions of pounds. It would mean putting on a spectacular demonstration of its power before China would buy, but he had all that in hand. He had planned just such an attack near to his British base.

Thirdly, he wanted to damage the country that had spurned him.

His plan had been to develop several weapons, ranging from a small assault type rifle, up to a multi-barrelled weapon, that could fire up to half a million bullets at one time. Then he would dismantle them, and ship them out from Italy as machine parts to a shell company in the Midlands. This plan was now well advanced and most of the weapons were in the UK.

He would then attack what he called high value targets around the City of Derby. He was planning a diversionary attack in the City Centre, but the main thrust of his attack would be both daring and lethal and would shake not only the country but also the world.

From the shell company in Birmingham the parts were to be either made up there, or transported to his headquarters at Walton Priory, near Burton, set in very large grounds next to the River Trent, to be assembled and made ready for the attack.

Dreadnought had put together a large force, and quartered them in the Priory ready for the final attack, but also to try to take out The Thirteen as well. They had already succeeded in killing two and injuring one of them, and were about to redouble their efforts to deal with the rest. He was very angry with his men who had failed in Cornwall. It was Bladon again. How could they have failed so badly? They had drawn attention to the possibility of the existence of the weapon, but little did he know that one of his guns had actually fallen into Bladon's hands.

The build up of his forces from places as far as Europe and North Africa was almost complete. They had been entering Britain by Eurostar and the ports, and then with the shocking state of the border forces, just slipping away. They were congregating in Walton ready to be joined by Dreadnought and his men from Italy.

However he did not want to wait until his return from Italy to take his revenge on The Thirteen. He didn't want his final assault to be hampered by having to deal with them as well, and he wanted to eliminate them straight away. Whilst finalising the transmission of the final weapons to England, he had given specific instructions to his number 2, Carla, (an impressive, Al-Qaeda trained assassin) for an all out attack, to try and kill the remaining ten friends who had thwarted his evil plans before. But, he didn't know that Stefan had almost fully recovered, and that Bladon, Lexi, Wilf and John were at that very moment on their way to Italy to try and find him.

He had many contacts still in the UK, some in the Government, some in the security services, several in the police and even someone in the SAS, and word had gone out to locate Bladon and his team. Waiting at Dreadnought's base at the Priory, in the little village close to the A38, south of Burton-on-Trent, was a crack team of eight mercenaries whose specific job was to locate and eliminate the rest of Bladon's team. The remainder of Dreadnought's forces had been stood down, ready for the final attack, with strict instructions not to leave Walton Priory, but some, particularly the Al-Qaeda warriors, were getting very restless. Abdul, in overall charge in Dreadnought's absence, sensed the Arabs were like a pressure cooker, nearing the end of its cycle, and so he took the potentially dangerous decision to use four of them in the search for Bladon and stand down the rest. He knew they were the most ruthless of his men, so he gave Carla one of his precious cache of super-guns, only to be used as an initial shock attack weapon.

Before the end of the day he started to receive hard evidence that something was afoot at a nondescript little place on the river Trent.

As more and more information came in, he realised this could be his best opportunity to eliminate all his main protagonists at one fell swoop. Surely it was too good to be true; but he had learnt over many years that you took your opportunities when they presented themselves, and what could go wrong whilst they had the protection of the super-gun with them?

He contacted Carla, and started to formulate a plan for an attack with lethal force on the Hotel and Spa.

Twenty One

"Do something please," Lexi shouted. "We're going to crash."

With less than 50 metres to go, Steve selected first stage of flap, and it was just enough to get the weight off the undercarriage. He flicked the undercarriage switch up, just as the concrete of the runway changed to grass. He held the aircraft level to build up a little more airspeed and they roared over the perimeter hedge of the airfield, with inches to spare.

"Everyone ok?" Steve called over the intercom.

"That was close," said Bladon.

"I'm glad I didn't bring my tooth brush," Lexi joked in relief. "We wouldn't have made it if I had."

"Quite right, I think we would have carved some topiary in the airfield hedge!" Steve laughed.

The aircraft was set on a course of 125 magnetic and dropped down to 200 feet as the speed built up to 180mph. They were close to East Midlands Airport and they needed to stay below their radar coverage. Steve eased the power back to about 75% to save fuel but it was going to be very tight indeed.

The sky in the east was just starting to brighten significantly, but there were a few scattered mist banks and they had to keep checking their position, to avoid slicing through power lines. The Garmin showed 4hrs 40 minutes to Urbino.

"Bladon," said Steve. "Would you retune the radio to

129.55, Luton airport radar, and keep very alert for me please?"

Lexi felt drowsy after the early start, and her eyes gently flickered as she fought off the enveloping veil of sleep. Wilf was deep in thought, glancing fitfully out of the window as the brightening morning showed more detail of the landscape.

The sun was now starting to light the eastern sky, but fortunately there was a bank of cloud on the horizon and that would hopefully stop the sun streaming straight into their eyes, which would have made flying low level really challenging. The air traffic controller at Luton was handling a number of early morning Easy-jet flights to Berlin, Amsterdam and Milan, and everything seemed to be running smoothly, so hopefully no one would notice a fast moving, primary radar contact, racing past the Airship hangers at Cardington. Normally the big jets would pick up small aircraft through their TCAS collision avoidance systems if they were closer than five thousand feet, but their system relied on the smaller aircraft using its transponder and Steve had switched his off for just that reason.

They turned onto a heading of 147 to pass between the Luton and Stansted's controlled airspace. If they were going to be detected this was one of the danger areas, close as it was to London. The morning had brightened just enough for Steve to drop down to 150 feet as they steered round Ware and headed for Stapleford. While close to London, suburbia still had a lot of open fields and golf courses, so low level flying would not wake the locals. They flew over the M25, where the morning rush was just gathering pace and the lines of vehicles slowly lacing their way along the motorway looked like a glittering necklace around north London.

As they passed over Stapleford airfield Steve switched fuel tanks to maintain the balance of the aircraft and Bladon carefully noted down the fuel used from the port inner tank. With such tight margins they had to make absolutely the best use of every litre.

The Thames was clearly visible as they approached the

Twenty One

Queen Elizabeth Bridge. Normally Steve would fly at fifteen hundred feet, not a hundred and fifty feet, and then the Thames was a beautiful sight, running through the centre of the great city like quicksilver, before lazily fanning out into the Channel. But this morning's view was very different; the river passed in a flash and Steve was busy avoiding the chimneys and cooling towers of the oil and power facilities that lined the Thames. Bladon retuned the radios to Farnborough Radar East. Again things were quiet, with some early morning Military Chinook movements the only real activity.

The chillness of the morning had left some mist banks around the low-lying land to the south of the Thames, and they climbed carefully over them. They looked white and billowy, as though you could reach out and touch them, and they cleared them by no more than twenty feet.

Bladon was fascinated. "You really get an impression of speed from the clouds don't you. They look so close."

With the rising land of the east end of the South Downs, they gently climbed past Rochester and then Canterbury. Steve hoped the rising ground would not show them too vividly on the primary radars, but they were now heading away from London and he hoped that any casual air traffic controller who noticed might think it was some form of atmospheric interference, and not a potential unidentified threat to London.

Bladon checked and read out the location and time, and they were a couple of minutes up on the flight plan; they must have picked up a stronger tailwind than expected. Fuel consumption also seemed to be in line with the plan as Steve changed tanks again to maintain the balance of the aircraft.

While flying very low, the English Channel was clearly ahead of them, as the cloud pattern changed over the sea. They went over the escape procedure, should they need to ditch into the sea. That really cheered Lexi up! Normally small aircraft crossed the Channel at two to three thousand feet. That helped with radio communication and also gave time to prepare, if a ditching was necessary. Flying low would give very little time to prepare if the engine suddenly gave up, so preparation was essential. With Bladon by the door, Steve was a little more relaxed, as he was certain he would stay calm and get the door open, regardless of what was happening.

As they flew over the White Cliffs, they dropped down as close to the sea as possible. Steve knew that the Coastguards used radar to monitor the shipping traffic in the Channel, and it would be impossible for them not to notice the radar response they would generate. Clearly moving at 180mph plus, they were unlikely to be a ship, but maybe they would assume it was some unannounced military exercise. Flying so close to the sea was a real challenge. The flatness of the sea and lack of peripheral objects in the eye made it difficult to judge height, but a Channel ferry suddenly came into sight and he decided to divert to the rear, rather than climb over it, and wake the bridge officers.

Half way across, Steve asked Bladon to retune the radios to Lille information. Bladon quickly retuned the radios to 126.475 and they listened carefully to what traffic was about. While the language of international air traffic control is English, the controller was using French for local traffic. This was where Lexi really felt she could be helpful. She had read French at University and was very fluent in the language.

They crossed the French coast just north of Boulogne, and moved into the wide-open spaces of agricultural France. With land firmly beneath her, Lexi relaxed into fitful sleep, although the occasional jolt due to turbulence disturbed her. Wilf passed some caustic comments about the EU farming subsidies, and the French preoccupation with them, and that helped to lighten the atmosphere, as they all laughed. This gifted doctor was not a fan of the EU!

Suddenly, Lexi awoke as the French air traffic controllers voice came over the radio.

"He's making an enquiry for a fast moving aircraft, north of Amiens, to identify itself," Lexi reported.

The first couple of calls were in French, but then followed by the same call in English. They were heading north of

Twenty One

Paris, but Steve turned the plane slightly and dropped down to fifty feet, over the low-lying countryside. The plane could not divert for long without using up precious fuel, but after a couple of further tries the controller stopped calling, so they turned back towards the next waypoint north of Rheims.

Had the controller given up, or had he passed the unidentified aircraft onto the military? It was a real worry. With the speed of the aircraft, interception would be difficult, as the Comanche was faster than most of the helicopters available, but was of course slower than an interceptor jet.

"Could you retune the radio to Paris approach, please Bladon," asked Steve. "I'm going up to one hundred feet as it is too demanding to fly at fifty feet for long. Paris is busy handling all the scheduled traffic that uses Charles De Gaulle airport, but please keep listening Lexi.

Suddenly, there was that ominous open broadcast again, which Lexi translated.

"Aircraft low level north of Rheims; please identify yourself".

"Does that mean they are on to us?" Bladon enquired.

"I think so," Steve replied without further elaboration.

He was busy working through all the possible scenarios in his mind, and there were not many. He turned north again, away from Paris, and dropped down to fifty feet once more. He realised he was gripping the controls very tightly; he had flown in many tough situations, but this was proving to be the most demanding by far, and he was pushing the aircraft and himself, to the limit.

After three or four open broadcasts the controller stopped, and focused on the scheduled traffic. They hoped their plan had worked again, but could not be sure. Someone must be putting two and two together, and working out that something was happening. Would they make it?

Twenty Two

Andy, Patrick, Phillip, Giancarlo, Sandy, Jeremy and Stefan, a formidable force, moved over on the ferry to the hotel early Tuesday afternoon. There was a small pedestrian ferry further downstream opposite the scout hut, but it was pretty primitive and only held two people. Andy had arranged with Willie that arms would be available for them when they arrived, including automatic weapons and smoke grenades.

Fortunately the Hotel was not very full that week but it had surreptitiously been denuded of most of its staff, and on the pretext of hosting the show and the visit of the PM, all of the remaining guests had willingly agreed to a rearrangement of their booking to a later date, with the promise of free dinner and champagne! The Spa had been closed, and the pool drained, because Bladon had reasoned that if the opposition should attack with their super-gun, then no walls would withstand it, so he had suggested to Andy that he shut the pool off, and use it as a possible shelter in the event of an attack. It sounded to Andy like overkill, but he was not the one who had seen the effect of the gun at first hand, as Bladon had.

Andy had actually started to put his planned surveillance operation into place around Trent Lock early Monday evening. It was really important for him to know as early as possible the direction from which the enemy's attack was coming, if indeed it came at all.

Trent Lock, near the town of Long Eaton, was an area of locks around the point where the River Soar (flowing northwards) meets the River Trent (at this point flowing east). Near this point two canals also met the Trent, providing a route for boats heading downstream avoiding a weir. The Trent at this point, was very wide and fast flowing, and could be very dangerous. A few miles before it reached Trent Lock from Burton-on-Trent, it was joined by the River Derwent, swelling further the force of water, before branching to the right at Trent Lock. Here it plunged over the large weir, flowing spectacularly under the main Derby to St Pancras railway line.

There was only one road down to Trent Lock, the one running from Tamworth Road in Long Eaton, over a railway crossing, and down between the Trent Lock Golf Club, to the large car park adjacent to the Trent Lock Inn. This was a feasible approach route for the enemy forces and so Andy had stationed watchers at a house adjacent to the rail crossing, and some more in a narrow boat moored close to the car park entrance. Harry and Anna would report any suspicious movements over the crossing from the house, and Aidie would do the same from the boat, also keeping surveillance on the towpath next to his boat.

Another access point for the enemy forces could be along the tow path by the Cranfleet Cut, the stretch of water which linked the Trent by a lock, and out onto the wide bridle path running alongside the river. An unmade road made its way over the fields from Long Eaton to its ultimate destination at Trent Valley Sailing Club. This road passed over the Cut, by way of a small bridge, and access from the bridge to the towpath was possible and then on to Trent Lock. It was feasible to drive motorbikes, or even quad bikes along here, so Andy asked Paul and Pam, members of the sailing club, to keep watch on the towpath from an upstairs window in the club.

This left, what was probably the best possible route for the enemy attack—the river. A large houseboat, called "River's Edge", was moored about three hundred metres from the Hotel and Spa, on the opposite bank of the river, and it had

Twenty Two

a clear unobstructed view of the river in both directions. As watchers here, he placed Pat and Carol, to keep watch from behind the lace curtains. He had also arranged an early warning system with Robin and Martin, and Selwyn and Janet, keeping watch further up the river, but he still felt he needed one more pair of eyes and ears on the same side of the river, close to the hotel. So he asked Terry and Andy, friends of John from Derby, to wait in the scout hut adjacent to the hotel as additional back up, but he didn't arm them; they were only there to observe and report back.

Later that night, back at Trent Lock, an inflatable raiding craft, small enough to be deployed from a van, (disguised as a Sainsbury delivery vehicle) was silently launched from The Trent Valley Sailing Club. The club was accessed by a long, winding, unmade road from the town of Long Eaton, through open countryside for about 3 miles, until it arrived at the sailing club. Four Special Boat Squadron marines unloaded the boat, and the van returned the way it had come, as if it had made a normal grocery delivery. A further six SAS men left the sailing club, joined the SBS, and prepared to launch the inflatable quietly onto the river. One of the SBS then took the SAS soldiers to the far side of the river, just below the hotel and spa, and returned to the sailing club. The other three SBS joined their comrades, and together they quietly crossed the river to the opposite bank, sailed under a little bridge giving access to the canal lock, and stopped in a narrow basin, just before the lock gate. They then manoeuvred their craft three metres under another small bridge, tied it up securely to the quayside and then flung a large tarpaulin over the vessel to disguise its appearance.

Meanwhile the six SAS men spread out on the far bank of the River Trent, taking up firing positions about a hundred metres away from the Hotel and Spa and the scout hut, and overlooking the riverbank. They then proceeded to build hides with great skill and expertise, until eventually as the dawn light started to peep through the darker clouds, they had vanished from sight, as if they had never existed at all.

Twenty Three

At Dreadnought's main base at Walton Priory the enemy had now received accurate intelligence about the VIP reception at the Hotel and Spa at Trent Lock on the Tuesday evening as Andy had envisaged. Carla, Dreadnought's number two, would lead the attack herself this time, and would use one of the new super-guns.

She left Walton Priory with eight mercenaries, just past midnight on Tuesday morning, in a fast inflatable boat. It had to be at night as they would have been far too conspicuous in their craft during the day. One of her men steered the inflatable along the River Trent using night sight goggles, and they soon passed Branston, famous for its Pickles factory, on the port side, and then, after a non-eventful journey, they began to approach the environs of Burton on Trent.

This old Staffordshire town was famous for its brewing industry, and one of the main reasons for this was the availability of copious amounts of water, due to the proximity of the wide-flowing River Trent. In fact the river was extremely dangerous here where it flowed under the long straight road bridge, which linked the Repton road to the town itself.

"Be very careful at this point," said Carla. "Just under that long bridge the river splits into two very wide and fast flowing currents. If you take the left hand fork it is very, very, difficult. There is a big weir right under the bridge to negotiate, and we will be in full view of the bridge most of the time, so it is out of the question. If you take the right fork, you will meet the weir and the mill further along, which are difficult to circumnavigate, but it is possible with the nine of us."

They moved carefully up the river, rapidly leaving the town behind them, moving through flatlands on either side, with stunted vegetation and boggy grassland. Eventually they reached a small stretch of pebbly foreshore, secured the boat, and clambered onto to the bank to survey the area. Opposite, the main stretch of the river was unnavigable to river traffic, as a large mill, now turned into luxury apartments, blocked access, but a small tributary joined the main river from the left and rejoined it further along, but this was effectively blocked to river traffic by a large and dangerous weir.

On the bank, was a small wooded area, beyond which another small stretch of foreshore enabled them to be able to re-launch their boat onto the tributary, on the other side of the weir. Carla went ahead to scout the best place to re-launch the vessel, and the eight mercenaries shouldered their weapons, and manhandled the assault craft the few hundred yards to the foreshore, where they quickly relaunched it.

They were about to climb aboard when Carla stopped them.

"Get down. Now."

Strident sirens rent apart the stillness, as two police cars blasted along the road at the side of the river from the direction of Burton. They skidded to a halt in the car park of the mill complex, and three uniformed PC's jumped out of their car, and four armed response officers leapt out after them.

"Keep down. Don't move," said Carla. "Give me those glasses and let me see what's happening. Get ready to leave the boat and escape towards the farm behind us."

She looked calm and in control but inside she was very worried. They were now marooned on a piece of rough ground that was effectively cut off by water on all sides. The only real way out was by water, but that would alert their pursuers to their precise whereabouts. How had they been located? How did the Police know they would be moving up the river? What on earth should she do?

She would wait.

Nothing would be gained by making a run for it. They would only be captured or worse still, wiped out. Surely it was impossible that their base, or their planned attack, had been compromised.

Sweat ran down the back of her combat suit despite the cold night air.

But then another police vehicle roared into the car park, the back door opened and two attack dogs jumped out.

She turned to her comrades and was just about to recommend that they withdraw when one of her men whispered to her.

"Look boss. I think we might be okay. I don't think it's us that they are interested in."

As Carla turned to look back at the mill car park, she saw that the uniformed PC's had run to one of the apartments with an 'enforcer' battering ram, smashed down the front door, ushered in the armed response team, followed by the dog handlers and their excited charges.

"Thank goodness", whispered Carla, "It's a drug raid. It's nothing to do with us. Quick, let's take advantage of all the sound and fury, and get in the boat and make ourselves scarce."

Mightily relieved at their close shave, they moved on down the tributary, until in silence they rejoined the main channel of the River Trent.

"It's a good job we didn't try to get by the mill or they'd have spotted us," said Carla. "What a relief. Thank you men."

They rejoined the main river again, and moved slowly onwards, close to the left bank, keeping as far away from the main road on their right as they could, until thankfully the river's course moved away from it. After a few minutes, the other main stream of the River Trent joined them, and the channel became much wider than before, cutting through desolate fields and grasslands, with a large sewage farm on the left hand side.

The river meandered through more prosperous arable land, passing the little village of Newton Solney on its right, and they started to feel more relaxed, particularly as they entered a more remote stretch of countryside, where the river meandered in wide loops, what the geologists would call a river in old age, and on to the larger village of Willington. All seemed to be quiet as they puttered along at low speed to keep their presence hidden from any prying eyes or ears.

They successfully by-passed the main village and started to pass through a more depopulated area, travelling almost due east, under a cloudless sky, towards the hamlet of Twyford. Carla became a little anxious as they neared Twyford, as they were again closing in on the main road from Willington to Swarkestone.

Little did Carla know, but her luck was about to run out as they approached a large country house set by the side of the river. Twyford was a tiny hamlet, really only consisting of a few farms and the occasional bungalow, but that house was in a very strategic position, and it so happened that it was owned by very good friends of Bladon's, Dr Selwyn Goodman and his wife Janet. He was a retired GP who was also a world expert on Alice in Wonderland, and he had only just returned from a lecture tour in the States that very evening. They were still suffering the affects of jet lag, and so instead off being tucked up in bed fast asleep, they were enjoying the last of a very fine 'medicinal' malt. They were relaxing in their conservatory, looking out onto the glistening sheen from the moonlit river below, when they heard, rather than saw, the discordant noise of an outboard motor, in the stillness. As they looked up, they saw the incongruous sight of a fully laden rigid inflatable boat, full of intimidating, heavily armed men, with a sinister, black clad woman, leaning watchfully over the prow.

"Down, quick, Janet," said Selwyn, and they both dropped to the floor, until the noise of the boat began to recede.

"Do you think they saw us," said Janet.

"No, I don't think so," replied Selwyn, rising slowly to follow their progress through the picture window.

Twenty Three

They watched surreptitiously for a few moments, until the river wound to the left, before reaching the tiny hamlet of Ingleby.

"Do we phone Andy now Janet, or wait until the morning," Selwyn asked.

"Well," said Janet, "it is rather early, so why don't you text him now, and then speak to him in the morning"

And so arrived the first piece of good fortune for Andy and his men, and it would join all the other intelligence that was being gathered at Andy's headquarters.

Carla and her men continued their slow but methodical progress down the river. They were passing through a very fertile vale in slow ponderous loops, and before long they passed Ingleby on the port side, and continued on past Barrow-on-Trent, Swarkestone, Weston-on-Trent, and on towards their immediate destination of Shardlow. The river meandered along the flood plain, between lots of flooded sandpits, passed underneath the A50, left the town of Shardlow on their port side, and travelled onwards towards Trent Lock. Clara checked her map again. It showed that the river flowed south, then east, then north again, then under the Cavendish Bridge beneath the A6. The bridge came into view, and as they approached it, Clara scaled back the engine revs and reduced their speed to a crawl.

"Do you see that marina basin on our left, with all those narrow boats and river cruisers moored? Well that's where we are making for. We must keep our eyes open for the entrance. It's along here somewhere on the port side."

She saw the entrance, which was rather tight on an awkward angle, moved further out to starboard, and then yanked the wheel of the boat as far as it would go, and slowly entered the marina.

This was Shardlow Marina, and they knew that they must be very careful during this phase of the operation. Patchy, heavy cloud partially obscured the moon, and the marina was in almost total darkness, except for some gently suffused light on the water.

As they entered the marina basin, they saw moorings for about a hundred vessels; but in the pale, diffuse light Clara saw their destination, on the far right of the basin next to the shore. A concrete slipway sloped down from a small shed to the water, and on either side of the slipway were two vessels. One was a narrowboat, which had seen better days with gaudily painted sides and chopped wood neatly stacked on the roof; and on the other side of the slipway was a large vessel, named 'the Avenger'.

This was Dreadnought's river cruiser, a New Haines 35 SEDAN, and it was a beautiful boat, made specifically for him at great expense for just this occasion. He had deliberately left it out in all weathers to disguise its beauty and power and exclusivity, as he didn't want to draw unnecessary attention to it when out on the river. The paint was peeling, the chrome rusting, and the window blinds dirty and bent. The wood was dirty too, and pitted, but all of these signs of neglect were only surface deep. The boat was in reality in pristine condition and ready for action. The engine option with this boat was usually a 50hp Nanni, but Dreadnought had fitted the top of the range 260hp Yanmar 6BY, which had fearsome power with no outward hint as to its prowess. Its displacement was three feet, making it ideal for the Trent, and it had twin 60-gallon fuel tanks and a 90-gallon water tank. It also had a bathing platform and swim ladder, and plenty of space above deck for sunbathing and eating.

They grounded the inflatable on the slipway, and all eight men jumped quietly ashore and went into action, while Carla made for the cruiser.

One of the men unlocked the padlock on the shed door, opened it and wheeled out a boat trailer onto the slipway. They pushed it down to the water where four others manoeuvred the inflatable aboard, and within seconds it was hidden behind locked doors.

Meanwhile, Clara unlocked and entered the aft cockpit of the cruiser, where two young women from Walton Priory met her. They had come during the evening, left their car in the marina car park, and settled down to wait for Clara and the eight men.

Within 10 minutes the cruiser was full to the brim with Clara, eight mercenaries, and two staff members from the Priory. Clara went over all the plans for the following day with them again, and told them to get as much rest as possible, for they had to leave the marina just before lunch for the attack on Bladon, his men, and the Prime Minister.

Twenty Four

Selwyn telephoned Andy as soon as they awoke, and explained to him what he had seen. Andy thanked him profusely, ended the call, and turning to Patrick, explained that this might be their first real piece of information about where the attack would come from. What Selwyn had seen could of course be unconnected to the gathering at Trent Lock, but he was pretty sure that it was relevant. But, if it did presage an attack up the river from Twyford, then why hadn't they got here by now? Maybe they had landed and were coming overland.

Andy had telephoned Robin and his brother Martin, close friends of Bladon, who were also fine painters and decorators. Bladon knew that they had a house on the banks of the river, at the confluence of the River Derwent and the Trent, where the river flow increased considerably. He had already alerted them to the possibility of an attack along the river, but he phoned them again.

"Hi Robin, it's me, Andy. You know that Bladon asked you to watch the river, well I would be really grateful if you could please let me know if anything significant happens along the stretch near your house in the next 24 hours. An inflatable full of armed men has been sighted in the early hours of this morning, and they may be holed up somewhere along the river, and if you see anything at all could you please let me know?"

"Yes of course Andy. We have got all the equipment round the back and we will put up some scaffolding and ladders, and anybody passing will think we are decorating the front of the building. If we see anything out of the ordinary, we will let you know. In fact, better than that, we can take pictures of any suspicious craft using the river on our mobile phones, and email them straight to you"

"Thanks," said Andy. "Here is my mobile number. I wait to hear from you. It could be very important."

After a late breakfast, Clara made her final dispositions for their leisurely cruise down to Sawley, and on to Trent Lock. They checked their weapons, whilst Clara took them all through the details of their attack plan again. She and six of the mercenaries were to stay below deck, hidden from view, locked down in the largest cabin, whilst the two girls from Walton and two of the more 'respectable' looking men piloted the boat down the Trent as if on a normal holiday trip on the river. The girls wore shorts and brightly coloured T-shirts from Ralph Lauren, and the men had designer shorts from Hugo Boss and very fashionable shirts from the Polo Ralph Lauren Jeans range. They looked the part they were playing; wealthy, fun-loving, young sophisticates, on a lazy holiday cruise down the river.

The wide, meandering river took them slowly to the east, but always with each bend in the river moving them inexorably to the north. After a while they floated serenely past the confluence of the Derwent and the Trent, and as they moved out into the middle of the now even wider river Robin took three photos with his mobile of the cruiser, and sent them through to Andy, with the innocent comment that it was a characterful boat if a bit neglected. Nothing caused any suspicion when Andy saw the photos. The cruiser travelled on, under a pipeline, through cultivated land and past large flooded gravel pits on their right and finally under the M1 motorway.

Here it began to get more tricky for them, as on the right a huge concrete works appeared, but to their consternation, the river's passage northwards was blocked by a line of marker buoys, guarding a large extensive weir beyond it. This was completely impassable to river traffic, and so they had to turn sharply to starboard though a narrow entrance, into a long

Twenty Four

narrow section of water known as the Sawley Cut. Halfway along they came to Sawley Marina, the largest Inland Marina in the United Kingdom, with a water space of 23 acres, with moorings for 600 boats.

They moored their craft, and had a leisurely snack in the restaurant, further consolidating their cover as just four friends enjoying a lazy day on the river.

Meanwhile Clara took a call on the boat. It was from a distorted voice but she knew who it was.

"The Prime Minister has arrived at Trent Lock Golf Club for a quick meeting with the local Nottingham Chamber of Trade, before he goes to the Trent Lock Hotel. I am expecting him to board the ferry across to the hotel at about 4 o'clock. I understand he is only taking two Special Branch officers with him, and the rest of his protection team is going back to London in two Range Rovers. He will go from here in his Jaguar XJ saloon and park at the car park by the river. I also understand that most of Bladon's men are over at the hotel now, but I haven't seen him. Do you still want to go ahead with the attack? "

"Yes," she replied. "If I know Bladon, he's arrived there by some devious means to try and fool any watchers, but he'll be there. You can bet on it. We have got him just where we want him."

As the clock in the restaurant reached three in the afternoon, the four men roused themselves from their torpor, walked languidly back to the "Avenger", and got back on board. They powered up the impressive craft, and slowly made their way along the remainder of the Cranfleet Cut, inching past canal boats and river cruisers on both sides of the channel, on through a lock, finally passing under the main road to Long Eaton, and back into the large body of fast flowing water that was the Trent. They slowly made their way northeast, until they came within sight of Trent Lock.

Clara called up to them in a low voice, "Slow down a bit and make for the scout hut on the starboard side. Tie up at their moorings, very leisurely, as if you've not got a care in the world, and then set up a table and chairs, and a barbecue, and start to cook some steak. Make it all very relaxed and slow, as if you're in no hurry."

The four of them set up as instructed, with their little table decked with a lace tablecloth, fine china and silver cutlery, and chilled wine, and whilst the girls prepared a green salad with French dressing, the two men fired up the gas barbecue.

Meanwhile the concentration on Clara's face was formidable. She had her eyes glued to the riverbank around the ferry and for thirty minutes she had not moved the binoculars away from her eyes for a second.

"There", she said, suddenly shaking two of her men awake who had drifted off in the warm sunshine filtering through the lace curtains. "The P.M.'s arrived. We can go. Get your weapons ready."

Pat and Carol, sitting watching the two couples barbecuing on the far side of the river, behind the curtains of their houseboat, were uneasy. The body language of the four was somehow not quite right. What was it? There was something incongruous about their behaviour, but it was difficult to pin down. Then Carol realised.

"For saying this is a relaxing peaceful scene, on a beautiful day, on an idyllic stretch of the river, they seem a bit jumpy; a bit ill at ease; and the taller of the two men keeps looking a bit too furtively back to the boat for my liking," she said.

"We'll I can't see it myself," said Pat, "but I trust your instinct darling. Let's phone it in."

"Hi Pat," said Andy, "any problems?"

Pat explained Carol's unease, and Andy thanked him profusely. "Right, I'm on it straight away."

Turning to Patrick, he explained Pat and Carol's suspicions. The PM had now made his way safely back to Downing Street so he called over Colonel Harry, ex-army, now with the Special Protection Service, who was acting as the Prime Minister's double, and explained his concerns.

They immediately acted on the tenuous suspicions of Carol, and ordered everyone away from the conference room at the side of the hotel facing the scout hut, where Andy's furniture exhibition, had been "set up." The few genuine visitors to the exhibition were hurried to a place of safety far away from the conference room, with the promise of a cream tea.

Apprehensively, Andy's men took up positions around the entrance hall and in the Spa area. It was so still. The scene outside on the river and around the pubs and lock gates looked restful and relaxed; the train to St Pancras from Derby Midland sped by in a blur of red and blue, and the little dinghies bobbed about on the fast running river next to the sailing club. It all seemed so normal. Was there really a deadly attack imminent?

After forty-five minutes the coals were hot enough to put four succulent steaks on the grill, and as they did so there was a fusion of flames and marinade and steak. It was to any casual observer an idyllic scene played out under a warming sun and clear sky. The swans made their leisurely way past the boat, the cattle grazed contentedly at the edge of the river, a brightly coloured narrow boat chugged slowly into the canal basin ready to negotiate the lock. All was peace, and all was well with the world, and the heron stood still and seemingly lifeless on the far bank waiting patiently to pounce on the next unsuspecting fish to swim by.

And then ... the heron sprang into life and speared a fish, and simultaneously the tranquillity was savagely destroyed, as pandemonium broke out from the river cruiser next to the barbecue.

A woman clothed all in black, leapt out of the cruiser and onto the bank, with a very strange multi-barrelled weapon, followed by six vicious looking thugs in combat fatigues, heavily armed with Kalashnikovs. They threw weapons to the two men on the bank, whilst the two women retreated to the boat. The eight stood back behind Clara as she trained her gun on the hotel. With a thunderous crash the gun was fired and the entire sidewall of the hotel facing her disintegrated in a shock of sound and fury, and dust and rubble, badly damaging the whole edifice. Carla, with the blood lust on her, shouting, "kill them all", stepped aside, waved her men on, and the eight mercenaries with blood curdling cries charged at the remaining ruins to finish off their task and kill every last person in the hotel. Andy and his men were at their mercy.

Twenty Five

The land started to rise a little as the plane approached Vitry and Saint Dizier. Steve went through his routine checks; two hours and six minutes into the flight and they were still a couple of minutes ahead of schedule, the fuel seemed to be on target, although the auxiliary tanks were effectively empty.

As they approached Chassey the note of the engine changed, waking Lexi again and snapping Wilf out of his thoughts. Steve guessed that he had finally emptied the starboard auxiliary tank, and he quickly switched tanks and flicked on the electric fuel pump, to speed the flow of fuel back to the engine.

Worryingly the engine continued to die, and the pump whirred as it tried to move fresh air, but then it finally picked up the fuel and reassuringly Steve watched the fuel pressure gauge climb back to it normal level and the engine quickly regained full power.

"Don't worry," said Steve. "Normally I would change tanks before they are completely empty, but every ounce of fuel is vital so I have no choice but to take every tank down to the bottom. It will happen again but don't worry."

Steve asked Bladon to retune the radios again to Luxeuil approach. Ideally they would tune into the military frequencies, as they would be carrying out any interceptions, but they operated on secure UHF frequencies and the Comanche was not equipped to this level. The Garmin 765 gps system fitted to the plane also connected it to a portable collision (pcas) avoidance system that showed other aircraft within a five-mile radius and two thousand feet in altitude. Nothing showed as they were flying so low. It was still quite early and most sensible pilots were not flying at 100ft. But then a quiet ping in his headset made him glance again at the 765. There on the edge of the display was the indicator of another aircraft, curving in on an arc that would meet up with them in about two minutes.

"Looks like we may have some gate crashers about to join us," said Steve, "so please keep a sharp lookout on the starboard side for incoming aircraft."

The indicator moved inexorably towards them, and was clearly moving much faster than they were, so it had to be an interceptor jet, probably a Mirage. Bladon was the first to spot it, as the sleek grey jet shot down their starboard side and arced into a climbing turn that took him into the clouds that sat at about fifteen hundred feet.

Steve tried not to show any panic, although the risk of them being shot out of the sky was now very real, so he pushed the aircraft lower, which was difficult as the ground was starting to become more uneven. Rocky outcrops kept appearing ahead and a few tight turns were needed to avoid them. The 765 showed that the jet was coming in for another pass, more slowly this time, but still probably 50 mph faster than they were travelling. The jet was struggling to get low enough to make eye contact with the Comanche, but he waggled his wings, the international interception warning, before again having to increase speed and go into another climbing turn.

"I don't like the look of that jet Steve. What are your thoughts," Bladon asked.

"We have three options," Steve replied. "Legally we should follow him, as he has given us the international signal, but he cannot be sure we have understood. Secondly, we could ignore him and risk being shot down; and thirdly, my favourite, is that we should try and disappear!"

The land was now starting to rise quite quickly as they approached the Alps and the cloud stubbornly stayed at about

Twenty Five

fifteen hundred feet, so that the ground slowly merged with the cloud. The original plan was to pop up through the cloud and get through the Alpine valleys flying visually, but this now looked impossible with their new friend in attendance.

Steve leaned over and selected the synthetic vision option on the 765. He had used similar systems on fighters, costing millions, but this one was based on a unit costing £2,000 and he had never used it in anger before. The screen changed to show a three dimensional view ahead of the aircraft, with potential collision points shown in red. He was still flying visually, but the screen seemed to give a good interpretation of the ground ahead, and it seemed to be pretty accurate. Should he risk everyone's life and try and get through the Alps using the system, or should they play safe and land as directed?

Twenty Six

Dreadnought's eight mercenaries pushed past Carla to finish their deadly task. They spread out to envelope the badly damaged building from a wide arc, six in black combat smocks and two in designer shorts and shirts. They opened up simultaneously with a vicious and sustained wall of fire from their Kalashnikovs.

In anticipation of the follow-up attack, after the shock of the disintegration of the side of the hotel, Andy reacted quickly to move all his men and staff to the far side of the building away from the carnage. Two of the staff were covered in brick dust with cuts and abrasions, but otherwise there were no injuries. Andy, Patrick, and Sandy, jumping into the empty pool for cover, returned fire. The eight mercenaries hesitated, rather like Napoleon's Imperial Guard did at Waterloo, but then encouraged by the paucity of defenders and rather frightened by the frenzied cries from the blood-crazed Carla, drove on with fresh resolve to overcome and crush their seemingly shaken, inadequately armed opponents. It was the critical point of the battle.

The tide of the battle suddenly turned. The hidden SAS sharpshooters announced their decisive presence, as six high velocity shots rang out over the embattled arena from their firing positions among tussocks of stunted grass, dotted about the far bank.

The three mercenaries nearest them dropped to the ground, and as the next two half-turned to try and comprehend where this maelstrom came from, they too were cut down.

Carla was the first to realise that the game was up.

"Back, back here, as quickly as you can," she yelled. "I'll cover you."

And with that, with no thought for her personal safety, she turned the super-gun on the SAS. Or rather, where she thought they were. The gun was really no use against well-concealed individual snipers. This was the strategy that Bladon and Andy had brilliantly worked out. It had succeeded beyond their wildest dreams. The attempts of Dreadnought to destroy all of Bladon's forces had failed miserably and they were now in headlong retreat.

Clara had only succeeded in blowing into oblivion a straggly hawthorn bush, and several clumps of grass, but not one of the SAS were threatened. However it did have the affect of warning off any further threat to her and her men and she was able to push the two girls and the three remaining dejected and sullen mercenaries below deck, while she fired up the massive twin turbo engines on the cruiser, turned the wheel hard to port and powered away from Trent Lock, back up the river towards Sawley.

Andy phoned the SBS marines on his mobile, and spoke to their leader.

"We've beaten back their attack. Will you please follow them, as it is imperative that we find the exact whereabouts of their base, but be very careful? They still have the supergun, and their leader is not afraid to use it. Try and keep well out of range."

The SBS boat left the lock basin, turned to starboard into the main river flow, and followed Clara and the "Avenger".

Clara was shaking with anger and adrenaline. How could their carefully worked out plan have failed so miserably. Dreadnought would not be happy. She now had the difficult and dangerous job of getting back to Walton Priory without giving away the location of their headquarters.

Twenty Six

She turned the craft and headed back westwards towards Sawley Marina. She poured on the power until the prow lifted perceptibly and they reached thirty-five knots, far beyond the legal limit and the bow waves arced out to the banks causing a mini tidal wave on both sides of the river. They reached the entrance to Sawley Cut and slowing the cruiser right down, went under the road bridge and carefully passed the marina until they returned to the river itself.

They continued west under the M1, and out into the main stream of the river, where Clara again opened up the throttle and powered down to the confluence of the Trent and the Derwent, where Robin and Martin's house stood. At this point the river turned sharply to the left, until it flowed in a southerly direction, and here Clara hardly lifted the power as she swung the wheel hard left, and for a moment she thought the boat would plough straight on into the bank, but it recovered and sped on down towards Shardlow.

Robin phoned Andy and reported the cruiser's erratic course, and Andy relayed the information to the following SBS men.

Clara retraced her route of earlier in the day, but not in so leisurely a fashion. This journey was now a race for her life, and a race to try and stop their implacable enemies from finding her headquarters, which would be disastrous. She could feel herself shaking with adrenaline, fatigue, and shock. Those snipers were devastating. They had turned what had seemed like total victory, into ignominious defeat. Over half of her crack mercenaries were dead, and they didn't even know what had hit them.

Who were they?

Surely not Bladon's men?

She may have to use the gun again, despite Dreadnought's warnings, for she could not afford to lose any more men. As it was, it was going to be very difficult for the remaining three men and herself to lift their inflatable out of the water and relaunch it on the Trent. They had only just managed it before with eight men.

She safely negotiated the winding river course back to the Shardlow marine basin, and tied up at the side of the bank, just outside the entrance. Clara and the three men jumped out of the cruiser and made their way to the shed, ordering the two girls to stay on board the cruiser until they had made good their escape in the inflatable. Then they were to make their way to the canal boat, stay hidden there until night, and then get their car and go back to Walton Priory.

Clara checked for any sign of pursuit, and satisfied there was none, she unlocked the shed door and the four of them manoeuvred the inflatable down to the water. Clara jumped aboard, started the engine as the three remaining mercenaries followed her. They made their way out of the entrance to the marina and back up the Trent towards Burton on Trent. They had passed under Cavendish Bridge, and were about to go round the next bend in the river taking them out of sight of the cruiser, when Clara looked back down the river towards the marina, and to her horror saw that an inflatable, full of marines, was about to reach the cruiser before the girls could make good their escape.

"We can't let those girls be captured", said Clara to one of her men. "They'll tell the enemy about our plans, or at least what they know about them, but more critically, they'll tell them the whereabouts of our headquarters."

"What do you mean?" said the mercenaries. "Surely you're not going to kill them. They are just innocent women."

Without hesitation, Clara trained the super-gun on the cruiser, and pulled the trigger.

One of the SBS marines saw Clara reaching for the gun, and slewed his craft off to the left, and back down towards Sawley as fast as he could. Even then, it was as if they had been hit by a hurricane. The sound and fury of the gun smashed across the river, completely obliterating the cruiser and its occupants, and narrowly missing the rapidly retreating SBS men. They waited a few moments, to restore their equilibrium, and turned the craft back to Shardlow Marina. They gingerly inched their craft back towards the cruiser and saw that

Twenty Six

upstream Clara's inflatable had disappeared from view round a wide loop in the river. They carefully manoeuvred their craft just downstream of the smoking remains of the beautiful cruiser and jumped out on to the bank. They saw to their horror that one of the girls had realised what Clara had intended, had tried to jump out of the boat, but was too late, and her lifeless body lay in the water. However, the other girl had somehow miraculously managed to escape from the terrible attack, and lay moaning, in and out of consciousness, on the river footpath. The marines rushed over to help her and assess her injuries.

"I can't believe that she tried to kill us both," she said. "Anything at all you want to know about that woman and her base, just ask."

"Just rest for now, we'll....", but as the marine held her he realised that she had lapsed into unconsciousness again.

The SBS captain phoned Andy and asked for instructions in the light of these new developments. He told Andy that the girl was now in a comatose state probably as a result of the trauma she had experienced. Andy consulted with Willie and Sandy and they agreed that it was far too dangerous for the SBS to follow Clara, as she seemed to have lost it completely, and was very, very, dangerous, like a wounded animal. They realised that they might have in fact been given a very valuable advantage with the surviving girl. She seemed willing to give them details of their base, without a dangerous river chase. She may also know something about a possible target. Sandy phoned the SBS captain and instructed him to transfer her to the Nuffield private hospital near Derby, and to put her in a private room. She was to be given the best medical attention and guarded round the clock. As soon as she regained consciousness Sandy insisted on being notified first. She obviously had a lot of vital information but her recovery could not be compromised by a rushed interrogation.

Andy did however think that he should put a land pursuit in place as well, so he deployed Willie with four SAS troopers in a Range Rover Sport, to follow Clara by road to try and reach Burton on Trent before she did, assuming she would have to go through the town. They sped through minor roads to Sawley, Shardlow, Weston on Trent, Willington, Repton, Newton Solney and finally to the outskirts of Burton. They left their car in Newton Road and walked up to the long bridge over the river into the town, the same bridge that Carla had negotiated the previous night, which spanned the two wide sections of the Trent. They hoped to be able to stop her there.

Twenty Seven

Clara continued her headlong flight back up the river to her base, all subterfuge and secrecy thrown to the winds. Devastating speed and aggression was all she looked for on the river now, and negotiating the weir near Burton. That was the most dangerous part, that and her passage through the large town of Burton, and particularly the passage under the road bridge.

She passed underneath the A50 again, on between fertile fields where the river toiled through long ponderous loops. As she approached Twyford again, little did she know that Selwyn was observing her boat passing at great speed by his house, and as she passed he took two surreptitious photos and immediately emailed them to Andy.

Carla continued her headlong flight towards Burton until she finally reached the point where the river divided, and here she slowed the boat. Checking her map, she took the left hand fork, and moved on to the most difficult part of the journey. She had to get this right; she only had the one chance. She slowly negotiated the river until she recognised a small footbridge crossing the river in front of her. This was where the tributary up to the weir turned off to the right, and she eased the boat into the narrower channel and crept onwards.

"There on the right Clara, it's that stretch of pebbles where we need to land," one of the mercenaries volunteered.

She steered the boat over, and the other three jumped out and pulled it onto the little beach.

"Hold it," said Clara. "That's not right. We're too far away from where we relaunched last time. The bank here is too high. We'll never lift it up that slope. Push us out again and I'll go further down."

She moved down the river twenty metres more and then at the very moment the craft was grounded, they heard the rotor blades of a helicopter coming in fast, and looking up she saw a police helicopter with camera starting to circle their position and slowly descend.

"Idiots," said Clara, and picking up the super-gun she shouldered it and pointed it in their direction. As she had hoped, she did not need to fire it again, as the mere threat was enough to deter any further attention, and with an exaggerated turn it flew back to base.

"With this," she informed her worried companions, pointing at the gun, "we have a good chance of making it back to base. Lets go."

Clara and the other three men manhandled the boat up the bank, and walked with it over to the other side of the weir with great difficulty, stopping twice for a rest. It was very hard work. Finally, they reached the far bank, relaunched the inflatable, and moved on to Burton and that dangerous bridge.

The river continued in a south westerly direction until they approached a large field on the left that led to the houses along Newton Road, which years ago the river regularly flooded. It then turned east once more, before bending round due south to negotiate the long river bridge, which Clara feared.

This was the danger point, and Clara and her veteran killers knew that any attack would come from here. Bladon, or whoever was in command, only needed to place snipers on that bridge, or the slope at the side, and they could pick her little force off at will. She let the craft's engine idle in midstream, whilst she weighed up her options.

She was very loath to use the super-gun again, as she knew that Dreadnought would be furious with her, but she had no other option. But still she dithered. This day had all been too much, even for her.

And then she saw something from the bridge through her binoculars that made up her mind. She saw in a millisecond, a flash of light reflected from a sniper scope. There were two snipers in place, ready to take her and her companions out. She knew they were good if they were the same men she'd encountered at Trent Lock. She indicated to one of her men to take the wheel of the boat, which was still idling on the bend of the river before the stretch to the bridge. She gave him specific instructions.

"When I've got the gun ready, I want full power, and don't stop until you're over 100 metres past that bridge. OK."

He nodded his assent.

With a surge of raw power, the inflatable shot forward, weaving from side to side to present a more difficult fast moving target, whilst the top part of the bridge disintegrated and fell into the boiling river, under the impact of multiple bullets from Clara's weapon.

Willie had indeed placed two snipers on the bridge, in fact they had hoped that Clara, as vicious as she seemed, would not dare to fire the gun again in such a public place, but when they saw her hand over the steering of the craft and go for the gun, they shouted a warning to the two SAS snipers to withdraw, but their own instincts had taken over and they were already in full flight.

Both men were knocked backwards into the road by the force of the attack, but fortunately the bridge itself had taken the full power of the guns volley, and they picked themselves up and ran back to their car. They piled into the Ranger Rover, all of them shaken again by the power and ferocity of the weapon, and they realised that their pursuit would have to be a lot more subtle and clandestine. They started the car and headed up Newton Road, towards the large junction at the head of the bridge, and when the lights changed, they moved straight across towards Stapenhill, a suburb of Burton, at the same time moving away from the scene of desolation on the bridge where Carla had tried to eliminate them, and so very nearly succeeded.

The road travelled alongside the river for the best part of a mile and Willie with his binoculars could just see Clara's boat disappearing round the bend of the river to the west and away from Burton. They sped along the road and saw to their delight that the river was now meandering back in a southerly direction towards the road they were on. They gunned the Sport to try and catch Clara, but they had to brake hard as they approached a large traffic island.

"Which way should we go?" queried Willie almost to himself. Straight on kept pretty much to the course of the river, but went through a complicated network of suburban roads and terraced houses, and so Willie reacted by instinct and flung the 4x4 violently to the right and sped down a long straight road over marshland and swamps.

"Right decision," he shouted to the others, but they were not so confident, and sure enough they found themselves in the town near to the station, with the river disappearing away to their left.

One of the troopers spoke. "I was born here sir. Go straight on towards the station and then when you hit the Branston road, turn left along a long straight road to Branston itself. Once you get there it's easy as the road follows the river for miles. They won't be able to get away."

They battled against the traffic and eventually found the road and sped to Branston, but Clara was long gone. She finally eased the boat next to the riverbank, and then she and her men pulled the inflatable up onto the left bank. Hidden in a little copse in the grounds of Walton Priory, was a boat trailer. They manoeuvred their boat on to it, and pulled it back a hundred metres to a large barn, pushed it in, covered it with a tarpaulin and bags of sheep feed, and made for the safety of the house.

After such a disastrous episode, she was dreading what she would say to Dreadnought.

Twenty Eight

Back in the plane their options were running out. The cockpit was filled with the roar of the fighter as it passed just in front of them, the slipstream causing the Comanche to buck like a mule. The next meeting might involve a missile. Steve chose option three with all its attendant risks, applied full power, and climbed quickly into the clouds, just as they entered the foothills of the Alps east of Interlaken. The synthetic vision showed the valley ahead, and Steve started to climb hard. The cloud enveloped the aircraft, and to their relief the threatening dot on the 765 appeared to turn away to the east, and then disappeared as it climbed to more than five thousand feet above the Comanche.

"Well done everybody. We have lost the Mirage jet," said Bladon.

The synthetic screen started to show vivid red either side of their track, and the distance between the red blocks started to narrow alarmingly. The map suggested there was a route through the valley, but were they in the right valley? Mountain flying in valleys was notoriously difficult, as they all looked the same, but as well as that Steve was relying only on a box of electronics.

He could feel the sweat starting to trickle down his neck.

"I'm going to climb hard up to six thousand feet and on to seven thousand feet. The fuel consumption is now much higher than planned, but we have no choice. The temperature is falling rapidly. It's just hovering above zero."

"Is that going to be a problem?" Bladon queried.

"A thin film of ice is starting to build on the windscreen and leading edges of the wings," Steve responded. "Ice is a real threat. It makes the aircraft much heavier, but more importantly it changes the profile of the wing aerofoil and reduces the lift produced by them. In simple terms the aircraft could stop flying and become a frozen brick!"

"What can you do?"

"I'm going to select hot air for the engine intake as the last thing we want is a frozen air intake, and no air to the engine."

Bladon updated Steve. "The outside air temperature has dropped below zero, and as we're still in the clouds, the ice has started to build up quickly. What does that mean?"

Steve replied, and the stress showed in his voice, "the aircraft has started to feel heavy and unresponsive and the climb rate has dropped to a little over three hundred feet per minute. There will come a point where the plane will not climb any more. The synthetic vision is showing we're in trouble as well, as the sides of the valley have closed in and an endless block of red is now extended across the screen."

Just as they thought they were all going to die the cockpit suddenly brightened and they burst into clear blue skies.

The rock faces were still too close for comfort though, so Steve banked hard to port to clear a rocky outcrop and through rapidly thinning ice on the screen could just see a break in the rock face. Another swift turn right to starboard and they just cleared through the gap and into the next-door valley. The sky was a brilliant blue, and the mountains, capped with snow, stood out against the beautifully billowing clouds in the valleys.

"Wow. That was close," said Bladon.

"You can say that again," Lexi responded.

"Can you just stop for a moment," Wilf added. "I'll take our blood pressures."

Steve laughed. "We have to continue climbing," he said, as he scanned the Garmin for any signs of unwelcome guests. "It looks clear though."

They continued along the valley, heading towards Italy, gently climbing to 12,000ft, just a few feet above the clouds. If they needed to, they could hide inside them.

Flying was now easier but they were about four gallons down on fuel. The plan showed they could not reach Urbino with the fuel that they had, as they would run out about ten minutes before their planned arrival. Steve stared at the plan and figures before him. Bladon sensed the calculations going on in Steve's mind.

"Is it going to be tight on fuel?" he enquired, trying to defuse the tense atmosphere that had built up in the cabin.

"Just a bit!" replied Steve, also trying to calm things down.

"How big's the bit," Bladon asked with a faint smile.

"About ten miles," Steve replied,

"A gentle stroll" laughed Bladon.

"It might be for you," chimed Lexi from the back, "but that's quite a hike for us mortals"

Spirits started to rise with the warm sun and Lexi and Wilf were soon in a semi-soporific state as the tension eased. As they started to descend more quickly, breaks started to appear in the valley clouds below and beautifully ornate little alpine villages were dotted here and there, in the dazzling green meadows that surrounded them.

They had about an hour to run, and a quick check on the fuel flow totaliser showed they had about twelve gallons left. Steve leaned the engine out a little further, which reduced the amount of fuel being used, not a good thing for the life of the engine, but that was the least of his concerns. Bladon retuned the radio to 133.45, Locarno military. It was still early, and a few local aircraft were calling requesting a basic service, the lowest form of air traffic control, basically collision avoidance advice if the controller had time!

All of a sudden the brilliant blue of Lake Como opened up below them, and they shot across the little village of Bellagio at the heart of the lake. It brought back fond memories for

Steve, as he had spent his honeymoon there nearly forty years before. But at 9000ft there was not much time to reminisce, and hugging the mountains really tightly, they flew on, past Bergamo, and on to Brescia. They kept a listening brief on the radio, but all seemed quiet and Steve hoped the mountains were providing a bit of radar clutter, to confuse any unwanted military interest.

Past Brescia, the mountains gave way to the fertile plains of northern Italy and it was time to drop down as low as they could again. South of the mountains they seemed to have picked up a bit of a tailwind, not enough to get to Urbino, but every little helped. The Comanche was now down to 50ft and with a ground speed of nearly 200mph Bladon and Steve had their work cut out looking for power lines. The early morning sun in the east made the task even more demanding.

Bladon suddenly shouted "ahead", and out of the sun the outline of a power cable mast raced into view. It was impossible to get the Comanche over it, so Steve dived to the left and pushed hard down, to less than twenty feet, slipping under the looping power cables, it was a close shave, but as the sun lifted a little, the forward view got easier. Passing to the south of Ferrara, they relaxed a little and climbed to 200ft. There were a lot of sports flying fields in the area, and it was unlikely anyone would notice them amongst the other traffic. Steve calculated they had seventy miles to run to Urbino, about twenty-one minutes at the speed they were flying, but the Garmin was still showing that they would be about five miles short.

Slipping between Forli and Cervia airports, the ground started to rise to the south and the ground also rose sharply to the west, and to the east. The Adriatic shone like a diamond-encrusted blanket, fading into a haze on the horizon.

They continued until the map said they were passing over Verucchio,

"Sounds like something I would dig out of your foot," said Wilf, in an attempt to diffuse the tension that was rising as they approached the end of their epic journey. They all laughed.

As they started to gently climb over San Marino, Steve rocked the Comanche and went through each of the auxiliary and main port tanks, to make sure they had used every drop of precious fuel. Each time the engine coughed a little as it drew air instead of fuel, and Steve quickly changed back the tanks.

The Garmin showed nine miles, and zero fuel.

"We'll push on direct to Urbino and if she coughs, I will put her down wherever I can, and we will just have to make the best of it. Bladon, when I shout, open the door please, so that it does not jam if we land very hard", Steve explained.

"Why haven't we run out of fuel, when the Garmin says we have none", Bladon asked.

"This is a first for me", replied Steve. "The general idea is to land with a bit of fuel left!"

At that moment, the fuel pressure started to die and the engine started to cough, as it became starved of fuel.

Urbino was now only a couple of miles away, and they could see a small field to the north east of the city, clear except for some bushes running in parallel lines. Steve selected undercarriage down, just as the engine started to die. The gentle hum of the undercarriage drive motor and the sound of air racing past the cabin were now the only sounds they could hear. As they crept over the hedge at the edge of the field Steve shouted, "Door open now," and Bladon quickly undid the locks and pushed the door open. The wheel hit the ground with a thump and the contents of the cabin, people and all, were thrown about violently, despite being strapped in. The field was only about 200 yards long, and Steve braked as hard as he could, but the hedge at the end raced up to meet them, finally burying the propeller and nose wheel ... but they had landed safely.

"Out out out", yelled Bladon, and in a flash he was outside the aircraft, crouching near the hedge, urging Wilf and Lexi to join him. They scrambled out, and finally Steve unstrapped and climbed out after them. The Comanche would fly again, but not from this field.

Twenty Nine

Steve looked at his Michelin map of Umbria and Marche, which although only 1:200 000 scale showed him that they were not too far from his planned airfield near Trassani a few kilometres north of Urbino just off the main Urbino to Pesaro road. They had landed in a remote field between the town of Gadana and the small village of Giardino della Galla, about two and a half kilometres north of the medieval city of Urbino in Marche. Now the problem was how to get the plane to the airfield near Trassani quickly and surreptitiously before someone discovered it, as it lay vulnerable with its nose in the hedge.

Steve still had some friends and contacts in the Italian Airforce, so he phoned Matteo who lived in the nearby coastal town of Fanu, and after fifteen minutes he turned to the others with relief and satisfaction.

"I have arranged for the plane to be taken to Trassani tonight, where it will be checked over for any damage, and then refuelled ready for our return."

"What is this airfield like Steve? Is it safe?" asked Wilf.

"The airfield was built in February 1945 with two large parallel runways, and at the time it had enough facilities to house two 15th Air Force fighter groups. It was turned over to the Italian government in late September 1945, and then dismantled after the war, and the land has largely been returned to agricultural use, except for one runway, which is still operational for occasional civilian use. I had planned to use it, and as long as Matteo can get it there, we should be fine."

"Thanks Steve. I don't know what we'd have done without you. Johnny assured me before we left that all your expenses would be covered by the Government, including any necessary repairs," said Bladon. "And one more thing. I think I'll ring Johnny before we return and ask him to contact Paris and have a few quiet words with Fighter Control, to keep inquisitive Mirage fighters away on our flight home."

"Brilliant idea, darling," said Lexi. "That will keep me and Wilf from heart failure on the way back."

Whilst Steve had been on the phone to Matteo arranging for his ministrations to the sick plane, Bladon had phoned Riley, John Parkin's son, who lived in nearby Urbino with his wife and twin sons. They had been anxiously waiting for his call, and he was now on the way to pick them up. He had originally intended to stay at a hotel recommended by Riley close to the city where his father had once stopped, but because of the crash and the problems in French airspace, he asked Riley if he could possibly put all four of them up at his house, in the centre of the city. Riley was thrilled to be asked and whilst he went to collect them, Gaia went to make up the three beds situated in a separate annexe attached to their home.

Riley duly collected them all, and they piled into his Volvo XC 60, with Steve fondly waving goodbye to his stricken aircraft. They reached the little village of Giardino, took the road to the right, signposted to Urbino, and reached the outskirts of the city fifteen minutes later. Riley continued round the ancient city walls, until he reached a large car park situated below the beautiful old walled part of the city and parked up. At the entrance to the car park, opposite the Gendarmerie, an old and lavishly painted section of the fortified city wall guarded the fine old cobbled street, leading steeply uphill to the city itself. At the top was a delightful little square where people met to while away their time in the cafes and Gelateria's, where the most delicious ice cream, or gelato, was served. There was a quaint little lift formed out of the cliff face, entered by a little office by the car park, which whisked people up to the square without any effort or struggle. Riley and his two sons, Leone and Arco, however, liked to walk up the ancient medieval street, stopping to sample the various delights in the plethora of fine shops found there. Jewellery shops, bookshops with comics for the boys, fine shoe shops, leatherwear shops, delicatessens, dress shops, opticians with Armani frames, and small coffee shops.

They went by lift on this occasion, because they didn't know whether the enemy had any of his watchers in the medieval city, and they walked the short distance to the square and found a table outside Riley's favourite coffee bar. They ordered a selection of cappuccinos, latte's and espresso's and gradually the horrors of the flight slipped away.

"Tell me about your town Riley," asked Steve. "Do you like it here? What's it like?"

"Well Steve. Where do I start? Dad spotted this description in the Daily Telegraph and it just sums it all up for me. This is what it says.

'It's an idyllic hill town where houses and palaces of weathered brick and pantiles cluster around steep, narrow streets, with misty mountains stretching mysteriously beyond, like the background of a Leonardo portrait. It was one of the cultural capitals of the Renaissance in the 15th and 16th centuries and Piero della Francisco came there to paint, as did Ucello and Raphael's father. In fact it was the birthplace of the famous Raphael, and also of the late-Renaissance painter, Federico Barocci, who had a new exhibition in his honour at the National Gallery in London in early 2013.'

"So, yes Steve, it's a great place, and I love it. We love London where the boys were born but both the boys go to school here, and we are all very Italian now!"

Wilf loved it here too. He also loved Riley, from when he lived in England with his parents and Wilf was the family doctor. It was also becoming very clear that the boys were getting very fond of Wilf too, and together they went all over the city. He even went down to watch them play football for their junior team in Urbino that evening, and when they got home all three just chilled out on a pile of cushions in the second floor den. Arco played his drum kit and his electric guitar quite brilliantly, and demonstrated his staggering array of dance moves; Leone spoke excitedly about his love of acting, and his part in a film, which the whole family had been to the cinema to see. Wilf also swopped stories and apps with Leo on his iPhone, and loved to hear his encyclopaedic knowledge of Italian and English football.

That night Riley's friend Giacomo arrived for dinner, and John, Riley's Dad, joined them too, having flown in to nearby Ancona. After a very convivial time savouring Gaia's excellent cuisine of chicken, mushrooms, sauté potatoes and green salad, they all held a council of war.

Giacomo had some news of a possible location where the enemy were holding his grandfather, Professor Lane. It was a house off the main road from Pieve de Cagna to Urbania, and had been attracting a lot of attention in the area. It was known as 'The Hill', and there had been a lot of traffic in the night down this isolated road, and on occasions loud bangs had been heard from its 100-acre woodland. It had, coincidentally, belonged to a friend of Gaia's, until sold two years ago, and Arco and Leone had often played there, and Gaia and Riley, and Giacomo and his wife and sons, had been to parties there several times. In fact John had accompanied him on one very special occasion, and remembered an idyllic evening eating al fresco outside the main house, with wonderful views down to the glittering pool, on to the valley below, and across to the mountains rising sheer from the meandering river below, up to snow capped peaks.

So they parted in good humour and decided that they would go and check out the Hill, but not until they'd had another day's rest, after their very stressful journey.

They all met for lunch at Antica Osteria da la Stella, an ancient inn that claimed to have hosted Raphael and Piero della Francisco. They ate in a quaint, beamed dining room with white linen table clothes, and tasted the house pasta speciality, cappelletti in chicken broth, and tagliatelle with white truffle sauce. After lunch, Bladon and Lexi decided to get some better Italian walking boots from town, while they were there. They walked firstly to the Square, the one with the fountain and the Gelateria, and sampled a delicious cornet each, then walked halfway down the steep cobbled street to a very fashionable shoe shop, where they bought a couple of pairs of Tods boots. On the way back, Bladon sensed that he was being followed. He stopped at the next shop and saw in the reflection of the window, two men acting suspiciously.

He steered Lexi away, back up the quaint street, and then quickly returned to Riley's house.

He told the others what had happened and strongly recommended that they leave at once.

"I think it's urgent that we check out The Hill immediately, as I'm sure that I've been spotted. We must get there before they move out."

Within an hour they were on their way, following Riley in their hire car. Bladon hoped against hope they would not be too late.

Bladon and Lexi, Steve, Wilf, and John, left the main Urbino to Urbania road and travelled towards Gadana. They had hired an Audi A6 and were following Riley's car to Pieve de Cagna. Bladon and Wilf had forbidden Riley to come down to The Hill with them because it could be dangerous, but Riley had insisted on taking them most of the way, because it was a very winding and difficult mountain road.

After a few kilometres they came to the small town of Gadana and took the first left turn up into the mountains. The road got progressively narrower and more winding and steep, but also more beautiful. They crossed old pack roads and deep ravines with scarcely any space between the precipitous drop and the side of the road, and climbed on and on, almost into the clouds. At last Bladon saw, perched on a craggy hill, the town of Pieve de Cagna. It was a friendly old town, and Riley had told them over dinner that this was the first school that Arco and Leone had attended. They turned left, and after a while they came to the small hamlet of Guidio, and just as they were leaving the environs they came to Giacomo's house on the edge of the village.

They went into the small house, and Giacomo excitedly gave them an explanation of the events up at the Hill that day. There had been several cars travelling up and down the road and also he thought he had heard the dull thud of a helicopter's rotor blades in the distance.

"Oh no," said Bladon. "We must have been spotted in Urbino as I feared, and now they are evacuating their base. I do hope we're not too late to rescue the Professor."

They ran to the Audi after instructions from Riley as to where to leave the car, carried on up the ever increasing gradient, until after five minutes Bladon spotted the pull in, at the top of a very steep unmade track running off down to the right, and he left the Audi there.

Thirty

Bladon, Lexi, Wilf, John and Steve got out of the car and listened.

It was quiet.

It was always quiet here, but somehow it felt different this time.

It was an unnatural quietness.

They left the car, and followed the wooden sign, pointing down the steep track to "The Hill".

They came first to a small farmhouse just below the road and except for a few scraggy chickens scuttling into the hedgerow there was no sign of habitation. While Bladon and Lexi kept watch, the other three searched the house, but after 10 minutes they rejoined their friends.

"There is evidence of people sleeping rough, but they seem to have cleaned up in a hurry and left nothing incriminating. Let's carry on," said Steve.

They continued along the unmade track, which descended rapidly towards another farmhouse built alongside a precipitous escarpment that the track followed. There was a sense of dread starting to pervade their very beings, despite the idyllic setting. They were high in the Appalachian Mountains and straight below them, past the farm that they were approaching, the track steepened and then fell vertiginously into dense and opaque woodland on either side. The woods covered many acres of ground, and yet to the right they could see the verdant ground sloping gently down to a stream, and to the left the scrubby land rose more steeply towards a large house next to the main road. They could see the valley bottom through a gap in the trees and then beyond that, on the other side, was a forbidding, dark massif, with a sprinkling of powder white snow capping it.

They reached the house and listened.

Nothing.

Even the birds were silent.

Bladon and Wilf opened the heavy wooden door and waited for a few moments until their eyes focused in the gloom.

Nothing.

The remains of a wood fire lay in the grate, but the charred wood was cold. They searched the rest of the house quickly, but found no evidence of recent occupation.

They rejoined the other three on the road outside the farmhouse and looked down the rough limestone track.

What awaited them down that tunnel-like passage through the trees to the main house?

"I don't like it" Lexi whispered, "there's something very wrong down there."

"I agree," John spoke in an almost distracted way. "Ostensibly this track through the trees is the only way down to the house, but I remember from a trip here in the past, in happier times, that there are a lot of hidden tracks in the woods. I suggest we walk down this track on the left for about a hundred metres, where if my memory serves me correct, the track bends sharply to the right; then we'll leave the roadway and try and approach the house from below. There is a large garage underneath the house and then an old grotto near the back lawn, and past that you reach the front door."

They stopped and checked their weapons, as a feeling of dread had descended on all of them. The four men had been provided with shotguns, which Riley had managed to purloin from the surrounding population, and Lexi had brought a small handgun, which she kept in her handbag. It wasn't much, but they weren't intending to engage in an all-out fight against what they assumed would be a vastly superior enemy. They must go very, very, carefully. Normally, Bladon would have preferred to split his forces and engage the house from two different points of access, but he didn't feel at all happy about splitting up their small force.

They were half way down the track when Steve heard it first.

"Quick. Get off the track. I heard something in those trees coming this way."

As they all leapt off the track into the bushes and trees skirting the rough track, they all heard it.

"Get down", whispered Bladon, and they all melted into the surrounding woodland.

Then they heard a noise like a train coming, or a crowd stampeding, and then crashing through the trees and making for the path came… a herd of wild boar. Two huge males smashed through the undergrowth, followed by three females, six babies, and bringing up the rear a massive albino boar, with lethal looking tusks, seeming almost to stare at the five, as he lumbered on.

"That was close," said Lexi. "Something must have spooked them? We must be very careful."

It took what seemed like a lifetime for them to carefully make their way down the track, much more tentatively than before, until at last they saw through the bushes the house known as "The Hill", standing in all its glory in the sunshine.

It was so quiet. The stillness was sinister and permeated the atmosphere with menace.

Bladon stared at the building for a full minute, almost willing his eyes to see through the walls and check its contents.

At last He seemed satisfied, and without a word, beckoned them slowly forward to the path surrounding the side of the house, on past the garage, and then onto the bottom of the lawn. Again he waited, and then they moved forward again. In single file they made their way to the top of a grotto underneath the house.

They congregated by the grotto entrance, none of them wanting to go down into that dark place, as not only could they sense terrible danger, but there was also a sickening smell of death rising from the oppressive atmosphere below.

"Oh no," said Lexi. "I do hope the Professor's all right. I thought I heard a faint cry"

Steve had had enough. He rushed in through the entrance to the grotto, and by the weak, filtered light from the roof, he saw that it curved to the left and then entered a larger cavern. The sight that met his eyes in that cavern sickened him, and stopped him in his tracks.

The Professor lay on his back, with hands and feet tied, and he had been severely beaten and brutalised. He was not yet dead for it was him who had tried to shout, but his breathing was very shallow and laboured.

What had upset Steve even more was the sight of two cleaning maids tied to two dilapidated dining room chairs, who had both been blindfolded, and then ruthlessly executed.

Steve called the others down urgently, and then went to check the pulses of the two maids just to make sure, but they were both dead.

Wilf was next down, and when he reached the Professor, he realised that he was very gravely injured, probably mortally.

"Help is here at last Professor; we're here to help you" said Wilf. "Can I call you Louis? Could you please make him comfortable Lexi? Just something under his head please, and I'll try and relieve his distress as best I can."

He always carried a small medical kit with him wherever he went, and he quickly took two morphine tablets from his pack, and with water provided by Lexi, the Professor managed to swallow them both.

His breathing had started to improve, but Bladon took Wilf aside for a moment, and said to him under his breath.

"Wilf, I know I'm not the expert here, but I don't think

he's going to make it, do you? It's desperately important that we try to get some information out of him, as long as we don't cause him undue suffering. Would that be possible?"

"Of course, let me just stabilise him first," said Wilf. "We'll try and make him more comfortable. I'll get a drip into him, and then I think he will feel much better with the rehydration. I still don't think he's going to make it, but I understand that time is absolutely of the essence."

Wilf worked expertly and lovingly on the Professor, until he felt able to let him respond to Bladon's requests.

"Who kidnapped you Luis?" Bladon gently asked him.

"Well that's the strange thing. I recognised his face although I thought he was dead. It was Morgan, the former Minister of Defence, but I was sure I read in the papers that he had died in a helicopter crash," the Professor replied.

"Oh no," said Bladon. "It's Dreadnought. He is alive after all. We were sure he was dead. Now it all begins to make sense."

"Where have they gone Luis?" asked Bladon.

"I've been down here for hours....." He was beginning to tire. "The last of them left about 30 minutes ago. I think I heard them say that they were going down the hill to the river."

"Why did they hurt you?" asked Bladon

"They forced me to work on the prototype guns, and to modify them until they were ready for theatre..... They've had me working on a special gun that fires incendiary bullets too....... I realised they would kill me when I had finished the task...... But I had no option, because they threatened to kidnap and kill my son and grandson..... I went along with them to try and protect them."

"Are all the weapons ready for use?" asked Bladon.

"Yes," said the Prof, "but, but ...."

He was clearly tiring.

"They have hand weapons, and helicopter born weapons,

and lethal artillery weapons, all using my invention. They intend to sell them and the blueprints to the Chinese, but they have insisted that they carry out a lethal demonstration of their capabilities first."

"Where?" asked Bladon

"I don't know for sure," said Professor Lane, "but I think it's somewhere in the central region of England. They have fitted one of the weapons to their helicopter, so be very careful, but I believe all of the others have been dismantled here, and shipped to Britain labelled as machine tools"

"Thank you so much Professor. You've been very helpful. You just rest and Wilf will take care of you while we try and stop them from getting away."

"But there's one more thing ...." The Prof tried to sit up.

"No," said Wilf, you must rest Professor, "or..."

He was cut off in mid sentence by the Prof, who was trying to reach a small medallion hanging from his neck.

"Take ... this," he barely had the strength to speak now.

He rallied a little, "I so wanted these weapons to help protect British and NATO forces....

But if they get into the wrong hands, like the Chinese ....

They will be deadly.

That can never happen. Take this medallion. Hidden inside is a small specialist transmitter I've developed."

He stopped, breathless, and Wilf made him more comfortable and gave him a shot of very strong painkiller. So much talking, although very important, was sapping his strength.

"This will ease the pain, but in about two minutes he'll feel very sleepy," said Wilf.

The Prof was able to continue. "All the weapons are powered by battery packs. It's their only vulnerability. I have surreptitiously inserted into every battery pack, as part of their design, a device that makes the weapon combust when you activate this little transmitter, as long as you are within

Thirty

a thousand metres range. It was all I could think of to stop my kidnapper, but I couldn't be sure I would live to pass on the information. Thank God you've made it in time. Here it is Wilf. Thank you for your care. Give my love to my son and grandchildren in case I don't make it. Don't forget. Within a thousand metres and then press the activation switch."

With that, he lapsed into a deep coma. Wilf gave the medallion to Bladon who put it carefully in his pocket.

"That's brilliant," whispered Lexi, "we have the ultimate weapon to neutralise the guns now."

"I wouldn't be so sure Lexi. Yes, it could be a great weapon against them, but we don't know how it works, or whether it does work or not. And the Prof is in no shape to tell us either. I think we must continue to fight them with conventional weapons and stealth, but keep this back as a last resort."

Bladon was restless. Wilf understood, and agreed to stay with the Professor and Lexi, so the others left the grotto and retraced their steps to the lawn.

"Riley and Gaia tell me that it takes about 20 minutes to get down to the river from here to the flatlands at the bottom. That's the only place that they could land the helicopter," said John.

"I know we're not well armed," said Bladon, "but we must try and stop them from getting away. It's desperately important that we learn where their base is."

Thirty One

They dashed down a narrow path through the wooded hillside. Halfway down, they heard a stampeding noise again, so they stopped their headlong pursuit, and crouched in the tree line, but it was only the wild boar again. Something must have spooked them again. Bladon, Steve and John resumed their chase, and then fifty metres from the bottom, they saw it.

The helicopter was ready for flight and six armed men were getting on board. All three opened up on the helicopter with their shotguns, and the enemy returned their fire. John hit one of the men in the leg, just a flesh wound, but instead of helping him to safety, one of his companions, with a snarl of rage, brutally turned his weapon on his own man, and would have finished him off if Steve had not distracted him by firing again.

The helicopter took off, leaving the injured man, then flew over the little stream and up towards the mountains.

Then it turned a hundred and eighty degrees and approached Bladon, Steve and John. Bladon realised what their intentions were, and frantically propelled the other two towards an outcrop of rocks nearby, flinging himself in after them.

The helicopter fired at the place they had just exited devastating the adjacent woodland. It then flew off over the mountains and away from the Hill.

"Wow, that was close," said Steve. "Thank goodness you realised what their intentions were. And who on earth was that man, he was totally merciless."

Bladon replied. "At least we're still alive, but we've lost them."

"That may be so," said John, "but we've still got their wounded man down there. Steve, could you go and bring him back to "The Hill" please, and we'll see if he'll talk."

Bladon and John retraced their steps back to the house, then with heavy hearts they saw the sadness of Wilf and Lexi, and they knew that the Professor had not survived.

"I'm sorry, Bladon. He was a good man," said Wilf. "But we have the medallion, for what its worth. I don't have great confidence in it. I think it's going to take more than that little device to stop them.

"Thank you Wilf, it could be useful. Lexi could you please keep it safe for me just in case? But now we must search the house and see if we can find any information on the weapons, or their base," said Bladon.

Steve had not yet returned with the wounded prisoner, so they hurried round to the front door to start the search of the house, but before they could enter the house they heard again the horrendous noise of heavy rotors that heralded the return of the helicopter.

"They're back. They must have changed their minds. I guess they're going to try and obliterate the house," yelled Bladon. "Quick, back to the grotto. It's our only chance".

They ran, and Bladon saw that the helicopter's circling pattern had stopped; it was about to attack.

"Quick," said Bladon. "They are about to fire."

They made it to the grotto entrance and ran down into the larger cavern.

The helicopter circled, raining destruction with its dreadful weapon. They even fired down the grotto, but couldn't reach them in the cavern. Then it headed back to the river.

"They are tidying up like a typical 'Black Ops'". Destroy

everything. Leave nothing standing," said Bladon, wiping the deposits of soil and moss from his brow. "But hopefully, we still have the man they left behind. I hope Steve found him."

Steve caught him as he was limping over the river. He was just about to restrain him when they heard, rather than saw, the helicopter. They both looked up and saw it unleash its fearsome weapon. With an ear-shattering roar the house disintegrated. Steve had never seen anything like it before. It was just as if it had evaporated. All that was left of this building was a pile of smoking bricks.

"Quick," said Steve, hurrying the prisoner away from the open land by the river, to a small copse of olive trees that had been left to go wild. They slipped under the tree cover and waited. Sure enough the helicopter returned and circled the place where Steve had caught him in the river.

"I am afraid they will fire into these trees," he said under his breath.

But then he saw with relief another small herd of boar disturbed by the noise of the rotor blades, running in headlong flight from some bushes fifty feet away. The gun on the helicopter swivelled, and annihilated them. Satisfied, the pilot turned and headed back to the demolished "Hill".

Steve wondered what would happen next, and if he was still in danger, but then he saw that the helicopter was ignoring the ruins, and flying back up the track. It stopped above the first farmhouse, and again a cacophony of sound heralded another destructive burst from the new weapon, and then they saw it move on finally to the first house, near the main road, and from the resulting metallic cloud burst, they realised that it too, was obliterated. Then they saw the helicopter slowly rising in the clear blue sky, like a buzzard in the air currents, and for one horrible moment Steve thought that it was returning, but with a burst of power it flew away in the direction of Urbino.

"I must get you attended to," said Steve, but the man cowered away from him. "I'm not going to hurt you. We have a doctor.

Do you understand?"

"I 'ave no English," he said. "Italiano."

"Ok, first we are going to patch you up chummy. Let's go."

Steve escorted the limping man back to the remains of the Hill, and with relief and joy, found the others all safe.

Wilf took over, and finding some shotgun pellets in the man's leg, which had made quite a mess, he carefully picked them out with forceps, and then cleaned and disinfected the area, and bandaged him up.

"Grazie," said the man, who was finding it difficult to understand the kindness given to him by his so-called enemies. He limped back up the hill with them to the remains of the house, only to find a pile of shattered bricks, stones and burning wood, where this once proud house had stood and sheltered him.

"It is so remote here," said John. "It will take a very long time for the emergency services to respond, but even so I think we should leave soon."

Bladon, Lexi, and John went straight to the home of Giacomo, to break the sad news of his grandfather's death. Lexi and Wilf took him and his wife into their small living accommodation at the back of the house, and gently told them of their grandfather's bravery and his help at the end. He had died with Wilf comforting him. Meanwhile the others took the injured captive into the kitchen to interrogate him. He seemed eager to talk, after seeing how pitiless his former employees had been. He knew they had tried to kill him too. However all he could offer was confirmation of what the Professor had told them, that the weapons had been taken to a base in central England, and assembled there ready for an attack.

He was the one who had recognised Bladon in Urbino. He admitted fleeing from Cornwall, but the only other interesting thing that he had heard was the word, Trent, and Burton. Could this possibly be where their base was?

Meanwhile, in view of the possible arrival of the emergency

Thirty One

services, Steve and Wilf limited their search of the remains of the three demolished houses. All they came up with in the short time available was a fragment of cardboard from a package, with an address in Birmingham on it, and also a bill from a restaurant in Staffordshire called The Waterfront.

"That's very interesting," said Bladon. "We've not had much success here in Italy. We nearly got blown up by a French fighter jet; nearly lost Steve's precious plane; arrived at their hideout too late; nearly got blown to pieces; and then saw them fly away to goodness knows where. But I know this restaurant. I've eaten there several times. The food is good. It's at a place called Barton Marina, next to the canal and the river, and the A38. Interestingly, it's near Burton-on-Trent. I think it's our second big break, since we captured one of their weapons.

But most important, if the Professor is right, Dreadnought is back. Somehow he didn't die in the helicopter crash and he seems to be masterminding this whole operation. It's not good news. He's a very dangerous opponent. I must tell the others back in the UK as soon as possible.

The big problem is that even if we find their base we've still got to stop them. We've had another very clear demonstration today of how lethal this weapon is, and if they have lots of them, what do we do?"

"One step at a time though."

Thirty Two

As the helicopter wheeled away from "The Hill", back at Walton Priory, near Burton-on-Trent, a chauffeur driven Bentley drew up at the impressive entrance. The rear door opened, a man got out with his scarf pulled up over his face, and shadowed by two burly bodyguards he hurried inside.

It was indeed Bladon's terrible nemesis, Dreadnought, seemingly back from the dead, and now back in England, after his successful sojourn in Italy. He had returned and was now ready to bring all his plans to fruition. Who could stop him this time? "Well," he muttered, "certainly not Bladon, nor his woman, nor his motley assortment of pensioned-off pals".

But Dreadnought was not happy at the attention that had been brought to them at their base at Walton-on-Trent. Bladon did not know where their base was yet, but damage had been done. Instead of carrying out a clinical operation miles away from their base, killing all of Bladon's men, and the Prime Minister, they had killed none of them, in fact it was far worse than that, but Clara had not yet owned up to the full extent of the debacle.

Still, he had all the weapons and Italy had been a very successful operation. His base was still secure, and his plans near completion for the final attack and the deal with the Chinese. All in all, he felt everything was still on track.

Meanwhile, Steve landed at Rangemore Aerodrome in Staffordshire the day after Dreadnought had arrived back in the UK, in total secrecy. Matteo had really excelled himself and had arranged for the Comanche to be transferred to Trassani, just north of Urbino, by cover of darkness, and within a day minor repairs to the front and the undercarriage had been done and it had been refuelled ready for take off. The return journey was uneventful with a refuelling stop in France, and as the light started to fail, Steve taxied to the hanger, dropped off his passengers by the car, and then thirty minutes later he joined his three friends.

John had flown back by British Airways with Riley, from Bologna. At Heathrow to meet him were his daughter Rachel and her husband Saul. They greeted them warmly, and then Saul set off in his Land Rover Discovery to drive them up to Derby. Saul and Rachel now lived in Kent, and with the three of them coming home for a visit it promised to be a very happy time for John, a brief time of relaxation before events reached a climax. Riley had offered to come back with his Dad, partly to meet his sister again, but he also wanted to meet the others in case he could be of help. His iPhone pinged as soon as they started up the M25 and it was Leone, Riley's son, with a message.

"Hope you landed OK Daddy, and Nonno. Be careful and keep safe. Love Leo and Arco."

Bladon, Lexi and Wilf waited for Steve in his VW Toureg, and then Steve joined them.

"It's all sorted out friends. Let's get you back to our house. Julia is preparing a delicious chicken dish and after that we can share all our news with Julia over coffee.

"My, goodness," Julia said over cappuccinos and truffles, "you've had a very exciting time. Whatever next."

"Well," Bladon replied. "I've been thinking about that on the flight back, and I think we must assume that Dreadnought got back before us, and is making his final preparations right now. I am suggesting that we hold a Council of War tomorrow, but not in our house in Kedleston, as it may be too risky. Would you excuse me please as I have a phone call to make?"

Bladon left them for a few minutes and took his mobile

into the snug. He was back ten minutes later with a satisfied grin.

"I have found the ideal place for our meeting tomorrow. I have a friend who has a large house right next to the River Trent, and in fact has already been helping Andy; he has kindly agreed to let us have the use of his house for as long as we want. Selwyn was quite prepared to move out, but I refused, as it will be great to have him and Janet around for their input as well. I just have to alert the rest of The Thirteen, and Sandy and Willie, and I suggest we start at 10.30am. Is that OK? We have a lot to get through."

Monday 10.30am

They met the next morning at Selwyn and Janet's large country house by the river.

Bladon spoke first. "May I introduce Sandy? As some of you know, Sandy is chief aide to the Prime Minister, and they have been discussing the current position. Over to you Sandy."

"Thank you Bladon. I've been having a long discussion with the PM about how to proceed, now that we are getting so close to discovering the enemy base. Wherever it is, it will be a very difficult job to attack it as we don't know how many of the super-guns they have there. On behalf of the PM, I want to thank you all for the wonderful work that you have done on behalf of the country, at great personal risk. Bladon is still a legend in the SAS, and between you all, your unique and special talents are so valuable, most of all your courage and bravery. This enabled you to defeat Dreadnought's last terrible plot to take control of the country. Not only that, you have been outstanding in the way that you have fought off enemy attacks in Cornwall, and eradicated their bases at Nancenoy Towers and in Derbyshire, after some fierce fighting. But back to Dreadnought, we thought he was dead, but I'm afraid from what Bladon tells me he's back.

Because of that, the PM and I both consider that now is the time to hand over to the professionals. We are very reluctant to do so, but we have available to us the resources of the entire armed forces, including Special Forces, and also the intelligence community at MI5 and MI6. We also have some quite revolutionary weaponry that we think could assist us in the very difficult task of taking the enemy base.

Bladon sensed the disappointment, surprise, confusion, and even anger arising among his friends. He interrupted Sandy before the situation became totally unrecoverable.

"Sandy, I understand your arguments, and that you want the best for us, our families, and the country, but may I just say something, and then ask the rest of The Thirteen for their views as well? We have been friends for such a long time, and have faced many dangers together. I do hope you'll forgive me for interrupting you."

"Not at all Bladon, go ahead. The PM and I are not suggesting that ours is the only way forward, just that it might be the best way forward. We really want to hear your views—all of you."

Bladon stood.

"I sense a lot of disappointment and confusion amongst you, my trusted and loyal friends." After affirmative nods all round, he addressed The Thirteen, or what was left of them.

"We have a big decision to make. Do we carry on and finish the task of stopping Dreadnought ourselves, or do we handover to Sandy and the SAS and intelligence community as he has suggested? The Government have far more resources available than we could ever have, and on the face of it, what Sandy has suggested would seem to be the most sensible solution, particularly as Lexi and I only got involved this time, when we were attacked in Cornwall; but since the later attacks in the Peak District and Italy, it's got personal. If Dreadnought is indeed alive and active again, as seems to be the case, our lives will always be in danger. None of us are now active soldiers, but we have a unique blend of expertise and experience, and more importantly we know how Dreadnought thinks and operates.

But, perhaps the most compelling reason for us to

continue and not stand down is the moral aspect. I think you will agree with me that Dreadnought, and all that he stands for, is thoroughly evil, and I believe that you shouldn't let evil flourish, if you can do something about it. What is it that Edmund Burke said? "The only thing necessary for the triumph of evil is for good men to do nothing". So, do we do nothing, and step aside?

I know you might think this is a strange analogy, but I have been reading the biography of C. S. Lewis recently, and particularly his Narnia Chronicles. I think they've got a lot to say to us about the situation we find ourselves in. For those of you that haven't read any of the seven books, four children, Peter, Susan, Edmund and Lucy, are evacuated from London during the Second World War. To escape the bombing, they are taken to an old house in the country, occupied by a genial, eccentric professor.

One day they are prevented from exploring the outside world due to heavy rain, so they decide to explore the corridors and rooms of the old house. They stumble into a room that is quite empty except for a big wardrobe. Lucy, the youngest, enters the wardrobe and finds herself in her words, "in a cold snowy land a world in which it is always winter and never Christmas." It's the land of Narnia, where the true king is Aslan the Lion, who has been absent for many years, and the land has been taken over by the White Witch, who is the very personification of evil.

I know what you're thinking. Am I losing it? What have lions and white witches, and fauns, and beavers, and unicorns, got to do with the deadly situation we are facing. Well, the four could easily have stayed in the safety of that old comfortable house. They were scared, but all four of them went into that strange land, leaving the safety of their world, to fight a seemingly all-powerful, dangerous, and thoroughly evil regime. I think it's so relevant to our dilemma today. It's about choices to be made, of right and wrong, and of challenges that must be faced. I believe the time has come for us to make just that choice."

Thirty Three

Bladon sat down to complete silence. Nothing at all stirred in the large room overlooking the river. Finally, Andy stood, and to cheers from the others, articulated what was in all their minds and hearts.

"Bladon that was inspirational. Thank you. I'm with you. Let's make that choice. Let's finish the task"

At that, the others all burst into shouts of agreement, and the long faces of moments before, were replaced by beaming smiles.

Sandy spoke when they had quietened a little.

"Well done friends. We thought you might want to finish the job. The PM is more than happy for you to remain in charge, subject to reporting back to him, but he does have some conditions.

Firstly, he is putting two squadrons of SAS at your disposal, for use at your absolute discretion. For those of you not familiar with how the SAS are organised, 22 SAS Regiment (two-two) has four operational squadrons: A, B, D and G. Each squadron consists of approximately 60 men commanded by a Major, and divided into four troops. Troops usually consist of 15 men, and each patrol within a troop consists of four men, with each man possessing a particular skill; signals, demolition, medical or linguistics, in addition to basic skills learned during the course of their training. The PM wants to put A Squadron and B Squadron on standby for you, so you will have at your command 120 of the finest

Special Forces in the world. Willie will act as your liaison officer.

Secondly, he knows that the attack on Dreadnought's HQ will be very difficult and very dangerous, as he will have at his disposal a large number of those new weapons, including presumably at least one of the artillery pieces that Professor Lane has made. All my expert advisers tell me it promises to be a fearsome weapon. The PM knows that you will all be turning your minds to ways to combat these weapons, but he wants you to consider using two of our top-secret developments, which he is sure will be of help to you.

The first is a miniature drone, or to give it its full title, a remotely piloted vehicle, and it is modelled on the Reaper used in many theatres of war already.

The second is a top-secret helmet that has been developed at a cost of millions for use in tandem with the drones. He will send two of each, together with the technicians, to be here later today.

Most importantly though, he has asked me to say to you all how grateful he is. He knows you all well enough to realise that you were never going to agree to back off; he apologises if he's upset you, but he's with you every step of the way."

Bladon replied with effusive thanks to Sandy, and to the PM for their confidence and support.

"We would not attempt an assault on Dreadnought's headquarters without back-up from the SAS, and those offers of weaponry are astonishing. Thank you. I believe that the odds have just turned quite decisively in our favour. I am sure that Dreadnought feels supremely confident of complete victory this time. Perhaps he's over confident."

"Now let me introduce the team in case there's anyone you don't know.

I've said how much we appreciate Sandy's support and how much it's meant to us all. He lead one of the attack groups in Cornwall and helped us capture one of the super-guns in Derbyshire. I cannot express my gratitude to him enough.

Thirty Three

Willie has already been a tremendous help in Cornwall and Derbyshire, and is a serving Major in the SAS. He's in charge of A Squadron, who are tasked to help us.

Terry is his Sergeant at A Squadron, and probably the most experienced, battle hardened, non-commissioned officer in the whole of the Regiment. We are so fortunate to have you both.

We are known by legend, as The Thirteen, and unfortunately since our last adventure we have lost two of our number Martyn and Greg, and we will miss them a lot. We are further depleted by the loss of Julian, who is in the middle of delicate negotiations to buy another company, and regrettably can't join us. This effectively depletes our numbers to 10. What I want to do is to get back to our original Thirteen, by appointing Steve, Willie, and Terry to our number. You will all be the "New Thirteen". Let me introduce everybody else.

We'll start with John who lives in Derby, just over the road from Steve, and he kindly sheltered me in his house when Dreadnought's men had badly shot me up in Derbyshire last time. He is a Chartered Accountant, with a thriving practice nearby, and not many of his clients know that he served in the elite Royal Marine Patrol Group. After this is all over, if you ask him nicely he'll sort out your tax returns. Sorry, he probably does that already!

Next there's Stefan, a North Londoner, and a keen Spurs supporter. He is a brilliant hairdresser, a great friend of John's, highly artistic, kind and voluble, and whilst he spent several years training at Sassoon's in London, he joined a Territorial Unit of the SAS. He's been on several joint missions in Northern Ireland, with SIS and Special Branch, and is a former member of 14 Int., Northern Ireland's very secretive SAS undercover arm. Sadly, he was shot on our lawn at Kedleston, at the same time that Martyn was killed, but he is now recovered and raring to go.

Phillip is an old friend of mine, from our days in the Regiment, and until recently he worked for the Ministry of Defence in London. He was one of the first to come across

Dreadnought's evil organisation and fought alongside me in Cornwall and Derbyshire.

Jeremy, before starting his security consultancy, had done a tour with the SBS and still works very closely with them; he is a very talented man, and advises on Royal protection as well.

Giancarlo is the leading academic in our group, and holds the Chair in Medieval and Renaissance English at Cambridge University. We went on many hairy missions together for the SAS in Northern Ireland, before he left for the fields of academe.

Next we have Wilf. You'll all know the beloved Doc. Few know at his surgeries near the Nottinghamshire and Derbyshire border, that this brilliant and likeable GP has been on many combat missions, and has also advised the American Delta Force on Special Ops from a specialist medical perspective.

Patrick was a very successful businessman, before retiring to concentrate on completing the renovation of his house in rural France. Not many know however, that he was a reserve member of an elite Marines unit and was called on from time to time for counter insurgency work.

Andy, an old friend of John and Patrick, full of fun and joie de vivre, started in the lace industry, but now heads a very successful and exclusive furniture manufacturing business in Long Eaton. Some of you may now him as James, but we know him as Andy.

And last, but definitely not least, is the beautiful Lexi, who has been such a brave and solid support to me and to you all. She's been threatened in Cornwall, kidnapped in Switzerland, nearly killed in Jersey, and almost savaged to death by a killer dog in Cornwall. She's saved my life on many occasions. What I have asked her to do is perhaps the most important job of all, and that is to be the Coordinator of a Brainstorming Group that I want to set up. She will be based at our house in Kedleston".

Thirty Three

"So, how do we proceed, because time is absolutely of the essence? I have spoken to Sandy and he agrees that there are three urgent questions we need to address.

Firstly, where is their base?

Secondly, how do we attack it?

Thirdly, what is Dreadnought's ultimate target?

I want to leave the matter of the third question to our elite Brainstorming Group under Lexi. I propose that you start as soon as possible Lexi, and I suggest, for reasons that will become apparent, that you have Jeremy and Steve. I hate to take you out of a possible assault on the enemy base but I think it is absolutely crucial that you bring your special skills to try to discern where Dreadnought will strike. You need to be able to look into his very soul."

"Is that OK Lexi?"

"Thank you so much for your kind remarks, and your confidence in me darling. I know we need to keep the group down to a small number, but I would like to ask the Doc if we can borrow his two sons for a week or so, to help us with the brainstorming. Faisal and Adam are such likeable young men, but with formidable intellects. They would be a tremendous help to us. They followed their Dad into medicine with outstanding success, and are incredibly well qualified with first class degrees at Oxford and Cambridge and postgraduate studies in Toronto and Harvard. Do you think they could help us Wilf?"

"That's so kind of you Lexi and I'm sure they would love to help," said Wilf. "The problem will be for them to get time off at the moment. It might be a problem."

"Perhaps I could help," said Sandy. "I'll phone the PM now and let him sort it."

"Better ask the boys first though," said Bladon mischievously.

Wilf phoned them and they both jumped at the chance to help their country, and following the intervention of the PM they planned to arrive at Lexi's house in Kedleston in the early evening, ready for a meeting the next day.

Bladon next concerned himself with the first two questions; where Dreadnought's base was, and how to take it?

"Before we start, I think we should have a short break for lunch. There are one or two decent pubs nearby. Shall we try one."

At this suggestion Janet leapt to her feet. "No need for that Bladon. It would be dangerous to all meet so openly, and so close to the river, so I have already prepared a delicious Lancashire Hotpot for you all. Shall I set up straight away?"

"Wonderful," chorused everyone, and Selwyn showed them through to the dining room.

Thirty Four

Monday 3pm

Selwyn and Janet's home was a magnificent old country house, on the outskirts of the small hamlet of Twyford, set in its own substantial grounds, by a bend in the River Trent, between the villages of Willington and Shardlow. It was known as "The White Rabbit", a nod to Selwyn's love of 'Alice in Wonderland'. Being a world expert on Lewis Carroll, he and Giancarlo immediately recognised kindred spirits. The house was set in two acres of lawned gardens, and was a very handsome property, comprising a large lounge, a snug, a dining room, and a very large kitchen. There were four bedrooms on the first floor, most with ensuites, and two bedrooms and a bathroom on the second floor.

But where the property excelled for Bladon's purposes, was a huge ballroom on the first floor that had been fitted out by Selwyn, at short notice especially for them, with a large oak boardroom table, comfortable leather chairs, and phones and Internet access. Outside, off the York stone patio, a large swimming pool glittered in the midday sun, tempting them to a dip. They had no time for leisure though, as Bladon called the meeting to order at three. Seated around the table were Bladon, Selwyn, Sandy, Willie, Terry, John, Stefan, Giancarlo, Wilf, Andy, Phillip, Patrick, Steve and Jeremy.

"Now our first job is to find their base. We have collected quite a bit of information as to its possible location. In our search of the remains of the house in Italy, we found a bill from a restaurant in Staffordshire, called The Waterfront. I know the restaurant myself; it's located on Barton Marina, which is near Barton-under-Needwood, and it is very close to the canal, and just over the A38 dual carriageway, lies the River Trent.

The closest villages on the river are Walton-on-Trent and Branston, famous for its pickles. Now I think we can rule out Branston, as their base must be on the river, because that's where we last saw their inflatable escaping from our Range Rover, but we lost them soon after Branston, so I think their hideout could be the next village along, which is Walton.

That's conjecture, but when the SBS team questioned the girl from the base who had nearly been killed, she said that she would tell us anything we want to know about the woman who attacked her, and her base. Well I've just heard that she recovered consciousness late last night, and Sandy told me about an hour ago that she's disclosed that their base is in fact at Walton-on-Trent, as we thought. It looks as if it's Walton Priory, just outside the village and very close to the river. We are getting satellite photographs, which should be with us in an hour.

Now of course knowing where they are hiding, and capturing them and the weapons, are two very different things. But it's a first step, so the next question is how to launch a successful attack? Ideas please gentlemen."

"Well", said Willie, "we can surround the place with SAS, and put up road blocks to stop them getting away, but we have to find a way round those terrible weapons they have. In a straight firefight we would have no chance. Also the woman has given us a rough idea of the floor plan inside the Priory, but we need detailed plans of the house and grounds and how they access the river. As a matter of priority, I suggest that we put a couple of four man SAS patrols in the grounds, to cover the drive and front of the house, and the river access."

Sandy spoke next, for he had come face to face with the super-guns at Warslow and at Trent Lock and won both encounters.

"I agree Willie. Let's do it. I want them in place straight

Thirty Four

away. However, back to the attack, with their supergun Dreadnought's forces are almost invulnerable. In a straight assault against fixed, well dug-in positions, it is almost impossible to take them out. Even a missile or a drone attack on their base would fail, as their new weapons would shoot them right out of the sky. But then I thought of the deadly duels with them in Warslow and Trent Lock. Maybe the way to defeat them could be to turn their invulnerability and confidence against them. Dreadnought must be so sure of ultimate victory; and is probably right now preparing for a head-on attack from us like at Nancenoy Towers, but he might not consider a stealth attack by a few, just as we did at Ilam Manor in our last conflict. He has been trying to wipe out The Thirteen out of revenge, not fear, and I think that Dreadnought is very dismissive of our abilities even now. We can use that complacency.

I think a small team should assault Walton Priory using those miniaturised drones that I talked about with the PM. They have been specially developed and use Smart missiles in a controlled environment. That is, they attack small areas and groups of men surgically. They have only been operated by two specialist electronics operators before in trials, but I am certain that we can get up to speed pretty quickly and be just as impressive as they are. The drones and helmets are coming in about an hour, and the technicians can take us through the operating protocols.

Remembering the lessons of Warslow and Trent Lock, how did we beat them? Well we did it by stealth, and by targeting the operatives, not the weapon. We can do that with the drones operating in conjunction with the special helmets, with back up by the rest of us with conventional weapons. Not all of the enemy forces will be using the super-guns, as Dreadnought would not risk losing control of them. We will set a perimeter of SAS troopers round the grounds, and a Police presence on the adjoining roads, and then a further SBS and SAS presence by the river and the surrounding countryside."

"Excellent idea Sandy," said Bladon. "Comments and

thoughts please anyone?"

"I think it's a brilliant plan", said Andy. "But we need to choose the operators of the drones and helmets carefully. I think Steve is a shoe-in for operating the drones, with his aeronautical and engineering skills, and Phillip too with his MOD experience and his engineering background. I think for the helmets we need great dexterity and lightness of touch, so who fits the bill there—Wilf."

"Well that just leaves one more to control the other helmet", said Bladon, grinning at Andy. "I think Andy you are the obvious choice, as you did so well in the ambush at Trent Lock. Are you game?"

"You flatter me Bladon old friend," Andy replied. "Of course I'll do it, if you think I'm the right man. That leaves you in overall control, Willie and Terry to coordinate the SAS; and Sandy to liaise with Government. We then have Willie, Terry, John, Stefan, Giancarlo, Jeremy and Patrick for combat duties, alongside the drone operators. I have the feeling that the drones are our ace in the pack, and the rest will just be mopping up, and search and capture operations."

So they had sorted the first two problems; the location of the base and the plan of attack. They were expecting the drones and helmets to arrive soon, whereupon they would start the next stage of the operation.

Thirty Five

At 4.00pm two prototypes of the new high-tech military helmet were delivered to the farmhouse by a courier with a heavily armed escort, direct from the dinghy back room of a Kent factory, followed by the drones at 4.30pm. The codename for the helmet was SpartanWarrior, and it was designed to provide ordinary soldiers with the kind of heads-up display once reserved for jet-fighter pilots. Allied Special Forces were already testing the system and it was expected that it would be on the battlefield in as little as three years.

"Let me explain this revolutionary piece of equipment to you all", said Sandy. "The helmet relies on its transparent, high definition screen, which has taken more than 10 years to develop. Detailed positional information coming from the helmet, allows computers to map data on the battle area, (in this case the building being attacked) and it shows where targets, the location of friendly forces, enemies, and other points of interest are. The helmet wearers, Wilf and Andy, can also see in total darkness, because an infrared camera beams footage directly into their line of vision. This will be of vital importance to our attack. To use this infrared ability, electronics experts from 'A' Regiment of the SAS are going to ensure that just before the attack is launched, there will be a complete blackout of power. These two helmets are even more special. They also have integrated some special software, which takes each image apart, pixel-by-pixel, and anything that represents a straight line, such as a wall, or a window, is ignored. So it can literally see through walls, and only heat sources with irregular shapes are displayed. The deadly weapons that Dreadnought will be using against us will show up as soon as they are brought into combat. They will be lit up like Christmas trees. However it has a limited range at the moment. This new software will only work in the immediate vicinity. Also the helmets can be linked to work in tandem with the drones; wearing the helmet you can give precise instructions to the drone operators through their headsets, so that they don't just see through their drone's eyes, but also through yours.

Sandy then turned to the two drones, which had been delivered thirty minutes after the helmets.

"Now Steve and Phillip, here are the drones that you will be operating. You've heard of Reaper drones, used extensively in Afghanistan. Well another British company has been working on miniaturising them. The missile targeting system, electro-optical infrared system, laser designator, and laser illuminator on the drone have all been successfully miniaturised into a fully operative micro version of the Reaper, which will fit in the palm of your hand. All of these components give the mini-Reaper and its operators, multiple ways to acquire a target in any combat environment.

The mini drone fires a laser, or infrared beam, from the nose of the plane, which lands on the target and pulses to attract the laser seekers at the end of each tiny missile. The on-board computer uses the beam to make calculations about trajectory and distance, and once a target is "painted", the mini drone can unleash its missiles to destroy the target. Working with Wilf and Andy with their helmets, they will be able to see not only by means of their cameras, but through walls, round corners and through windows. They can then target and fire miniaturised missiles, or any other armaments you want. The two drones are almost ready to go, they just need some technical adjustments before handing them over. They both carry cameras and two miniaturised missiles each. These have been specially chosen for this environment, so that specific areas like a room or a corridor can be attacked surgically, and their missiles can be replenished very quickly. You can methodically take out room after room, including all

Thirty Five

the weapons and operatives, until you've cleared the house."

"That's brilliant", said Patrick. "Very exciting, but I see a major problem here. We have two of these very expensive, deadly mini drones, but what happens when we first deploy them in the building".

"What do you mean Patrick?" asked Bladon

"Well if they are deployed and one of Dreadnought's men immediately uses his super-gun on it, before we can set up the laser on a target, it will destroy them. We will then be forced to revert to a very dangerous and costly hand-to-hand conflict against their far superior weaponry. The helmets won't be much use either if the drones are taken out."

Sandy spoke up immediately. "Well said Patrick. This is the one major flaw in our attack plans, but Bladon and I have thought of a way of preventing Dreadnought's men taking out our best weapons in this way. You may think it's a bit 'Heath Robinson' but we think it will work."

"What is it then?" said Patrick.

"A lot of commercial organisations are using drones. For instance EasyJet use one for examining their plane engines. It saves them so much time. But that's expensive. We've sourced from Amazon some 'mini toy drones'. You can get a variety from retail outlets, but we've tested, and bought, some 'Hubsan' Mini Drones with cameras fitted, for under £100. We've bought twelve, so that after linking them electronically with the helmets, we can put them up before the Reapers. They will be delivered to Selwyn's by courier tomorrow morning. We will deploy them in order to try and build up a clear picture of the enemy dispositions, knowing that we will lose some, if not most of them. Our thinking is that they will probably blaze away at them with the super-guns initially, but after they've shot down a few we're hoping that they will lose interest, and in the heat of battle won't notice that we're putting up two altogether different beasts—the mini Reapers."

Giancarlo interrupted him, "Sandy, I hope you don't mind if I throw another spanner in the works. I wonder if we are over complicating things with the helmets and the drones. They are going to give us an incredible advantage in the attack, maybe even compensate for our lack of firepower against their super-guns, but why don't we simplify things and let the ones who wear the helmets also operate the drones. There would be no necessity then for the man wearing the helmet to tell the drone operator what he could see, he could act on the information and pictures he was getting live, there and then. Also it has the advantage of freeing up two men for our attack. Could I suggest that Steve and Phillip wear the helmets and operate the drones in forward positions just ahead of the rest of us? Wilf and Andy could then be released to stay with Steve and Phillip and protect them as best they can with conventional weapons. It will be very dangerous for the four of them though."

"No, Giancarlo, please don't apologise. You're absolutely right. It's obvious really. Why duplicate the tasks and tie up two of our best fighting men. Willie, what do you suggest for weapons for Wilf and Andy?"

"Thanks Sandy, and I must say I agree with Giancarlo too. May I suggest a Heckler & Koch MP5SD suppressed sub machine gun for them both. Despite its integrated silencer element, it has the same length and shape as an unsilenced submachine gun. The integrated silencer element suppresses the muzzle flash extremely effectively, as a result of which the weapon is also excellent for night operations using low-light amplifiers. We reckon, in the SAS, that it's one of the most accurate, silenced, submachine guns, of its type.

I don't want to get too technical, but I think that they should also carry a Heckler & Koch HK417. The 417 is a gas-operated, selective fire battle rifle, which we use to complement lighter assault rifles. Its greater accuracy, range, and penetration complement the MP5SD, particularly the 20" 'Sniper' Model. Wilf and Andy would then have the flexibility of a heavy weapon and a sniper rifle as well. We found in the attack on The Trent Lock Hotel that the sniper rifle is the only way to effectively deal with the super-gun—besides the drones of course."

Thirty Five

"Thank you Sandy, Giancarlo and Willie. We are eternally grateful to you all," said Bladon. "I suggest that Steve and Phillip, Andy and Wilf, after dinner go to an isolated barn that Selwyn has found, for some preliminary practice with the new equipment. Are there any questions, because if not, I'll close the meeting until tomorrow? Many thanks all of you."

Thirty Six

It was 6pm when Dreadnought and Clara slipped away from Walton Priory, as his men were sitting down to dinner, prepared in-house.

They found a table in a secluded corner of a nearby, quiet little pub, the Shoulder of Mutton, and ordered their meal from the bar.

Dreadnought had first met Clara when he was trying to set up his base in Italy for the production of the super-weapons. A friend had recommended her on the basis of her extensive experience with Spetsnaz, the Soviet Special Forces outfit. These elite units of the Russian Federation were mostly controlled by the military intelligence operation GRU, but she had spent the last three years of her time in the Special Forces, with the FSB, formerly KGB, known as the Spetsnaz Intelligence Unit.

In parts of the Le Marche province of Italy there was an ongoing problem with the Albanian Mafia. The area Dreadnought had earmarked for his forward base and manufacturing unit was in that province, around Urbino, and it meant that the mafia had to be dealt with first.

Dreadnought had grown to like Clara, and looked on her almost as his "heir apparent", in fact on first meeting her, he was so impressed with her, that he let her pick her own men to tackle the Mafia, and within a month she had completely broken them and eradicated their influence in the area. She was a ruthless, vicious, hard-nosed killer, used sometimes by al-Qaeda, but she also had a warm, exuberant, and bubbly character, which belied her lethal skills set. She was also a fearless warrior and a brilliant strategist.

When he was sure he could not be overheard Dreadnought started to explain his Grand Design to Clara over their starters. It was well away from any listening ears back at base. She already knew how Bladon and The Thirteen had previously foiled his plans for domination of the UK. However, until now, she hadn't realised his utter hatred of Bladon and his wife Lexi, and of his absolute obsession with eradicating all of The Thirteen, together with the current British Prime Minister, Johnny Hanbury. It was not just part of his grand plan for takeover of the country, it was more than that. It was his major objective and if it coincided with making him a fortune, and at the same time taking over the Country, then so much the better.

He explained his plans in detail to Clara, confiding in her totally.

"From our base at Walton Priory, you and I and four of our elite gunmen, will travel to our respective targets. It has to be a small elite force to be able to move freely. Firstly two men will make a diversionary attack in Derby City Centre, but the main target, which we and the other two men will attack, is Kedleston Hall, an impressive Stately Home, owned by the National Trust, and extensively used in several blockbuster films."

"I want to completely destroy the Hall, as a means of shock and awe to the whole country. I have reliable intelligence that the Queen will be visiting the Hall next Monday with several VIP's, and I am going to unleash a lethal attack with the super-gun on the private quarters of the Hall, where they will be meeting with the Curzon family. This will take them all out, and part of the building too. It is one of the conditions of a deal that I made with the Chinese Government in return for two billion pounds. They want conclusive proof that the weapons work, and this attack on Kedleston Hall will provide that proof."

"Once the private wing of the Hall is destroyed, the

Chinese will land their helicopter, take delivery of the weapons, including a lethal helicopter mounted gun, and I will then hand over not just the weapons but also the blueprints for the weapons themselves; whereupon the £2billion will be electronically transferred to my secret bank account overseas. Once the helicopter has been fitted with the super-gun, the Chinese will then obliterate the rest of Kedleston Hall, and as a personal favour to me, they will also wipe out Bladon's residence nearby. It will be a lethal attack and I am sure that nothing will stand in my way this time."

Clara thought that now might be an opportune time to confess the full extent of the debacle at The Trent Lock Hotel and Spa.

"I am afraid that Bladon's men outwitted us at Trent Lock. They must have known we were coming and when we attacked they killed several of my men and I had to extract my force very quickly to avoid capture."

Dreadnought's countenance changed from being supportive to one of dark anger. "How stupid of you Clara. How can I ever trust you again? What if they tracked you back to our base here in Walton?"

Clara was shocked at the vehemence of his response, but composed herself sufficiently to reply. "There is no need to worry sir. I completely destroyed the cruiser we used, and also killed both the two women on board with one blast from the super-gun, and stopped Bladon from finding our base. Furthermore, when an SAS team tried to stop me by attacking from the main road bridge into Burton-on-Trent, I destroyed them with the gun, before escaping to Walton. I am sure I was not followed, and that the integrity of our headquarters is still intact."

Dreadnought, however, had not got so close to success by taking chances. He made a quick decision and told Clara that they would be leaving Walton later that night. He phoned Kurt who he had left in charge of a narrow boat.

"There's been a change of plan Kurt. You have some new orders. We will be bringing the weapons up to you on the narrowboat, but not where you are at the Marina. It's too dangerous, as Clara ran into the SBS at Shardlow earlier. I want you to move the narrowboat out of Shardlow Marina then go down the Trent and Mersey Canal, and wait for us on the canal, just before you reach Swarkestone.

You will see on the map that the road from Swarkestone to Chellaston turns right just after the bridge over the canal, signposted to Weston-on-Trent. If you follow that road on the map, you will see that after about a mile, there is a small bridle path on the right that runs down to the canal. The path is tree-lined, and the bank has good tree cover as well, and you can moor the boat there. I've just googled it and it's a pretty lonely spot. I'll meet you after midnight and we'll load up the guns, and six of us will come on board. You can then use our transit van to get to the other narrow boat that I've moored at Sawley Marina. It's all stocked up with food. We'll meet you at the Marina tomorrow and we'll be staying there in both the boats until Saturday. Whatever you do, don't move from there until we've left. You'll get further instructions later. Is that understood?"

"Yes boss. No problem. I'll start out straight away and be there before 10pm."

"Kurt, whatever you do, don't rush. You'll only draw attention to yourself if there are any watchers still around. We'll be there before midnight."

Clara had heard his instructions and asked him how their plans would change.

"Well, I had intended to go up to Shardlow Marina with the men and the guns, stay for a few days, and then make for Derby and Kedleston; but I think that's too dangerous now. Our base at Walton may still be secure but I can't risk it. The six of us will sleep tonight on the narrowboat, and then take a leisurely journey up to the River Trent and on to Sawley Marina, the largest inland marina in the UK, where we'll stay until Saturday evening. How are you at working lock gates Clara? Then we move slowly up the canal on Saturday, through Long Eaton and Sandiacre, a very densely populated area, but no one will give us a second glance in a narrowboat. They'll just think we're on holiday."

He seemed to have forgiven Clara.

"We'll get to a little place called Stanton Gate, between Sandiacre and the large town of Ilkeston, by Saturday evening. We'll stop there, transfer the guns to some transport I've arranged, and then we'll make for Kedleston, after dropping off two of the men at the Holiday Inn Express in Pride Park, Derby, to prepare for their diversionary attack."

"The rest of us will make our way to the Kedleston Hotel, a derelict and boarded-up building not far from the Hall, which will be our forward base for the attack on our main target.

After our attack I plan to retreat from Kedleston Hall grounds, first back to the Kedleston Hotel, and then on to London by helicopter, to mobilize the takeover of the country. The bulk of our forces can stay at Walton Priory. I don't think they have tracked down our base at Walton, but I am leaving them some of the weapons just in case, to repel any attacks, until we're in London, when they can join us.

Meanwhile, after dinner, Steve, Phillip, Andy and Wilf drove the short distance to the isolated barn that Selwyn had found for them for some preliminary practice with the helmets and drones. Sandy came with them too, as he had been fully briefed by the technical gurus who had developed the Reaper drones and the helmet. As agreed, Steve and Phillip would wear the helmets and also operate both the 'toy' drones and the deadly Reaper 'mini' drones, and Andy and Wilf would act as guards to them both. It was necessary however, that Phillip and Wilf should also become familiar with both the helmets and the drones in case Steve or Phillip were incapacitated during the attack.

With Sandy's expert tuition they soon grasped the intricacies of operation.

"These drones are fun," said Steve. "It's just like flying my plane only even more technical. It's brilliant."

"These helmets are really futuristic," replied Phillip. They just take warfare to a new level. I can see through walls, round corners and can even distinguish different types of weapons. I'm sure their super-guns will be a doddle to identify. It was tricky at first for me to correlate the movement of the drones with what I see on my screen, but you soon get used to it. It's like a heads up display on expensive motor cars."

Andy and Wilf were similarly enthralled by the two brilliant technological breakthroughs, and soon became as expert as the other two.

"We can't fail with these gizmos," said Wilf. "When it comes to close quarter fighting we have a major advantage, even against their terrible weapons."

As the clock reached eleven they loaded the car with their precious cargo and headed back to base tired but exhilarated.

Monday 11.15pm

Back at Selwyn's house Bladon yawned.

"I don't know about you Lexi, but I'm tired out after the day we've just had. I think it's time we went home now, don't you?"

Bladon drove their car out of Selwyn's drive and made their way towards their home in Kedleston. After a companionable silence Lexi spoke.

"I thought you were magnificent in there," she said, "when the government wanted to take it all over from us. You completely swung the argument over and won the day. But I would love to hear what your feelings were at that moment. Was it all about justice, or were there any other considerations."

"Well," said Bladon, "that's a difficult one. You know that I'm a pretty complicated sort of guy in many ways, but I think the answer to that question is multifaceted. What I mean is that yes, I am really concerned about justice, and bringing this monster Dreadnought to book, and stopping him from committing another atrocity. It's so unjust what he's been doing, both previously and in this latest attack. Someone has to stop him and we are better placed than anybody."

"If I am really honest with you though sweetheart, there is an element of revenge about it too, as I told you down in Cornwall. I know that revenge is not a good thing to keep for a long time, as it makes you bitter and twisted inside, but I also feel it can be harnessed to bring Dreadnought down. After all, it was he who killed, or gave the order to kill Sarah in cold blood. You didn't know her, but she was a wonderful woman, did no harm to anybody, and he ruthlessly took her out."

"I suppose there's also a part of me that feels guilty that I was not able to protect her. She was really scared about him catching up with her, and nobody knows this, but I shadowed her when she went on that last tour in Norfolk with her pottery business, even staying in the hotel room opposite, to watch over her. But you can't keep close to someone in a situation like that all the time, and Dreadnought tricked her. He somehow lured her out to a deserted beach in Norfolk, and had her viciously killed in the driving snow. I found her too late. So yes, there is a big part of me that longs to avenge her."

"But I also want revenge for all that he's put you through, especially his attempts to try and kill you; your vicious kidnapping in the Swiss Alps, and his attempt to murder you in Jersey, and many attempts since. Also another element besides justice and revenge is protection. I just long to keep you safe and free from harm. That is the main reason that I get so upset when you get yourself into difficult situations like the one at Nancenoy Towers. However, I realise that I'm being a bit overprotective, and I'm quite prepared to let you be part of the assault team on Walton Priory, if you want to be, that is."

Bladon pulled the car on to the verge and stopped. He squeezed Lexi's hand and tenderly kissed her. "You are so precious. You are everything to me."

"But why does it have to be you that always sorts it out?" said Lexi. "Why can't you leave it to the PM and Sandy?"

"Well I don't want to get into the psychobabble business, but I think it goes back as far as Junior school Lexi, where I was always in fights, and they nicknamed me Randy, after the British boxer, Randolph Turpin. I've always had this sense of justice, and I may have got into trouble so much because I was the son of two teachers at the school, and in fact my Dad was deputy head. I'm sure I must have been picked on.

I've always been like that with bullies right through my life. You know how some poor souls are cowed and frightened by bullies, well I seem to be the opposite, and it seems that when I'm bullied it makes me very aggressive and makes me want to stand up to them. I remember being bullied by two older boys with a knife on my first day at senior school. It was pretty scary, but when they tried it again later in the week I was so outraged that even though I was smaller than them I turned on them, and I never had any trouble with them again.

My Dad died when I was 16 and I had to grow up very quickly. I think the grief made me a bit depressed for a while, and as a consequence I rebelled at school, and finally the teachers lost patience and expelled me. I think the final straw for them was when I took exception to a bully attacking verbally, and then physically, this rather delicate and withdrawn young girl in the playground. No teachers took any notice, but I just flipped at the injustice of it all and put him in hospital. I lied about my age and joined the army, and when I was accepted by the SAS I knew I had found my true vocation.

I have always had a quite advanced sense of justice. For instance I hate queue jumping, and when Mum and Dad took me to Switzerland on holiday once, I remember queuing for the train and being infuriated by the Germans and Swiss, who refused to queue and just tried to walk past us. We formed a line across the platform and refused to let them pass! I was one of the best recruits the Regiment ever had, because I was quite ruthless and very determined and single-minded.

But you'll be pleased to know that I settled down finally when on leave in Norfolk. I was staying in this small seaside town and there was nothing to do, so I went to the local dance at the Women's Institute Hall, and met this beautiful young woman who was serving the tea. I fell for her straight away. It was love at first sight, she was such a kind, generous, compassionate, Christian lady, but at the same time I saw in her a strength and purpose that I recognised in myself. She was my first love and Dreadnought snuffed out her life. Who would have thought that another beautiful, wonderful woman would have saved my life, and that I would find love again. I am not going to let Dreadnought take that away a second time Lexi."

They reached their home in Kedleston, and as they passed the reassuring presence of two SAS guards, Lexi kissed Bladon gently on the cheek.

"Thank you," she whispered and walked into the safety of its comforting presence, hand in hand with her husband.

Thirty Seven

Monday night

Dreadnought and Clara returned to Walton Priory and called an immediate Council of War. They explained that they would be taking a few of the men by river, to attack two unspecified targets. The rest would wait for their triumphant return and then join him in London to assist in his coup to take over power.

The total forces of Dreadnought sequestered in Walton Priory included 45 combatants and additional back up staff. Some of them were his old guard; veterans recruited from the armed forces and secret services of Britain and Europe. The rest formed a less cohesive and less disciplined force, but nevertheless brutal and effective. Many were from the Balkan nations particularly Serbia and Croatia, and others from Ukraine, Germany and Northern Italy.

Dreadnought addressed them.

"Clara and I are leaving tonight with a few men and some of the weapons, so that we can take out our main target. I'm not disclosing what that is, for security reasons, but its destruction will strike fear and shock throughout the whole country. The rest of you will remain behind to defend our base here. There is a remote possibility that the enemy may discover you here, but I want to reassure you that you have all the firepower necessary to keep them at bay.

For defending the inside of the Priory I am leaving six of the super-guns with you; they are specially adapted weapons, lower powered for close quarter fighting, and lighter, so as not to destroy the superstructure of this building, but just as devastating. They will totally decimate any opposition forces that manage to get into the Priory, and of course you have access to the entire armoury in the Priory itself. This includes small arms, sniper rifles, grenades and automatic weapons.

This is only a fall back position though. I do not expect you to be attacked. I am putting George in overall charge, with Olav in command of our friends from Europe. You will have plenty of warning of an attack, because I have lots of people in various places in government, including the Police.

However the most important defence is located on the roof. I have fixed there our biggest, multi-barrelled gun as a defence against any attack on the Priory from the air or the ground. It will destroy anything sent against you. However, early warning of such an attack is imperative and I've been able to source a portable surveillance system, which is also set up on the roof adjacent to the gun. I consider that we have sufficient firepower from the super-guns to deter a land-based attack. I have set up the surveillance system to stop any major aerial threat to our base from land based missiles, attack drones, and air to ground missiles launched from attack aircraft or Apache helicopters. The portable Tracker has 360° Integrated Sensor Surveillance of all surface targets. Automatic clutter processing allows the operator to perform multiple tasks and not focus on tuning the radar. The clutter processing automatically adjusts as storms and other environmental conditions change and the radar processing enhances the detectability of small targets. You can be confident that you will not be defeated from the air.

Clara and Dreadnought left Walton-on-Trent in a dark blue transit van after loading the weapons on board, including big multi-barrelled guns, in order to transfer them onto the narrow boat under cover of darkness.

"This is possibly the most dangerous part Clara. If Bladon's has discovered the location of Walton Priory, they may be coming for us right now, so we must be very vigilant".

They drove slowly down the drive of the Priory, turned

Thirty Seven

right onto the narrow road into the village, and then turned left towards the river and the quirky old bridge across. They had no idea that the SAS watchers in the Priory grounds had spotted the little group leave. The observers had only been given a watching brief, so they immediately informed Willie, and asked for back up. As Dreadnought approached the bridge, little did he know, that three Range Rovers full of heavily armed shock troops had been alerted, and were at the same time converging on the little village of Walton, as well as the local Police who had also sent a couple of cars, with their usual accompaniment of blues and twos.

The bridge was very narrow, and traffic-light controlled, and they pulled up on the south bank of the river, just behind a Royal Mail van, and waited for the lights to change to green. The original bridge was built in 1834 and lasted for over one hundred years before being replaced in 1948 by a temporary Bailey bridge. This was erected by the Royal Engineers over the top of the old bridge, part of which was removed to allow a support to be built on the Staffordshire bank of the river, the temporary bridge had to be built due to flood damage to the old bridge after the severe winter of 1947. This bridge had to again be replaced in 1974 by a more modern version of the temporary bridge, so there was no wonder it looked quirky.

The lights changed and Dreadnought moved over the river and headed for the A38 dual carriageway. From there Dreadnought headed north, making for the major exit just after the large village of Willington, where he intended to join the A50 east bound, and on to their floating bolthole waiting patiently for them. That was his plan, but as they passed the exit to Burton-on-Trent, they saw joining the southbound lane, a Police car in a headlong rush in the direction of Walton.

"I don't like the look of that," said Clara.

"No, I don't," replied Dreadnought, "but it could be just a routine incident they're attending. Let's keep our eyes peeled for trouble though."

As they passed the turn-off to Stretton a few miles later, they saw another police car following the first in pursuit, and then much more disquieting, a couple of black Range Rovers with darkened windows, following on.

"That looks like the SAS to me. I'm worried. They've not spotted us yet, but if I know them, they'll have stationed another car on the island we want to exit from, to cover the A50, as well as the A38. We got away from Walton just in time, but how did they spot us?"

Before setting out Dreadnought had pored over maps of the area, and Google Earth, for several hours, in case of just such an eventuality, so he slowed as he approached the petrol station, just before the turn-off to the A50. He left the A38, and then turned next left, onto the road to Willington. He approached the centre of the village, and at the small island, he turned right at the Co-op store towards Repton.

"Surely that's not the right way boss," said one of his men. "If you go straight on, the road leads directly to Swarkestone, and the road off to Weston that we want."

"You're quite right Cameron," replied Dreadnought, "but it's a long, straight, road with nowhere to hide, and if they catch us there, we're done for. I want to approach Swarkestone by a more circuitous route."

Dreadnought pressed on through Willington, past the church on the left, over the River Trent, and into the ancient village of Repton, a village on the edge of the River Trent floodplain, in South Derbyshire. It was a very historic village, dating back to A.D. 653; it also boasted a prestigious public school founded in 1557. They made a left turn along a narrow road signposted to Milton where they turned left and approached Foremarke, well known in the area as the location of the preparatory school for Repton. It was set in an idyllic position on the site of the old stately home, formerly known as Foremarke Hall.

As Dreadnought reached the small crossroads leading to Formarke Hall on the right, he glanced down the road that he was intending to take down towards the river, and saw to his dismay a large Black four by four racing towards the little village of Ingleby, and on up to his present location.

Thirty Seven

"That looks like our pursuers," Dreadnought shouted to the men in the back. "This is no place for a fire fight. I hope they haven't seen us."

He yanked the steering wheel of the van viciously to the right, and started down the lane.

"This is no good sir," shouted Cameron. "This road we're on is a dead end."

Dreadnought stamped on the brakes. And the van came to a dead halt just outside the gates of the preparatory school. He looked down the drive towards the car park at the front of the school, and his spirits lifted. The short drive down to the car park was completely covered from view, both from the road and from the air by a small copse, which the road passed through. Dreadnought made his decision quickly.

He drove down the drive to the school car park, but spotting a gap in the tree cover he took the van off road, and pulled in behind the trunks of the large oak trees, where he saw to his delight that he was completely invisible from the drive.

Cameron leapt out of the back of the van, and made his way quickly to the entrance to Formarke Hall. He found a suitable hiding place in a ditch at the side of the road, and waited to see whether they would be discovered.

At length the black Range Rover came up to the crossroads, stopped and waited. They were obviously discussing their next move, and eventually the car turned to the left and approached the school entrance. After a pause, the Range Rover turned down the drive, through the woods, and into the school car park. In the middle of the tarmac was a large immaculately manicured circular lawn, and the Range Rover slowed to a halt next to it. Three SAS troopers jumped out of the car to search the cars parked in the car park. Another ran to the end of the car park, followed the road to the right down to the school itself. Here were some more car parks dotted around the school campus; but after a search of 30 minutes they found nothing and returned to their car, reversed down the drive, and at the crossroads turned left towards Repton.

Cameron watched the Range Rover for some time, until sure that it wasn't going to return, then ran back to the dark blue van, hidden in the wood. Dreadnought, clearly relieved, reversed the van back up the drive, onto the road. Taking a right at the crossroads Dreadnought drove down the hill to Ingleby, set by the side of the river, and then followed the road on to Swarkestone. He turned left onto the bridge over the river, passed the Crewe and Harper Arms, turned right onto the road to Chellaston and made his way finally with great relief, to their waiting hideaway by the canal.

Thirty Eight

At 9.00am the Brainstorming Group met in Lexi's house in Kedleston Park, sitting around the dining room table. Like the lounge, it had breathtaking views of the garden and beyond, over green, gently undulating fields, and rising up to the far ridge where stately oaks rustled in the evening breeze.

Faisal, Adam, Jeremy and Steve had collected a coffee each and looked up expectantly as Lexi cleared her voice.

"Thank you so much for agreeing to join this small and exclusive team. Identifying the target that Dreadnought is planning to attack really is the most important task we have. I feel sure, and so does Bladon, that Walton Priory is just the launch pad for a large and deadly operation. Of course, if we can catch Dreadnought and Clara in our attack on the Priory, then they will not be able to activate whatever plans they have, but I fear that Dreadnought is far too slippery to be caught in the Priory when the attack takes place; and in any case he may have some other forces already in position to carry out the attack, if he fails to arrive. So it is of paramount importance to discover what his target is."

"Jeremy and Steve, I don't think you've met Faisal and Adam before, but of course, you know their father Wilf very well. They both arrived last night, and I've brought them up to speed on the scale and importance of the task facing us. Of course the attack group who are meeting at Selwyn's house will want to know any conclusions we come to as soon as possible. I've known Faisal and Adam for about a year, and not only are they the nicest young men you could wish to meet, with a fierce loyalty to our country; but they also have formidable intellects, which we want to harness for this difficult task. Thank you both for agreeing to join us, and welcome.

I did give you both some background information on Steve and Jeremy last night, and you were suitably impressed; but I want to say how honoured we are to have both of them on the team. Jeremy is one of the original 'Thirteen' that foiled Dreadnought's last heinous attempt to take over this country, and he has recently been appointed Head of Close Protection for the Royal Family. Steve is a neighbour of your Dad's good friend John Parkin, another member of the 'Thirteen', but he is much more than just a neighbour now. I was privileged to have flown with him to Italy, with your father, where against all the odds he got us unnoticed into Urbino; in fact he managed to get us out of a very dangerous situation in the Alps, when we were buzzed by a French Mirage jet. He's now a full member of the new 'Thirteen'."

Enough of introductions, let's get down to our task. Where does Dreadnought intend to attack next, when will it be, and how does he intend to do it? We have to find out urgently what the target is."

Faisal spoke first. "The attack could come in Derby, where all the activity seems to have centred around, and it could in fact be against a nuclear facility like the one at Rolls-Royce. This would cause great loss of life, significant damage to one of the country's industrial power houses, and set back our arms industry at the same time."

Adam thought it could be a prominent, historic building such as Haddon Hall or Chatsworth in Derbyshire. "I love Haddon Hall and it's one of the finest examples of a mediaeval manor house in the country, and has been the locale for quite a few blockbuster films in the last few years, including Jane Eyre, and Pride and Prejudice, and it has welcomed visitors for hundreds of years. It's a stunning English Tudor country house, one of the seats of the Duke of Rutland, and its loss would be an absolute tragedy."

"Even more of a tragedy would be the loss of Chatsworth

though," Faisal said.

"I'm not so familiar with Chatsworth, Faisal, nor for that matter Haddon Hall," said Jeremy. "I know the Queen visits and stays there, but not in my time. Where is it? Is it close to Derby?"

"Chatsworth House lies about three and a half miles northeast of Bakewell. It is the seat of the Duke of Devonshire, and has been home to his family, the Cavendish family, since Bess of Hardwick settled at Chatsworth in 1549. It's in a stunning setting on the east bank of the River Derwent, in expansive parkland and backed by wooded, rocky hills rising to heather moorland. It's a wondrous, captivating place and contains a unique collection of priceless paintings, furniture, Old Master drawings, neoclassical sculptures, books and other artefacts. It's been selected as the United Kingdom's favourite country house several times. Sorry, I'm sounding like a tour guide. But it would be a terrible loss, not only to the country but the whole world."

"I see," said Jeremy. "Please pardon my ignorance. I didn't know it was such an important place. But you've reminded me, and this is in complete confidence; I could be taken to the Tower for telling you this; the Queen is doing a quick tour of the Midlands, starting this Friday, and including a stay at Chatsworth. An attack there could not only wipe out a fantastic building and resource to the nation, but kill the Queen."

Steve had been deep in thought whilst the others brainstormed the problem, but he finally spoke up.

"I think the target could be closer than that. As an important manufacturer in Derby, I've had a top-secret invitation to lunch, with unspecified important dignitaries, at Kedleston Hall on Monday. Jeremy, do you think you could get some more firm information on where the Queen is going. Is she going to Kedleston, because if so, it could be a prime candidate for the target? You can be sure that Dreadnought will get to know because he seems to have his own people insinuated in every walk of life and every government department. His tentacles stretch in much the same way as the mafia does in Southern Italy, although from what I've heard lately they are beginning to infiltrate in Milan and Northern Italy too. I understand from Sandy that Dreadnought still has many people in places of power in this country. They weren't all rooted out last time I'm afraid."

Adam spoke again. "He could very well attack multiple targets to disguise his main attack."

Lexi had let them talk without interrupting, but at 11.30am she brought the meeting to order. "Thank you so much. We've made a tremendous start, let's have some coffee, and pull all our ideas together. Steve and Jeremy will concentrate on the possibility of an attack on Haddon Hall, or Chatsworth, or even Kedleston Hall, and the Queen herself. Faisal and Adam will look into the possibility of other targets in the Derby area and whether they will be major attacks or diversionary ones."

Tuesday morning 9 am

Whilst the brainstorming meeting continued at Lexi's house in Kedleston, Dreadnought, Clara, and the four men still slept on the narrow boat, moored at the side of the canal close to the Swarkestone to Weston-on-Trent Road.

The boat was named 'Aquinas', and although from the outside it looked as though it had seen better days, with gaudily painted sides, and chopped wood stacked on the roof, inside it was very well equipped. It was a 57-foot long, steel-hulled craft, with a 42hp diesel engine, with a light, stylish and spacious interior. A large rear deck provided an enjoyable place to sit and take in the views, and it had a small, light, open-plan area inside, with comfy leather easy chairs and side tables. It had three single beds in the large rear cabin, with ample wardrobe and storage space.

Another private room was equipped as a bedroom with a further three camp beds set up there. It had a fully equipped galley, and a breakfast bar with seating for six.

They unloaded the Transit Van and transferred the handguns, and the big multi-barrelled gun for the helicopter, with the help of the pulley, into the boat as they embarked at midnight. Then Kurt drove the van away.

When they awoke, they had breakfast of cereals and cheese, and found Dreadnought in a more expansive mood, explaining his plans in detail to the men as well as to Clara again.

"We're going to take a leisurely journey up the River Trent and on to the canal network. Apart from two of us who will steer and deal with the locks, it's vital that the rest keep hidden below deck. We're going to stay for a few days in a large marina at Sawley. I've reserved a luxury berth for us, and on Saturday I intend to take the 'Aquinas' slowly up the canal, through Long Eaton and Sandiacre, to Stanton Gate, just a road and a few houses. It's just before the huge industrial complex that used to be owned by Stanton Ironworks. No one will even give us a second glance in a narrowboat; they'll just think we're on holiday. We'll take our time and aim to get to there by Saturday evening. We'll stop there, transfer the guns to a large van I've organised and then we'll make for Kedleston, after dropping off two of you at the Holiday Inn Express in Pride Park, Derby, to prepare for our diversionary attack. The rest of us will make our way to the derelict Kedleston Hotel, not far from Kedleston Hall, which will be our forward base for the attack on our main target."

Thirty Nine

Bladon reconvened the meeting at Selwyn's for nine o'clock, in order to finalise the plans. Steve, Phillip, Andy and Wilf had been out to the barn until late the previous evening. They'd familiarised themselves with the helmets and the 'mini' Reaper drones, but this morning the 'toy' Hubsan drones would be arriving, and tonight would be more intensive, using the attack drones and helmets and some of the toy drones under 'battle conditions'. Also they had obtained the original architectural drawings of Walton Priory, which would be used for their attack plan.

They pored over the plans of the Priory and the latest satellite photos that had been couriered to them from London, and began to put together a detailed plan of attack. They noticed that the Priory was set in beautiful grounds, and a gravelled drive wound its way through deep woodland until it met the environs of the Priory itself, where it ended in a large, enclosed, circular driveway in front of the main building.

The south aspect comprised a line of ornamental wrought iron railings, broken in the middle by two huge and imposing five metre stone pillars, with lavishly sculptured iron gates opening onto the lawn with a centrepiece copied from Greek mythology in white marble. A large stone portico enclosed the entrance doors to the Priory itself with columns on three sides, and a huge slab of stone stood outside the portico, previously used by the landed gentry for mounting their horses. This could prove to be a very useful place to protect them during the attack.

On the east side of the house, the dense woodland abutted

right up to the circular gravel driveway, giving them an ideal means of approach to the main entrance unobserved. On the west side of the drive was a raised terrace, running the whole length of the enclosed drive, with a stone wall running from the side of the drive up ten metres to the terrace. The attack would be two-pronged, by way of the two doors at the front and the side, but they each held particular problems.

The main attack group could insert themselves into the portico relatively easily without detection, from the woodland abutting the drive, but they would meet the fiercest resistance from the enemy forces once they gained entry to the Great Hall.

The other attack, against the southwest door, would be a much more difficult approach, as any movement of men along the west wall would be very visible to watchers from the Priory.

After a lot of discussion, Bladon decided that the best approach for the smaller of his attack force was to emerge from the woodland to the south-west of the Priory and then carefully negotiate the rhododendron slopes up to the terrace, cross over to the top of the west wall, then run quickly along to the south eastern corner of the house, where they would rappel down to the drive, right next to the side door.

The Priory was a very imposing building. The main point of entry was through heavy, double wooden doors, strengthened with iron and black nailed studs leading into the Great Hall, a magnificent baronial edifice measuring about 25 metres long by 10 metres wide with a massive fireplace along the east side. The far end of the hall led into two wide corridors, one gave access to the west wing and the other the east wing.

The west corridor ran for about 20 metres before turning to the left into a large kitchen, which itself held the door to the enclosed gravel drive on its southwest corner. This was the other point of entry. Around this west corridor lay six rooms of differing size, some north facing and some south facing.

The east corridor led first to the foot of the main staircase and then turned 90 degrees, from which various rooms, both large and small led off.

The first floor opened up from the staircase, into a magnificent stately room named the Long Gallery, measuring 50 metres long and 10 metres wide. It was like a huge corridor, but at the same time so much more. You could imagine previous generations of the privileged promenading here, or their children playing cricket, or whatever heights their imaginations soared to. The Long Gallery ran the whole length of the south elevation of Walton Priory, and from here various rooms led to the north.

The grandest of these was the State Room, which measured 25 metres by 10 metres, and according to Lydia, the girl who was so nearly killed by Clara, this was where the majority of the men slept, about 30 in all.

Adjacent to this room was the Library, again a large room about half the size of the State Room, and the quarters for the rest of the combat forces, about 15 men.

There were two more rooms facing north, one large and the other a lot smaller, and these were used to sleep non-combatants, such as cleaners, cooks and gardeners etc.

On the east side was a smaller room where Dreadnought slept, and next to this, a spiral staircase led down to the ground floor, but also up to a large flat area of the roof.

The recent satellite photographs of the Priory showed some images of great concern to Bladon's team, and confirmed what they had suspected right from the initial planning stage. Dreadnought had indeed installed on the roof a formidable defence against aerial and missile attack. What looked like one of the biggest multi-barrelled super-guns they had ever seen, was situated on the roof, partially covered by a tarpaulin, and next to it a portable radar surveillance system, with two operators. It was not only a powerful deterrent against aerial attack, but Bladon feared it could be also be used against a ground attack, if they were careless enough to let it.

Lydia was really helpful to their attack plans. She had been outraged that Clara, Dreadnought's number two, and someone that she had faithfully served and looked after at Walton Priory, should quite callously try to kill her. Lydia told them, "when I left the Priory, Dreadnought's men were using five of the first floor rooms as dormitories, which were accessed only from the Long Gallery. The main access from the ground floor is the main staircase next to the Great Hall. I must warn you to also be aware of a spiral staircase in the east wing when you attack. Guard duties during the night are from 9.00pm through to 6.00am, and the defenders work three-hour shifts, which means that at any one time, only 15 are defending the ground floor and the other 30 are asleep in the rooms above. In the rooms to the east they are not fighters, so please be careful not to hurt them. Many are my friends."

This was really important information from Lydia, because it confirmed that their plan to attack at 3am needed fine-tuning a little, and so they decided to attack at precisely 2.45, just before the end of the second shift. It would have to be timed precisely, but if they got it right, they would be attacking the Priory at the precise moment that the third shift were still asleep, and the defenders would be at their lowest level of preparedness, ready for their sleep.

Based on the plans, photos, and inside information, they all agreed the plans for two separate, but simultaneous attacks, one through the main doors into the Great Hall, and the other through the side door on the southwest of the property. Phillip and Andy would force entry by the side door in the southwest corner of the house with a small force of five men. Their plan was to go in very aggressively and secure the rooms nearest the door, then deploy the drones to destroy the super-guns, and kill or capture the men. Then they would move through to the Great Hall to join up with Bladon's group.

Simultaneously, Bladon's group would attack through the main doors, where Steve and Phillip would deploy the drones until the super-guns were neutralised. Then Jeremy would enter the Great Hall with the sniper gun L115A3, the Army's most powerful sniper weapon, much feared by the Afghanistan Taliban, to take out the other more conventionally armed men. Steve and Wilf would then clear out the other rooms to the east of the Great Hall, destroying any super-guns, whilst the rest of Bladon's force guarded the staircase against any counter attack.

Phillip and Steve's men would then join Bladon's force, and together they would attack the first floor where the majority of Dreadnought's forces would await them. They planned to climb the stairs, use the drones to destroy all the super-guns in the main rooms, and then finally destroy the big multi-barrelled, super-gun on the roof, secure any prisoners for interrogation, including Dreadnought and Clara, and search the Priory for information about the target.

Stefan suggested that the Police should be warned that there would be activity around the Priory, and to set up roadblocks for Tuesday, Wednesday, and Thursday nights, but both Bladon and Sandy were concerned that if they let the local police know too early, then it could be leaked to the defenders of the Priory. Little did they know that Chief Superintendent Fordingley was indeed one of Dreadnought's men, and he was in overall charge of the Walton-on-Trent area now.

They decided instead to surreptitiously deploy elements of A Squadron SAS around the Priory and its grounds on Tuesday night, and also secure the circumference of the Priory down to the river frontage. North of the Priory, where the grounds reached the River Trent they were heavily wooded, which would enable the SAS to infiltrate without being seen.

By Wednesday night, they intended to deploy the whole of A squadron to the north and south of the Priory. Elements of B Squadron would cover the east and west side of the grounds, with the rest of the squadron forming a reserve close to the river and the main road through the village, before the attack began in the early hours of Thursday morning,

As they broke for lunch, they all expressed satisfaction with the attack plan, although from experience they knew to expect the unexpected.

Forty

Tuesday 10.30am.

Cameron manoeuvred the boat away from the side of the canal, but first they had to turn the boat around. Dreadnought and Clara estimated the length of the boat to be close to 60 foot and realised that it was not as easy as they thought, as the canal was only about 30 feet wide at this point. How could they turn the boat around? None of them had any experience with narrowboats; in fact none of them had ever even been on board one before. Dreadnought consulted Google Earth again and saw that the canal widened considerably past Swarkestone, where the canal branched to the right, and a mini marina gave plenty of room to turn. However it was longer and would delay them. They would have to pass through a lock immediately ahead of the marina, negotiate the lock, turn, and renegotiate the lock. This would draw a lot of attention to themselves which they didn't want. Clara meanwhile, realising the problem, was reading from a useful manual that Kurt had left by the steering wheel and shouted to Dreadnought excitedly that she'd cracked it.

"We need to find a winding hole."

"What on earth is that Clara?"

She read from the manual. "Where the width of a canal channel is less than the length of a full-size canal boat, it is not usually possible to turn a boat in the canal. Winding holes are typically indentations in the side of the canal, allowing sufficient space to turn the boat. A winding hole usually consists of a "notch" in the canal bank opposite to the towpath. A turning boat inserts its bow into the notch, and swings the stern round."

"Well then," said Clara. "We just need to find one, and the sooner the better."

Cameron pushed up the speed to three knots, and just around the corner of the canal, still in tree cover and well short of the road to Swarkestone, they saw a winding hole. Dreadnought took the steering and carefully turned into a large, inverted V, gently touched the bank before selecting reverse, and after two attempts, turned the boat round and started their journey proper.

They travelled along the canal running alongside the Trent for a short distance until the canal diverged to the north as it approached Weston-on-Trent. They continued on their way, passing a large gravel pit on their right, under the A50, and below Shardlow where Kurt should have left the van. They passed two more gravel pits on their right, then two small marinas below Great Wilne, and finally the canal met the Trent.

They joined the fast flowing river under the M1, and where the river turned left they saw a weir that had been buoyed off, so they headed up a man-made waterway to the right to avoid it, and on into the part of the canal named the Sawley Cut. The main entrance to Sawley Marina lay ahead, but Dreadnought slowed the boat to negotiate the narrow entrance to the Platinum Moorings, where with his usual careful pre-planning Dreadnought had reserved a mooring for the boat some six months before. The platinum moorings were in an exclusive small basin in a gated area. Strictly, it was limited to boats up to 55 foot long, but Dreadnought had used his powers of persuasion and Aquinas had been allowed to use it. They found their reserved birth, tied up, and Dreadnought at last allowed himself to relax. It had been a close run thing, but they had made it.

Dreadnought had ordered Kurt to take the dark blue transit van in the early hours of Tuesday morning along the quiet road through Weston-on-Trent, Aston-on-Trent, and on to Shardlow. He was to leave the van in the car park at Shardlow Marina, where the transit van would not be noticed among all the other commercial vehicles there. Dreadnought told Kurt to spend some time in the back of the van, where a sleeping bag and mattress had been provided, and then to make his way on foot as surreptitiously as possible to Sawley Marina. The van still had some logs in the back, loaded at Walton, which would help to demonstrate that he was delivering fuel to the canal boats, if he were to be stopped

Kurt arrived at Shardlow, but decided not to stop there as instructed. It was the middle of the night and he didn't relish the thought of walking another three miles. He thought it would be easier to take the van to Sawley Marina and dispose of it nearby, thus saving a walk, and also eliminating the risk of being picked up by the Police in the early hours. He knew it was a dangerous ploy as Dreadnought was ruthless, and if he found out, the consequences could be severe, but he just thought he was using his initiative.

He drove the van over Cavendish Bridge and on to Sawley Marina, and as he turned into the safety of the entrance to the Marina he breathed a sigh of relief.

"There, that was easy enough, and it only took me five minutes. Now to dispose of this thing," he muttered to himself.

The road wound around the marina and then turned sharp right and ran straight as a die across lonely fields, under a bridge with a railway above, until it emerged on the other side where a water filled gravel pit glittered in the moonlight to the right of the road. It was large and isolated, and Kurt thought it was the ideal place to get rid of the van.

He noticed that the first part of the gravel pit seemed quite a bit shallower than the rest, so he followed the road around the water until it got deeper. At a suitable place, he took the van off-road and drove towards the water's edge. This seemed to be an ideal place to dispose of the van. The bank was about 6 feet above the water level of the gravel pit, and so he stopped the van about 50 feet away from the edge.

He left the engine idling in neutral, opened the rear doors of the van and took two large logs out. He placed a short piece of plank carefully over the accelerator, and then the two logs, until the revs rose to 4000rpm. He reached in and pushed the gear lever into drive. The van shot forward like a rocket and he only just managed to stumble out onto the bank before it plunged into the water. Kurt got up, brushed himself down, and looked into the turbulent water below.

To his horror, he saw that the van was suspended half in the water and half out, on a shallow shelf at the side of the bank. Devastated, he looked around for some means of pushing it further into the deep water. Just as he was beginning to lose heart, he saw to his relief that the inertia and weight of the van had tilted it sufficiently for it to float down into the water. He heard the engine cut out, and watched as the van slipped under the surface.

He walked back to the marina, round the east and south side, and entered through the main entrance and on to the west bank. He found location DD and the mooring he was looking for, and saw Dreadnought's second boat, 'Caroline', a 45ft cruiser style, narrowboat Saloon, moored at the end of the mooring peer, very close to the exclusive Platinum Moorings where Dreadnought was arriving in the narrow boat 'Aquinas' later.

He boarded the 'Caroline' and took a look around. It had two single bunks, a shower room and WC, and another bedroom with a double bed.

He settled in, rather pleased with himself that his foresight had saved a long walk and the prospect of discovery. He made himself a cup of tea from the well-supplied kitchen cupboards, and then relaxed after the long, stressful night. At midday he started to prepare for the arrival of two of Dreadnought's men who would be staying with him on the 'Caroline'. One of them was Cameron, who he knew, but he had never met Aaron before. He hoped they would be good company, but at least the woman was staying on the 'Aquinas'. She scared him.

On the larger boat, 'Aquinas", four people would be staying

and as Clara could be recognised after the abortive raid on The Trent Lock Hotel and Spa, she would not be leaving the boat and neither would Dreadnought. It was too much of a risk.

The others could do any shopping that Dreadnought required, and keep an eye out for any trouble. All in all, it was a perfect hideaway. Who would be looking for them here?

On Wednesday morning all of Bladon's Forces met together after breakfast, including the Brainstorming Group who had been meeting at Bladon and Lexi's house. Steve and Wilf, and Phillip and Andy, reported on a very successful second practice in the old barn. They were now totally proficient with the handling of both the camera drone and the Reaper. Jeremy had spent some time too practising with the L115A3, the special sniper gun, and was delighted with its performance and capabilities. Most of the attack group were familiar with the weapons they would be using, but even so had taken the opportunity to test them, and dismantle and clean them again ready for action. The rest of the day was spent in relaxation and mental preparation for the battle ahead. The results from the attack on Walton Priory would be presented to the Brainstorming Group as soon as possible afterwards.

Forty One

Bladon's group assembled on the drive some way from the Priory at 2.15am and met one of the SAS demolition specialists, Dominic, who would lead them in to their target. They left the gravel driveway before the Priory came into view and disappeared into the dense woodland. After a very circuitous route, where Bladon had the impression they were going round in circles, they reached the edge of the wood and Dominic signalled for complete silence.

"Follow me and do exactly what I do," he whispered. Then he took a tentative step forward onto the gravel, being careful to keep the noise to a minimum, at the exact spot where the east side of the Priory met the woods. Crouching, he scurried sideways like a crab until he reached the safety of the front portico and beckoned the rest of the team towards him. With Bladon in the lead, Stefan, Sandy, Steve, Wilf, Jeremy, Patrick, Lexi, and Giancarlo all safely made the shelter of the front of the Priory, by 2.40am.

Meanwhile Phillip, Andy, Willie, Terry and John, safely clambered up onto the terrace after negotiating the rhododendron slopes, and ran quickly along the top of the east wall to the south eastern corner of the house where the other SAS demolition expert awaited them. He had rigged up two ropes already and the six of them rappelled down to the drive, right next to the side door.

The two SAS demolition specialists had provided the charges for both doors. They were sophisticated explosive charges, which were cone shaped and which delivered a very exact, cutting explosion, with minimum destruction to the doors themselves; they would just completely take out the locks and enable the 'Thirteen' to enter, without huge damage to the building. The two SAS specialists placed their charges on both doors, detonating them at precisely 2.45 am, the exact time that another SAS sabotage team cut off the electricity and power inside the building, plunging it into complete darkness.

At the west door, Andy, equipped with PVS-7 night vision goggles, as were the others, leapt through the now open door, straight into the kitchen. He laid down a fierce barrage of fire from his Heckler & Koch, MP5SD suppressed sub machine gun, at the fearsome rate of 700 rounds per minute down the corridor to his left. He also had as back up, a Heckler & Koch HK417 20" Sniper, gas-operated battle rifle, to complement the sub machine gun. Phillip followed immediately behind him and prepared to deploy his first toy drone. Willie, Terry and John followed on into the kitchen, and found straight in front of them, three men still seated at the kitchen table in a state of shock. Looking down the barrels of three MP55SD's two of them did the sensible thing and flung their arms up in surrender. The other went for his weapon that was lying on the table and was cut down by a double tap from Terry's gun, straight through the heart.

Willie ran through the kitchen to the smaller room on his right, but it was empty. The two who had surrendered were restrained and pushed into the smaller room until back up arrived. John meanwhile, in accordance with their pre-planned strategy, pushed past Phillip and Andy, and approached the doorway of a room on his left, pulled down his S10 gas mask, tossed in a stun grenade before raking the interior with a prolonged burst of fire from his Remington 870 shotgun. Before Phillip launched his drone, Andy threw a fragmentation grenade into the small room ahead on the north side of the Priory as a precaution, and looked back to see if Phillip was ready to launch. It had only been a matter

Forty One

of seconds, but they had already taken four rooms in the west wing, killed or captured three of the enemy, and seemingly shocked the rest into silence. They were doing well, and it looked as if they had taken the enemy completely by surprise.

They might have done ordinarily, but their opponents had been carefully chosen by Dreadnought; Luca, a veteran ex-Italian Special Forces soldier, and two of his men, still held two of the larger rooms in the west wing. The one furthest from Andy, adjacent to the Great Hall, had an unusual entrance that curved back at an oblique angle. This made it very difficult for attacking forces to gain entry safely, but at the same time gave defenders good cover, and Luca waited until the noise of grenades and bullets quietened.

Then he surprised his attackers by taking the initiative back. He jumped out into the corridor, saw Andy who was standing at the head of the corridor guarding Phillip, who was preparing to launch the drone. Before Andy could react, Luca aimed and fired his super-gun. He was a bit too hurried in his aim, half-expecting a vicious response, and fortunately for Andy his jerked action slewed the gun barrel to the right, but the lethal blast from the multi-barrelled gun still destroyed much of the west wall of the Priory, and Andy fell to the floor under a hail of bullets and falling masonry.

"Man down," shouted Phillip. "We need some help here." His helmet was now fully operational and he could see that Luca had retreated back into the comparative safety of his room. Luca could have gone on the offensive with his superior weaponry, but he couldn't be sure of the number or location of his attackers, so he decided to let them come to him.

"We need back up quickly, and some medical help for Andy," Willie yelled. "He looks to be badly injured."

John threw a smoke grenade down the corridor, closely followed by a fragmentation grenade opposite the entrance to the room that Luca had retreated into. Willie and Terry meanwhile clawed frantically at the pile of bricks and rubble covering Andy, and pulled him out.

A four-man SAS patrol heard Willie's shout for assistance,

joined him and together they carried Andy out onto the lawn at the side of the Priory. They kept under the lee of the wall and two of the patrol covered the windows of the priory to discourage any attack. Fortunately for Andy, having soldiers who are medically trained is vital to all SAS operations. Within every four-man patrol will be a soldier trained in the field of medicine to an advanced degree. A hospital doctor in London might see a massive injury from a high velocity rifle bullet once in his career, yet the combat medic in the SAS could treat dozens in the space of an hour.

The medic quickly examined Andy.

"I'm afraid he's not going anywhere sir. Bullets have damaged his thigh and ankle, and he has compression injuries to his neck and shoulders from the wall collapsing, but he is going to be alright."

Willie re-entered the Priory taking two SAS soldiers with him where John met him in the kitchen.

"We have a problem," said John. "Andy has been shot, Phillip has still not been able to launch the drone, we have two prisoners, and there are still three hostiles out there with super-guns. We've ground to a halt and I'm concerned that unless we counter-attack very quickly they may decide that we're not a threat, and attack Bladon's force through the east door and into the Great Hall."

"Don't worry John, it's just a small setback," said Willie. "We'll escort the two prisoners outside and you take up position in the corridor to guard Phillip. Take care though, and I'll bring another two soldiers to supplement our force."

Will and Peter joined Willie and Terry in the kitchen and waited for Phillip to deploy the first drone, the 'toy' one.

Forty Two

Meanwhile, the charge on the double doors into the Great Hall had done its job, and the two massive doors swung open, to reveal a magnificent, stately room, with wood panelled sides stretching up to a delightful vaulted ceiling. Unlike the attack on the west wing, Bladon did not plan to storm the Great Hall immediately, in fact as soon as the doors were blown open he expected a massive blast of lead to come their way from a super-gun, so they kept well back from the now open entrance to the Great Hall.

The Hall was in complete darkness, but Bladon could see clearly through his night sight glasses and the roaring fire on the east wall almost blinded him until he adjusted the intensity. They were all instructed to stay outside the Hall under cover, until any super-guns had been eliminated. Dreadnought's men, eleven in total, including the leader Ryan, were in the Great Hall and adjoining rooms to the east, but the two super-guns in the Great hall were operated by ex Special Forces veterans, who seeing no targets held their fire.

From comparable safety, Steve fitted his helmet and prepared to send the first 'toy' drone in. Wilf stood beside him as guard in case of any attempt from the enemy forces to attack them. With the helmet he could actually see through walls, and identify the weapons, but it was not a lot of help, as the two super-guns had a clear field of fire on anyone entering the Great Hall.

The first Hubsan 'toy' drone flew through the open front doors, and the camera had hardly focused on the interior before it was blown apart by one of the guns. The second attempt to infiltrate the drone was better, and Steve manoeuvred it close to the floor, where it began to transmit pictures; but when Steve moved it in an upward trajectory to about ten feet off the ground, again it was shot down and destroyed.

This continued until the guns, causing extensive collateral damage to the Great Hall itself, had destroyed four drones. However, the drones were managing to stay up longer, giving very good information to Steve through his helmet, showing the precise locations of the two guns. The rest of his men had still not been deployed, but had been kept out of danger until the two guns had been destroyed. Bladon consulted again with Steve, and they agreed to put up one more Hubsan drone to try and lull the enemy into a false sense of security, and to persuade them that they were only using them for observation, and after a much longer flight time, they shot it down yet again.

Risky or not, it was time to put up the mini Reaper drone, fitted with two missiles, but Steve only had one chance at this. He launched the Reaper, fired the laser, the on-board computer 'painted' the targets, and both missiles were fired in quick succession at the super-guns, destroying both guns and their operatives.

"Well done, Steve, now we can take the Hall," said Bladon.

Before the shock and confusion of the drone attack wore off, Bladon ordered Jeremy into the Great Hall, with the special sniper rifle L115A3; he fell to the floor killing four with his accurate sniper fire, whereupon the other two surrendered, and were hurried out to join the other two prisoners.

Steve and Wilf hurried to the door at the back of the Hall on the right, to clear the rooms in the east wing and to secure the spiral staircase leading up to the first floor. Patrick, Bladon, Lexi, and Giancarlo followed them, but stopped at the bottom of the main staircase, taking up defensive positions and cutting off any escape for the remaining enemy force upstairs. Bladon had asked Stefan, Jeremy, and Sandy to try the door from the Great Hall to the west wing, to see how

Forty Two

Phillip and his team were doing, but very carefully. He felt that the tide of battle had turned decisively in their favour. Steve and Wilf went to secure the east wing.

But then it all changed.

Bladon's Revenge

Forty Three

Wolfgang, a ruthless German, and one of Dreadnought's best leaders, appeared suddenly at the top of the stairs and fired his super-gun down in a devastating volley, which destroyed the bottom of the stairs, completely blowing away the first six steps. Stefan, Sandy, and Jeremy forgot about the door to the west wing and rushed to the debacle at the bottom of the stairs, where a scene of utter carnage met them. They found a pile of steaming bricks, broken and twisted wood, dust, blood and the smell of lead, and no sign of their friends.

Back in the west wing, Phillip manoeuvred one of his 'toy' drones out into the corridor. The manufacturers insisted it was not a toy, but a camera drone, but when compared to the lethal mini-Reaper drones, that's how Phillip liked to describe it. Staying close to the ground, the drone flew down the corridor, stopping where a door led into the Great Hall, and returning to Phillip. It was a strange sight, hovering just above the floor with a little squat body, from which four legs protruded, with propellers set on each leg. It looked very ungainly on the ground, but once in flight it was a revelation of grace and manoeuvrability. This first pass was just for reconnaissance purposes. Phillip knew from the read outs and heads up display from his helmet, that two men were hiding in the first room on the left of the corridor, and they had one of the super-guns, a smaller pistol type weapon, but the small room next to it was unoccupied. A wall of the kitchen ran along the right hand side of the corridor, but next to it was a large room, originally a chapel, and this was where

Luca waited with his formidable weapon, which he had used so effectively already.

Phillip turned the drone round to repeat its flight at eye level, and this time he flew it into the first room with the two men in almost tempting them to take it out. The drone buzzed round the perimeter of the room and its camera relayed pictures back to John of two terrified men, trying desperately to decide what to do about this intimidating little object zipping round the room.

"It's a drone," shouted the smaller man, called Sahab. "It could have weapons. We are sitting targets in here. Take it out."

His friend panicked, and blasted at the drone with his super-gun, destroying the Hubsan drone and most of the door and doorframe.

So far so good, whispered Phillip, and launched a second 'toy' drone, and sent it down the corridor, this time towards Luca. It entered the room and Luca eyeing it suspiciously watched it circle for a few minutes, before turning his gun on it and blasting it out of the air. The gun blast partially destroyed the wall near the door but also blew a hole in the wall to the kitchen, at about eye level, in the corner.

"That could be very useful," Phillip whispered to Willie. "That gives you a way to attack Luca with conventional weapons. Can I suggest you go back to the kitchen, wait under the new breach in the wall and I'll put another Hubsan drone in. Let's synchronise our watches. In exactly one minute I'll put the drone in, and then you throw in a smoke grenade, followed immediately by an M33 fragmentation grenade, and then saturate the room with lead from your sub machine gun.

The drone went in and before Luca could respond Willie threw his grenades into the room, and then emptied a full clip from his Heckler & Koch MP5SD, into the room.

Phillip turned to John. "That's one down, and the most dangerous, so just two more to go. I suggest we take no more risks. They must be so scared and disorientated in that other room, but I see no signs of them surrendering. I'll give them an opportunity to surrender but if they refuse I propose to put the Reaper in, fire one of the missiles and remove the threat entirely. Willie, can you distract them by a small explosive charge on the wall of the room next to them, well away from the doorway? Thanks."

Willie placed the charge against the wall. He then shouted to the men in the room, giving them just a minute to surrender, but all he received in reply was a burst of automatic fire through the door into the corridor. So, the rest of the small force stood ready as the Reaper mini drone took its maiden flight along the corridor, and hovered just outside the doorway into the room. At the precise moment the charge exploded, the drone slipped into the room, fired the infrared beam onto the man holding the weapon, the on-board computer used the beam to make its calculations about trajectory and distance, and once the target was "painted", the mini drone unleashed its missile and destroyed the target, all within less than a second.

It had taken much longer than they had anticipated, and had almost ended in failure, but Phillip's force had cleared the west wing, and captured two men who could prove to have some very valuable information.

Phillip, Willie, Terry, John, Will and Peter lead the way down the corridor to the door into the west wall of the Great Hall, ready to join Bladon's force.

Forty Four

Meanwhile, at the foot of the stairs, Sandy immediately realised what had happened.

"They've used one of their super-guns. Nothing else could cause this much damage. Stefan, Jeremy, give me back up. I'm going to see if anyone's alive in that rubble."

Stefan and Jeremy immediately moved to the hole where the steps had previously been, and laid down a massive hail of lead from their Heckler & Koch MP5SD's to dissuade the gunman from firing again. Sandy ran to the pile of rubble to see if he could save any of his four friends, including Bladon and Lexi.

Whilst he clawed at the debris from the stairs he summed up his options. He assumed Bladon and Lexi were dead, he had no idea how the attack on the west wing was going, almost half of his force had been wiped out, and he only had Steve and Wilf to deal with an unknown force of men and weapons in the east wing. Also there was still a deadly threat from upstairs as he couldn't use the drone against them for the rooms to the right had still not been secured. What a mess!

He pushed such thoughts aside and concentrated on rescuing his friends, although it seemed a hopeless task. He lifted a large piece of solid oak panelling, now rather worse for wear, and to his delight he found Bladon curled in a foetal position underneath, a bit shocked and dusty, but OK. Next they found Patrick, badly hurt but still conscious. They pulled him from underneath a pile of bricks, cleared his airways, made him as comfortable as they could, and returned to look for Giancarlo and Lexi.

"Why did I let Lexi come inside with us? I should have kept her safe," Bladon lamented.

"Because she insisted, that's why," Sandy replied. "She deserved a chance to come with us and she's as strong mentally and physically as any of us. Don't give up hope yet Bladon."

They both dug furiously with their bare hands to remove the debris and to their delight found Giancarlo, but with extensive cuts and abrasions and covered in blood. Sandy found an undamaged leather chair nearby, and Giancarlo flopped down to recover.

Bladon was desperate to find Lexi. His mind went back to their first adventure at the top of a Swiss mountain, and he remembered how distraught he was when two thugs kidnapped her at gunpoint and bundled her onto the departing alpine railway. He was inconsolable, but this was even worse.

"Why is everybody safe but Lexi? I should never have let her come with you Giancarlo."

"Wait," said Giancarlo. "She's the reason we're alive. She spotted the gunman first, and shot him in the knee with her sniper rifle, and that's why he didn't take us all out. In his pain his gun skewed to the right as he fell. That's why the damage, as bad as it is, is not worse."

"But where is she?" Bladon cried. "Is she dead"?

The shattered doorway of a small room close by shuddered open.

"I'm here," she shouted. She had managed to crawl into the doorway of a small cubbyhole, just off the corridor and the staircase, and she was fine. A bit winded and shocked, but fine. "The bullets missed me, but as the wall and staircase collapsed, I crawled in here for safety."

"Well done Lexi, you have saved the day yet again," said Bladon beaming from ear to ear. "But you've had a big shock. I have a feeling that you still have a crucial part to play here, so please go back to the Great Hall and see how Patrick and

Giancarlo are. We'll try and finish off here. How wonderful that you're safe. I love you."

Meanwhile Steve and Wilf followed the corridor in the east wing round to the left of the stairwell into a small hall. Steve pulled on his helmet and studied the heads up display. The helmet could see through all the walls in the wing, and he saw to his right a small unoccupied room, which led on to a larger room, where he saw a gunman and the unmistakeable outline of a super-gun. He looked to his left, where a door lead into another large room, again empty, and then on into a small room where the spiral staircase was located. He saw another man standing by the door into the room, with what looked like an AK47 in his hand.

"So there are only two men left down here Wilf," Steve whispered. "I think a grenade should sort out the one near the staircase, but the other's a different proposition. He's got a super-gun, but he doesn't know we can see him. I think I'll target him with the drone, but if you could disorientate him with a smoke grenade, it will give me time to target him."

Wilf took a smoke grenade out from his webbed belt, tiptoed out of the hall and into the corridor beyond. To his right was a small vestibule leading to the room and he saw the door was open. He looked back to Steve and saw that the drone was airborne and hovering ready for the attack. He threw the smoke grenade into the room and backed off further down the corridor. Steve flew the drone into the smoke-filled room, targeted the man with the gun, and fired the missile, destroying man and weapon and leaving a five-inch diameter hole in the wall adjoining the Great Hall.

Steve joined Wilf in the corridor and together they entered a large room on the southwest corner of the house. Wilf took the drone from Steve, and using his helmet, Steve exited through the French doors, walked round the corner of Walton Priory to the east facing wall, and there in front of him was the small room where the man waited with his rifle, completely unaware of Steve's presence. In the wall facing him, Steve saw a small open window with frosted glass so he took out a stun grenade, threw it through the window, and immediately followed with a fragmentation grenade.

They retraced their steps to the corridor, Steve returning to the bottom of the staircase, and Wilf checking that the man in the room with the spiral staircase had been put out of action. Satisfied that he had, Wilf dropped another grenade onto the bottom of the staircase to take it out of commission, and hurried back to the others.

"Wilf, Could you have a look at Patrick and Giancarlo please? They're both struggling," said Bladon.

Steve, Bladon, Stefan, Jeremy, and Sandy considered their next step.

"We can't attack Dreadnought's men on the first floor after the losses we've taken," said Bladon. What's happened to Phillip's group? We need them desperately."

As he spoke, to their unalloyed joy, the door on the left of the Great Hall opened and out came a smiling Phillip, followed by Willie, Terry, John, Will and Peter.

"Welcome all of you. We were just wondering how we could take the first floor with only five men, but now we have eleven and two Reaper drones.

"Well let's make a start," said Bladon. "Both staircases are out of action now, and their only way out is either to jump out of the first floor windows, or surrender. There are about thirty combatants in the big State Room and the Library; the leaders are in the small room in the east wing, and the non-combatants are in the bedroom to the left of the staircase. How many Hubsan toy drones do we have left, and how many missiles?"

"We have about six Hubsan toy drones left, but plenty of missiles for the Reapers," said Steve.

"Sandy, before we attack could you please order A and B Squadrons to tighten their circle around the Priory so that none of the enemy get away when we go in? But please ensure you warn them so that they don't present too easy a target for a super-gun; they may have several left."

Forty Four

'A' Squadron SAS started their manoeuvre, but unfortunately one of the hostiles in the State Room, keeping a careful watch out of a window on the north side, noticed some movement, and clambered up what was left of the spiral staircase to the large super-gun on the roof. He alerted the men there, who fired and decimated part of the woods to the north, from where the SAS had emerged. Sadly five SAS were killed or wounded, and their Commander immediately ordered them to retreat back into the woods, disperse and keep under cover. Fortunately however, a lot of them had already reached the perimeter of the Priory, and about twenty melted into the undergrowth near the front of the house in case they were needed for the attack.

The SAS casualties were a setback, but Bladon and Sandy were now confident that their attack would succeed. The initiative had passed decisively to them, and they had the men and the drones to take out the super-guns upstairs. Destroying the main staircase was a major own goal for Dreadnought's men, as it effectively trapped them upstairs. But before their attack was launched Bladon shouted to the enemy above.

"It's not too late to surrender. You are trapped and have no chance of getting out alive. If you come out now and hand over your weapons, you will come to no harm. You have five minutes to decide."

The reply was immediate. A torrent of abuse, coupled with a hail of automatic fire down the stairwell.

Forty Five

Phillip and Steve deployed the Hubsan toy drones on the first floor, along the wide corridor known as the Long Gallery. Both drones flew up through the stairwell and entered the Long Gallery, for reconnaissance purposes. Phillip deployed his drone left to the east wing, to verify the occupants of the various rooms, which according to their information, should house the non-combatants. Steve turned right to the west wing, to check the Library and the State Room where he expected to find some strong opposition.

Phillip flew his drone past a small room, which he thought may be where the leaders slept, and turned left into a smaller corridor, and then right into a large bedroom and smaller adjoining room, which their information suggested, held only non-combatants.

It did not.

One of the ten men and women in those rooms was hiding a super-gun and as he saw the drone enter the room, he panicked and fired quickly. He destroyed the drone but also killed two of the kitchen staff and punched a large hole in the north-facing wall.

When Steve learnt of the demise of Phillip's 'toy' drone, he piloted his Hubsan much more circumspectly down the Long Gallery. He cruised the corridor checking through the camera and his helmet through the walls without going in, and identified both men and weapons in both of the large rooms. On the way back to the ground floor Steve flew the drone into the other small room on the east side where the spiral staircase was located, and followed it up to the roof. Here the camera spotted two men manning a very powerful super-gun on the roof, the same gun that had attacked the SAS in the woods. He hastily tried to recall the drone, but was too late, as the men spotted it and blew it out of the night sky.

"Very well," said Bladon. "Release the Reapers."

Both Reaper drones were guided up through the stairwell, and out into the Long Gallery. Phillip again turned the drone towards the east wing, and from outside the door of the small room that the leaders were using, targeted and released a missile, destroying the room completely. He then continued into the room where the spiral staircase was located, and followed it up to the roof of the Priory.

He was very much aware, from the clinical destruction of the toy drone, that the super-gun was handled by two of Dreadnought's most experienced men. Therefore as soon as his Reaper drone reached the roof, he directed it rapidly to the side, behind the huge chimney that rose from above the Great Hall. The drone fainted to the left of the chimney, attracting a torrent of fire, then slipped back to the right of the chimney, targeted the gun with the laser, and released its missile, destroying everything on top of the roof including the men and their weapon. With both missiles used Phillip returned the drone to the ground floor to re-arm.

Meanwhile, Steve had arranged with a four-man SAS team outside to launch a diversion in the State Room and the Library, before he attacked with his drone. He moved the Reaper halfway down the Long Gallery, but hovered low on the ground, just to the right of the entrance to the library. Exactly on time, two stun grenades were thrown into the State Room and the Library from underneath the windows. Steve utilising the period of confusion moved first to the entrance to the Library, and then to the entrance to the State Room, and targeted, and then launched his missiles at the super-guns that he had located on his helmet screen, destroying them all.

He brought the drone back down the Long Gallery and

down the staircase, to re-arm. Then with both drones re-armed, Phillip and Steve flew the Reapers up the staircase and on down the Long Gallery, and prepared to launch their missiles again. To their delight they saw stumbling out of the Library, and then the State Room, a file of dishevelled and disorientated men, plainly surrendering. They piloted the drones back to the head of the staircase, only to see another file of men and women, holding a white flag, and also preparing to surrender. Reporting what they'd seen Bladon arranged some strategic planks of wood, between the floor on the staircase and the seventh step, so enabling the surrendering enemy to come down.

Sandy had called for support from 'A' Squadron SAS, and 12 troopers joined him in the Great Hall, ready to take charge of the prisoners. They would be taken under armed guard to the lawned area at the front of the Priory, where they would be restrained, and ordered to wait until transport arrived to take them to SAS headquarters for interrogation.

Those men who had fought in the State Room and the Library negotiated the stairs first, and out of the 45 men in those two rooms, only 11 negotiated the stairs into the Great Hall. None of them had any of the super-guns with them. Six SAS troopers led them to the lawn, where they were restrained. Following them even more gingerly, trembling, with pale complexions, and looking very fearful, came the non-combatants, and they too were ushered into the Great Hall. Meanwhile, Steve and Phillip had left the house and walked round to the east side of the Priory out of sight of the others with their drones, in case any further action was required.

Bladon asked Jeremy, John, Will and Peter, to search all the Priory thoroughly, particularly the sleeping quarters upstairs, to make sure that none of the enemy were hiding, that all the guns were accounted for, and especially for any documents or other objects that might provide any information as to the ultimate target for Dreadnought's attack.

Among the non-combatants was a man called Felix, the

same man who had hidden amongst them and taken out the drone with the super-gun. He walked slowly and dispiritedly, with his head down, towards the door with the others. He was wearing a long coat, but hidden underneath its copious folds was the last remaining super-gun. As one of the SAS troopers started to handcuff the non-combatants, Felix took his chance and ran to his right, pulling out his gun at the same time grabbing Bladon who was next to him, and pulling him away as a hostage.

"Put your guns down all of you, and don't try anything or your leader dies. He has a date with Dreadnought, who has been looking forward to meeting him again for a long time."

Forty Six

Bladon's men placed their weapons on the ground, and kept their eyes steadily on Bladon and his captor, looking for an opportunity to intervene. What Bladon's captor had not noticed however, was that Lexi was not amongst the others, either in the Priory, or outside with the rest. She had in fact, been resting from the strenuous efforts of the day, and her near fatal demise by the staircase. When she heard the commotion, she peered around the corner of the Priory and saw to her horror Felix with the super-gun pointed at her beloved Bladon. Were they never going to have any peace and security in their lives?

Sandy spoke to Felix, as Lexi wondered what she could do to intervene.

"What's your name sir? We can't talk unless we know who we're talking to?"

"It's Felix; why do you want to know?"

"Well Felix, how can we sort this little problem out in an amicable way? We aren't going to let you get away but I'm sure we can agree a solution."

"Well I'll tell you what sort of amicable solution I want. I want you to bring a car round, so that I can take Bladon away with me, and if he is very lucky he may get out alive."

Sandy was playing for time, and Phillip and Steve hidden behind the east wing realised this, and they had earlier seen Lexi walking towards the gardens next to the west wing. She must have heard Sandy talking and perhaps she was hiding around the side of the Priory away from them. Yes, they could just see her rifle barrel.

As they watched, Lexi lifted her sniper rifle. Felix had his back to her, but was still too close to her beloved husband, and to fire would be too risky. What was needed was a diversion to allow her to take Felix out, before he took Bladon away to certain death. Phillip and Steve still had some Hubsan toy drones left, and surely they could create a diversion with them.

They launched both drones, and as Lexi watched she saw them both climbing round the east wing corner, and separating in front of Felix.

"Wait, wait," she told herself, "until Felix spots them."

Felix looked up, and saw both drones hovering in attack formation, and the horror of the devastation they could cause came flooding back to him. Not knowing that they were harmless toy drones, he pushed Bladon down to the floor, and brought his gun up, to shoot them out of the sky. He destroyed the first with a blast from his super-gun, and swivelling to take out the second, he fell to the ground, shot twice in the head by Lexi.

Bladon and Sandy rushed over to her, and she collapsed into Bladon's arms.

"I'm so sorry darling. I'm sorry Sandy. I hated having to do that. But I had to stop him didn't I? Please, Sandy, when will this business ever end?"

"You saved your husband's life again, and you saved our lives too Lexi. He could have wiped us all out with that gun, but we distracted him just enough to allow you to nullify the threat in your usual decisive way. Thank you. Thank you so very much."

The prisoners were searched, handcuffed and made to kneel together on the grass in two groups, combatants and non-combatants, all under the watchful eye of Bladon's men, with loaded sub machine guns.

Some of the prisoners were interrogated as to the

whereabouts of Dreadnought and Clara, before being transferred to SAS Headquarters. They were not among the prisoners or the dead bodies, and Willie confirmed that his men had not seen anyone else trying to escape. After an intensive interrogation of one of the leaders, Willie and Peter finally made a breakthrough. He confirmed what a cleaner had also reported, that late on Monday night, Dreadnought and Clara, with four of his elite guard, had loaded several weapons into a Transit Van and disappeared.

So he had escaped and was still on the run.

As Willie walked towards the damaged front doors to tell Bladon the news, he stopped suddenly. Four Police cars, including two armed-response vehicles, followed by two Police vans, roared into the front drive of the Priory and skidded to a halt. The cars disgorged eight constables and eight heavily armed officers from the specialist firearms unit, chosen from the Derbyshire and Staffordshire Forces. The armed officers surrounded Bladon's men holding the prisoners, levelled their guns at them and waited for a pompous, self-important Chief Superintendent in full dress uniform to get out of the leading car.

Bladon, whispered to Steve, "Watch out it's Fordingley."

"What do you want Fordingley. This is not a Police operation."

"Chief Superintendent Fordingley, to you Bladon. And don't try to pass off any more false Special Branch documents on me. I've sussed what you're up to. These so-called prisoners are now under my jurisdiction, and I am going to take them away for questioning myself."

Steve, Wilf and Jeremy stood beside him, as Bladon replied coldly, "No way Fordingley, back off."

He noticed Sandy striding towards him.

"I repeat," Bladon said. "You have no jurisdiction. Now leave immediately and I'll take no further action."

"You'll take no further action," shouted Fordingley, seething with uncontrollable anger. "I refuse, you cretin.

I've been in touch with Special Branch and they have never heard of you. We are taking the prisoners into custody, and furthermore we are arresting all four of you for criminal damage to the Priory, and for murder."

Sandy approached Fordingley, and brandished his identification in front of the Chief Superintendent's face.

"I work directly for the Prime Minister and have full authority here, and I tell you that neither you, nor your men, have any authority whatsoever in this situation, and have no right to be here."

Fordingley did not back down. "Get lost, Government lackey. I've got the power here in my own patch, and my authority is those guns. That's all the authority you need. So back off. Johnston, start to move those prisoners to our patrol wagons."

There was an apparent stalemate, but then Sandy raised his voice and shouted, "Willie, bring the men out, and if the Chief Superintendent or any of his men make a move, kill them."

It was an outrageous threat, but the situation was desperate, and to back it up out of the surrounding trees and the Priory came fifty heavily armed, SAS veterans.

"Arrest him Willie," said Sandy coldly, "and interrogate him in the Priory before we move out."

An instant change came over Fordingley, like all bullies when defied, and he pleaded with Willie. "No, please don't hurt me. It was just a mistake, an honest mistake. I didn't know this was a security operation. No one told me. I'm not to blame. We'll keep well away in future now that we know who you are."

"OK," said Sandy. "Your men must return to their vehicles immediately, and all of you move away from this area and don't bother any of us again. The Prime Minister has put Bladon in personal charge of this operation and I am informing him and the Chief Constable of your actions here today. You will assist Bladon whenever he requests it. Is that clear?"

"Yes sir, I understand."

"Sandy, I don't trust him. Don't let him go, I feel he could yet play a significant part in this operation," said Bladon.

"I'm sorry Bladon, you could be right, but we must follow procedure and go through the usual disciplinary channels. But, Chief Superintendent, consider yourself suspended."

Fordingley, very chastened, drove off with his entourage, and ten minutes later with a mighty roar, an Apache AH 64 flew low over the river and hovered over the Priory, whilst a Special Forces Chinook CH 47D followed and landed on the croquet lawn a hundred metres from the Priory. Another Apache followed it in, and took up a holding position above the Chinook, whilst Bladon's men moved the prisoners on board. Inside they were manacled, and then the Chinook took off for 23 SAS Headquarters in the West Midlands, with its two attack helicopters as protection.

Forty Seven

Thursday 11am

Bladon joined Faisal, Adam, Jeremy, Steve and Lexi and she welcomed everyone to the Brainstorming Meeting after they'd all got a coffee.

Their last meeting two days ago had decided that the probable target for Dreadnought was a stately home in Derbyshire, either Haddon Hall or Chatsworth in the north of the county, well away from centres of population, or Kedleston Hall which was close to Derby. Faisal and Adam also were looking into the possibility of another simultaneous major attack, in the manner of Al-Quaeda, or a diversionary attack somewhere close to the main target. There was a strong possibility that the Queen would be visiting an unspecified House on the following Monday, and Steve and Jeremy were working on that problem.

In fact, Jeremy had established through his contacts that the Queen would be staying at Chatsworth on the Saturday and Sunday night. However Steve had some even more startling news, which was that the Queen would be coming to Kedleston Hall on the following day under strict secrecy and security for lunch with the Curzon family, the owners of Kedleston before the family gave it to the National Trust many years before, and a select group of industrialists and charity workers, about thirty in all. The Royal family had insisted the visit should still go ahead, even though the threat of an attack from Dreadnought was still a very real possibility. The Prime Minister himself had allowed it, as long as it took place in complete secrecy, and no press or media were notified.

Bladon listened and then spoke. "If the visit does go ahead, then we must have total control of the security arrangements. There must be a Police presence, but not in the precincts of the House itself, and I think the whole of 'A' Squadron SAS should guard the main House, the private quarters where the Queen will go, and the outbuildings and immediate grounds right down to the lake. Also "B" Squadron should cover the surrounding area and all the approaches to Kedleston; but it's imperative that they all keep under cover. We don't want to scare Dreadnought away. We want to arrest him this time. However tight our security is, it will still be risky for the Queen though. I am not happy about that aspect at all."

"With respect we are all getting a bit ahead of ourselves here." said Steve. "We don't know that it's definitely Kedleston and we could be denuding ourselves of the protection of the SAS somewhere else just when we need them there."

"I agree with you Steve, and unless we get some more tangible information to link Kedleston with the attack, we should keep all other options open," said Lexi.

"Well, our search of Walton Priory may very well help us there," said Bladon. We've found nothing yet, but I'm certain something will turn up. Also I'm hoping that our aerial search for the van will turn up some clues. Let's meet again late tomorrow when we've more news."

Bladon left the meeting, phoned Sandy on his car phone and updated him on the Group's progress. The most disturbing aspect of the attack on Walton Priory was that Dreadnought and Clara were not there. When did they leave? It could only have been in that dark blue van late on Monday night. The Police and the SAS had found no trace of either the van or the occupants. They had just disappeared. Bladon wanted to intensify the search for the van and so when Sandy answered, he explained what he wanted, and asked him to by-pass Fordingley completely, and phone direct to Police headquarters in Ripley, North Derbyshire.

Sandy was put through urgently to the Deputy Chief Constable, who he knew by reputation, and he asked him to intensify the search for the van and for Dreadnought; this meant scrambling two more helicopters from neighbouring forces. They had succeeded in taking Walton Priory with so few casualties, but still Dreadnought had evaded them, presumably with a large supply of his deadly weapons, and they had no certain information about his target.

Three helicopters were airborne on Thursday morning and they began to search an area from Walton-on-Trent in the south, to Chatsworth House in the north; and from Uttoxeter in the west, to Nottingham in the east. Sandy had asked the DCC to instruct the pilots to concentrate on the area around Derby and the Trent Valley. He had a hunch that Dreadnought would not risk travelling too far in the van. He had a suspicion that as he had used the river and canal networks before, he would do so again.

At 5pm that night Sandy phoned Bladon in a state of high excitement.

"Bladon your hunch was right. They've found a submerged van in a gravel pit very close to Sawley Marina. As the water was very clear they could see it from the air."

"Well done Sandy. Tell the pilot not to draw attention to himself though, as they may be hiding nearby. Just stand all the helicopters down and tell them to return to base. Could you please speak to the local acting Chief Super and ask him to put up Police roadblocks around the Marina but not too close? We don't want to spook Dreadnought if he's holed up in the Marina. Also I want that van recovering and I want a search team to check it over with a fine toothcomb, but we shouldn't start the recovery until after we start the search of the Marina. I suggest we start at 5.00am tomorrow. I'm sorry to put you under so much pressure, but I must have the results of the search of the van by midday tomorrow."

Bladon put the 'phone down and arranged for Willie to put fifty men from B Squadron on alert immediately to search the Marina the next day. There was to be no activity at all until 5.00am, but then they would carry out an extensive search of all the boats, vehicles, and buildings at the Marina, starting with the pitches closest to the main entrance on the south-west side. The acting Chief Superintendent would be asked to remove any Police officers in the vicinity of the Marina by 4.45am.

However, none of them knew that Fordingley was not just a pedantic, annoying, little bureaucrat only interested in his own advancement in the force, but he was Dreadnought's man. He had been turned several years ago, and he was one of his most useful undercover assets. He had overreacted at Walton Priory, and very nearly blown his cover, but he was still around the force headquarters as his suspension had still not yet been ratified, although the acting Chief Superintendent knew what had happened. Fordingley heard the instructions from Sandy relayed to the units out on patrol, and although it was very risky, he sent a text to Dreadnought from his office at 5.00pm, but on an untraceable pay-as-you-go phone he had purchased earlier in the week.

"Van discovered nearby. Searching 5am tomorrow, Friday. Suggest clean up and leave ASAP. F."

At 5.30pm Dreadnought recalled Cameron and Aaron from the 'Caroline' immediately, whilst the others made ready to leave. He met Cameron by the Bistro next to the towpath and gave him instructions about Kurt. Dreadnought realised now that Kurt had placed the whole project in jeopardy. Ten minutes later Cameron returned and nodded quietly to Dreadnought that the deed was done, and took his place with the others, ready to leave as soon as darkness fell. Bladon had arranged for two squadrons of SAS, under cover to watch the Marina for any suspicious activity, but they were too late to see Cameron returning to the 'Aquinas'. The narrowboat left the Marina in the dead of night, moved into the Sawley Cut, the only means of getting to Trent Lock, and on to his ultimate destination. Dreadnought's boat carefully negotiated the "Cut" and moved slowly past the narrow boats moored by the canal bank. The biggest obstacle to them getting clear away from Sawley Marina was the double locks at the entrance to the fast flowing River Trent. They would be extremely conspicuous as the only boat negotiating the locks so late at night. Dreadnought ordered Cameron to remove the name plates from the boat to prevent recognition, and as he drew close to the lock and the moment of biggest danger approached, he saw to his relief that a 26 foot Cabin Cruiser had already entered the left hand lock and was preparing to close the lock gates. Fortuitously the cruiser's owner looked up just in time, and beckoned Dreadnought's boat into the lock, and the Aquinas slipped alongside the cruiser with a wave of thanks from Cameron in the wheelhouse.

The moment of greatest danger for Dreadnought was over. They were through the lock and out into the river's strong flow, and in a short time they were approaching Trent Lock, where the river flowed straight on, unnavigable to boats. A canal known as the Cranfield Cut turned to the left. Immediately before this, the Erewash Canal cut back almost at a right angle to the river, to travel on to Long Eaton, Sandiacre and on to Stanton Gate.

It was here that Dreadnought proposed to spend the night, before moving up the Erewash Canal. There was only one place they could safely lay up overnight and this entailed a rather tricky manoeuvre. Immediately past the entrance to the lock leading to the Erewash Canal, the river curved left and on to Cranfield Cut, and here several narrow boats were moored. Opposite was the Trent Valley Sailing Club, and it meant Cameron would have to carry out a difficult manoeuvre in the midst of the fast flowing river in order to place the boat on the north bank ready for a quick and easy start in the morning.

Cameron had, however, become remarkably proficient at steering the boat, bearing in mind his limited experience. He carried out the manoeuvre with alacrity by steering into the entrance to the lock on his left, and then just allowing the boat to float back with the current for a short distance, before applying full power and pulling in safely to the bank.

Forty Eight

Friday 5am

At Sawley Marina, in the early hours of Friday morning, the SAS started a systematic search of the whole area, including every boat, whether occupied or not, every building and vehicle, laundry, toilets, showers, and restaurants. In the Marina basin, and on the river moorings, there were over 500 boats to search, so it was going to be a long job. At about 11.00 am, a four man squad approached the narrow boat 'Caroline'. The SAS Captain, George, knocked on the door to the galley.

No reply.

They knocked again.

Silence yet again.

The four of them searched the outside of the boat which seemed normal, but on closer inspection they saw from fragments of splintered wood that the bolt on the galley door had been forced, and a new bolt fitted.

"This looks very suspicious," said George. "Can you see anything through the curtains, Jon?"

"No, it all looks absolutely fine."

"Well I don't like it. I'm going to investigate". He kicked the door hard, which gave way and fell back on its hinges against the wall of the galley.

"Cover me, Jon. I'm going in."

Whilst the other two soldiers secured the outside of the boat, George jumped down into the galley and in one movement was into the sleeping birth.

He found Kurt lying on the bed, with a single red hole in his forehead, staring at him obscenely like a third eye. "For some reason, Dreadnought had no further use for him," said George, as he reported back to Willie.

"Either that, or he has displeased him or lost trust in him. Maybe he was the one who dumped the van in the gravel pit."

Willie deployed a forensic team to go through the boat methodically and see if they could find any incriminating evidence. They found nothing. Dreadnought's organisation was impressive. The SAS continued their search of the Marina and the river, but they found no further trace of Dreadnought, or his men. Dreadnought was out there somewhere, and still just as dangerous, and they still had no certainty of the time or the place of the planned attack. All that they could do was hand the matter back to Bladon for referral to the Brainstorming Group.

Friday 9.00am

After a good night's sleep on the boat, Dreadnought, Clara, Cameroon, Aaron, Vladimir and Hussein all met over breakfast to discuss their next move. Aaron suggested moving down the canal and the river to Beeston, to the east of Trent Lock, a large town on the outskirts of Nottingham. They could take a leisurely cruise down to a pub he knew by the river at Beeston Rylands and then just before the large weir, turn round and head back to Trent Lock. They could then make the trip up to Stanton Gate the next day as planned.

"That has some merit," said Dreadnought, "but I'm reluctant to agree, as we need to keep under cover, and also because it means staying for a further two days on this very dangerous waterway. We know that the police and the SAS will be searching the Marina right now and I'm just wondering how long it will be before they realise we may have got away on the river. In my opinion the quicker we can get off the river and canal and to our base in Kedleston the better."

"I think I am inclined to agree with you, Dreadnought," said Clara. "I think that the quicker we get away from here and into the more populated areas of Long Eaton and Sandiacre the better. We can hide there in plain view. We will just be holidaymakers on a leisurely relaxed journey, pottering down the canal. The only problem is that you have made all the arrangements for transport for tomorrow night and not tonight."

"We'll see," said Dreadnought, and gave instructions to Cameron to negotiate the Lock onto the Erewash Canal.

Dreadnought had already thought of this problem. Unknown to the rest of them, just before midnight he had risked a 'phone call to a secret contact who lived in Derby, with a rather strange request—to order an Ocado food delivery for later that day.

Cameron started the engine of 'Aquinas', and moved the boat forward and slightly to the right, under a footbridge, under another smaller bridge, and into the basin before the lock opposite the Steamboat Pub. Aaron and Vladimir jumped out of the boat and started to open the lock gates. The level in the lock itself had to be lowered to the level of the river, where the 'Aquinas' was waiting. Fortunately the last boat to negotiate the lock had come from the north and out onto the river, and so the level was already low, which meant they had no difficulty in opening the gates. Boaters approaching a lock are usually pleased to meet another boat coming towards them, because this boat will have just exited the lock on their level and therefore set the lock in their favour, thus saving them some work. Their narrow boat chugged slowly in, Aaron and Vladimir closed the gates and ran back to the towpath and held the ropes thrown up by Cameron and Dreadnought.

When a boat enters an empty lock, the lock chamber is filled by opening a valve that allows water to enter the chamber from the upper level. When the filling process was complete, Aaron and Vladimir hurried to the gates onto the Erewash Canal to open them.

So far, so good.

However, for some reason Aaron and Vladimir were not finding it very easy and were really struggling to get the gates open. One of the patrons of the Steamboat Pub called out and asked if they wanted any help. From inside the boat Dreadnought gesticulated to them not to accept and just get on with the job, but the patron, a little worse for wear even at this time of the day, was having none of it and moved over to the gate to give them a hand. Vladimir, not being too well endowed when it came to the social graces, told him in no uncertain terms to clear off back to the pub. This started a very unseemly fracas that if not nipped in the bud would bring undue attention to their flight to safety.

Much against his better judgement Dreadnought signalled to Vladimir to get back in the boat, and he jumped onto the bank and tried to calm things down with the disgruntled patron. After a heated response from the drinker, Dreadnought managed to persuade him to help him to open his side of the gate while Hussein joined Aaron to open the gate on the other side.

With the gates open, Cameron gratefully steered the boat through into the canal and tied it up temporally at the side of the canal. Aaron and Hussein returned along the towpath to re-board the 'Aquinas', but Dreadnought with his arm around the shoulders of the aggrieved man, went back into the pub with him, bought him another very welcome pint of bitter, and after 10 minutes of friendly chat bought him yet another pint and left a very happy drinker in the bar. He left money behind the bar for four more pints for the man, and left to rejoin his boat knowing that if questioned later in the day the drinker would remember little of what had happened, and hopefully the barman would remain discrete with the large tip he gave him.

He waited until they had negotiated the lock and were safely travelling along the canal network, and then found a long stretch of the canal, just before it went under two railway bridges. At the side of the canal were a large number of narrow boats moored, so he stopped behind one of them, a bright red barge with coal and logs on top, and they moored up.

"I think it's time that I explained my timetable in detail," said Dreadnought. "As you know, once we get off the canal network, we will be splitting our forces up in Derby. Four of us will be carrying on to our new base in Kedleston. I still intend to travel slowly up this canal, through Long Eaton, stopping at Sandiacre for a while, and then moving on until we get to Stanton gate, at about 9.30 pm.

There is an old coal yard there, and I have taken out a ten-year lease on it under the pretext of starting up a haulage business from the yard. It's ideal for unloading the guns from the boat, as the yard runs right down to the canal and is shielded from the road by thick bushes and tree cover, so the transfer can be done in complete secrecy. I have stored inside one of the deceptively decrepit industrial buildings on the yard a stolen Mercedes Sprinter van. I've had it painted in Ocado livery, in raspberry, as I thought an Ocado delivery vehicle would blend in well on the journey we have to take through little villages, and between town and country.

I have asked a friend who lives in Derby to order an actual Ocado food delivery for Saturday evening between 10 and 11. You probably know that Ocado deliver Waitrose food all over the country. What you probably don't know though, unless you've used them before, is that they always confirm deliveries by text at about 2 o'clock in the afternoon, before delivery later in the evening, and in that text they give details of the delivery van, the name of the driver, and most importantly, the registration number of the van. The biggest risk with a stolen car nowadays is ANPR, the Police automatic number plate recognition system, so when we get the text from Ocado my men at the yard can mock up number plates, which correlate to that genuine delivery van. What do you think?"

"Brilliant," said Clara. "Well done."

Friday 6.00pm.

They moved out again into the middle of the canal and made their way north towards Long Eaton and Sandiacre. They passed under two railway bridges and a road bridge until eventually they reached New Sawley on the outskirts of Long Eaton. As they moved in leisurely fashion up the canal, they passed a large park on the left, and an old mill on the right, until finally crossing beneath the main Derby to Nottingham Road into the centre of the market town of Long Eaton. They continued through heavily built-up areas and deserted post-industrial landscapes, until they moored again for lunch. They set off again, stopping for some rest at Sandiacre, and finally, with great relief, they approached Stanton Gate right on schedule and tied up at their moorings by the side of the yard at 9:30pm precisely. Clara jumped out of the boat to reconnoitre the area, whilst the rest of them stayed on the boat. The yard could not be seen from the road, and seeing nothing untoward she unlocked the door of the barn, checked that no boats were in sight on the canal and drove the Ocado van down towards the boat on the side of the canal bank.

The van had been carefully adapted, so that on opening the side door the inside looked just like a normal delivery vehicle, with crates full of provisions ready for delivery. Carefully hidden on one side of this compartment though, was a small area which could hold at least five people, and on the other side a smaller compartment capable of storing the weapons. They moved the weapons out of the boat and into the van, whilst Dreadnought checked that the number plates were correct. A text sent by Ocado to a Mr Williams, who had ordered a delivery for that night, had been forwarded to Dreadnought during the journey from Trent Lock to Stanton Gate, which read as follows.

"Dear Mr Williams. Georgio will deliver your 10pm-11pm order in Raspberry van number TT63 OTV. You have no missing items."

This was vital information for Dreadnought. The same friend who had received the text from Ocado had arranged for plates to be made up for TT63 OTV, and the plates had been made and fitted to the van. It was a smart move, for who would think of stopping an Ocado delivery van on its normal business, with a genuine number plate.

With the weapons loaded, Cameron drove the van out of the yard, and along narrow country lanes and through small villages finally reaching Pride Park in the Derby City Centre, where Vladimir and Hussein jumped out of the van and settled into the Holiday Inn Express, after carefully stowing their two weapons under the bed.

Cameron drove on from Derby in a north-westerly direction, past the University, on to Allestree, and finally just before the entrance to the Golf Club and Kedleston Hall, pulled in on the right to the deserted and boarded up Kedleston Hotel, which before its demise, was a popular eating place. He hid the van in an old barn round the back, after transferring all the weapons into the safety of the hotel.

Friday 9.00pm.

Meanwhile, Lexi called another brainstorming meeting for 9.00pm that Friday night, this time at Selwyn's house.

"A lot of additional information has come in that I want Bladon to tell you about."

Bladon, in an exuberant mood, shared his excitement. "Our extensive search of the first floor of Walton Priory had yielded absolutely nothing until about two hours ago, when we found under a mattress in the small bedroom, the stub of a visitor's ticket to Kedleston Hall. It was so small it had been missed before, but the new search team found it. But it gets better. In the waterlogged remains of the transit van that we reclaimed from the gravel pit near Sawley Marina, we found under the front seat a guide book to Kedleston Hall."

"Wow," said Lexi. "It looks very much like it's Kedleston. It confirms what we have been thinking"

"Yes Lexi, it looks like it, but knowing the target, is still a long way from stopping Dreadnought. Let's all meet up early tomorrow to discuss your conclusions with the others.

Forty Nine

Saturday 7.30am.

As everyone drifted slowly into the big meeting room at Selwyn's house with their coffee, Bladon commenced.

"Welcome everyone and thanks for all your incredible efforts, those involved in the attack on Walton Priory, those who have been on the Brainstorming Group, and those of you involved in back up. We've taken some hits; Andy has fractured some bones, and sadly we've taken some SAS fatalities, but otherwise the assault on the Priory was successful, except that Dreadnought and Clara escaped. As I've already explained to the Brainstorming Group the search of Walton Priory finally gave us some important information. They found the stub of a visitor's ticket to Kedleston Hall in the Priory, and in the abandoned van they also found a guide book to Kedleston Hall."

"That's brilliant," said Lexi. "Is it a good time to fill you in on the results of our brainstorming so far? It is relevant to these two findings."

"Go ahead Lexi," said Bladon, with pride and affection.

"All of our team are here today, including Faisal and Adam who have been really helpful. Let me tell the rest of you how our deliberations have gone, and you can then judge for yourselves whether they are helpful and whether they fit in with your information.

We had come to the conclusion that the probable target for Dreadnought was a stately home in Derbyshire, either Haddon Hall or Chatsworth, in the north of the county well away from centres of population, or Kedleston Hall closer to the City of Derby. Faisal and Adam also feel quite strongly that there is either the possibility of another simultaneous attack, in the manner of Al-Quaeda, or a diversionary attack somewhere close to the main target. We picked up on a strong rumour that the Queen would be visiting an unspecified House on Monday, and Steve and Jeremy have been looking into that possibility. Well, Jeremy has established through his contacts, and this is still highly confidential, that the Queen will in fact be staying at Chatsworth on Saturday and Sunday night. Steve then received some even more startling news. The Queen is planning to come to Kedleston Hall the next day, on Monday, in strict secrecy for lunch with the Cavendish family, and also a select group of industrialists and charity workers, about thirty in all. The news that Bladon gave us last night about finding a ticket and a guidebook for Kedleston Hall, confirms our theory. The target is Kedleston Hall."

Bladon listened carefully and then added, "Thanks Lexi. Your group has done really well. Thank you all so much. We must have total control of the security arrangements, including the SAS and the Police, but I'm still very uneasy about risking the Queen's life.

"May I make a suggestion?", it was Faisal who spoke. "I've been thinking about this problem since our meeting on Thursday. Have you seen the film 'The Queen'? Well Dame Helen Mirren plays Her Majesty brilliantly. Why don't we ask her to understudy for her for real? They could whisk the Queen off to safety from Chatsworth on Sunday, and Dame Helen could take over her duties on Monday morning. She's a real sport. I'm sure she'll be up for it."

"But we can't leave her and the thirty dignitaries in the line of fire. It wouldn't be fair", said Lexi.

"No that's true," said Adam, "but we could evacuate them immediately after they've gone into the private quarters on the east wing of the Hall, and take them all under cover, into the safety of the stable basements, or even down to the lower floors of the main part of the House, or some of the buildings in the grounds."

"Thanks Adam, I like that," said Sandy. "I think that could work, as long as we put some of 'A' Squadron in the stable or lower floors in the early hours of Monday morning before any other security is set up. They can then guard those areas and the VIP's when they arrive. And no autograph hunting from your men Willie", he said with a smile.

"Don't worry sir", said Willie. "The mere sight of Dame Helen will be enough for us thank you. On that subject though, she will of course have to be very expertly made up. They will need some padding, heavy make up and a wig, but there's nothing we can do to disguise her height. We will have to leave that to Dame Helen, and her consummate acting skills."

Bladon summed up. "That sounds excellent. We have thought of everything we can to protect Kedleston. We will also have a strong Police presence in the grounds, quite visible as a deterrent, and a large SAS cordon in and around the Hall, but all under cover. If Dreadnought brings his big super-guns in to attack the Hall and kill the 'Queen' then I propose we deal with his attack in the same way that we attacked Walton Priory, with snipers, and with the two drones. The drones will be a total surprise to Dreadnought hopefully. We will also have some rocket propelled grenades and Stinger Missiles, but I think Dreadnought will be prepared for those and blast them out of the sky. I will have some Apache helicopters in reserve too.

An attack on Kedleston is bad enough but I hope that Adam and Faisal are wrong about simultaneous or diversionary attacks on Derby. It could mean great loss of life."

Bladon's Revenge

Fifty

Monday 10.00am.

Unfortunately, Adam and Faisal were not wrong, and Dreadnought had planned a devastating attack on the Cathedral Quarter, in the heart of Derby City Centre. Dreadnought had devised his lethal diversionary attack, after reading about an accidental fire, a year earlier, on the top floor of the Assembly Rooms car park, where 70 firemen and 15 fire tenders had attended, together with many Police officers from the City and County forces. If so much panic and devastation could be caused by one accidental blaze on the top floor of a car park, then how much more devastation and panic could be caused by simultaneously attacking two major targets in adjacent locations at the same time. By carefully timing the attacks, he could effectively bring the whole of the City Centre to a standstill, and draw away most of the Police presence from Kedleston, leaving him a clear field for his devastating attack on the Hall and the Queen herself. He had originally intended to launch his twin strikes at 4.30 in the morning, but on reflection he had ordered Vladimir and Hussein to attack at 10.00am instead. He anticipated that the later start time would cause so much fear and pandemonium so close to the time of the Queen's visit to Kedleston, that the City Centre turmoil would cause untold panic and fear among the Derby City Police, and seriously compromise their effectiveness. The two targets chosen by Dreadnought were the Quad, and the nearby Assembly Rooms.

Vladimir and Hussein left the Holiday Inn Express car park

in a small Fiat 500 that Dreadnought had left for their use; it was old, scuffed, and inconspicuous. Vladimir dropped off Hussein at the Derby mainline railway station, and Hussein bought a ticket to Nottingham and moved onto Platform One with a small rucksack. It contained nothing more sinister then Lego building sets, but no one was to know that. Vladimir left the station in his car, after dropping Hussein off, and returned through the city centre, moving out towards the north of the city, making his way through the one-way system to the block of flats in the Handyside area of the city. In Handyside there was a mixture of housing, including some imposing terraced Georgian houses, and some attractive semi-detached post-war houses, but there was also some sheltered housing and high-rise flats. He left the car in front of just such a block of flats, and walked back into the city by the Catholic Church, over the new pedestrian bridge and into the heart of the Cathedral Quarter.

Meanwhile, Hussein approached a group of school children, and sat near them on a seat by the side of the railway track to Nottingham, and removing his rucksack, placed it under his seat. After a few minutes he rose from his seat, left the station with a ticket provided in advance by Dreadnought, and walked into the City to rejoin Vladimir. Twenty minutes later, he too was very close to the Cathedral Quarter, and the two men met in the Brewery Tap Pub, close to Exeter Bridge over the River Derwent. Dreadnought had provided an escape route for them both, by leaving a small boat with an outboard under the bridge, which could easily be accessed by steps down from an entrance next to the bridge.

Hussein slipped out of the pub, took his pay-as-you-go mobile from his coat, walked onto the bridge and phoned Derby City Police headquarters in the City Centre. He informed them that he had left an explosive device inside a rucksack on Platform 1 in the station, and then he threw the phone into the river.

After about 15 minutes, pandemonium broke out in the Derby City centre, with police and fire engines rushing out to the station to the southeast. With their weapons safely stowed in their large sports bags, Hussein and Vladimir made their way towards the Cathedral Quarter, allowing themselves ten minutes for the short walk to the Central Square, adjacent to the Assembly Rooms car park and the Quad. They placed their bags on the floor directly underneath the giant TV screen on the edge of the square and looked over to the Quad building.

Derby Quad is an arts centre opened about five years ago, a steel and glass design by Bath architects, Feilden, Clegg, and Bradley. When it was chosen by Derby City Council, it was considered to be a very controversial design, but the people of Derby had grown to love its quirky lines, and it was now very popular. It provided an art gallery, two cinemas, artists' studios, a cafe bar, and the centre also had available spaces for people to create their own artwork. At ten o'clock it was starting to get busy, and in particular the early matinee at 10.30am was attracting a lot of interest.

Vladimir and Hussein were aiming to make two lethal, pre-emptive strikes, in tandem, with Hussein attacking the Quad main entrance, an imposing glass edifice adjacent to the café bar; and Vladimir launching an attack on the Assembly Rooms entrance and booking hall, and the ground floor of the car park. Hussein had one of the super-guns that Clara had used to create such havoc on the river Trent, but Vladimir was using a specially adapted weapon for use with incendiary bullets. Dreadnought had discussed this with Professor Lane, the gun's inventor, under duress, who had pointed out that one or two incendiary bullets do not start a fire—it needs hundreds. This new weapon that Vladimir was using, was based on the same design as the other weapons except that it fired multiple rounds of incendiary bullets, making it a lethal weapon in the confined space in which it would be used.

At precisely 10am they launched their attacks. Hussein walked slowly and deliberately towards the Quad, steadied himself whilst people bustled in and out of the cafe and gallery totally unaware of the danger nearby, and then emptied two pods of bullets into the main entrance and the tinted glass walls of the cafe. The glass disintegrated under the assault, decimating the north side of the building, and causing great loss of life and major structural damage.

Vladimir meanwhile walked the few steps towards the Assembly Rooms, took the previously untried incendiary gun, and fired it first at the ground floor entrance, and then at the car park. He saw to his delight that immediately two major conflagrations broke out, in fact the heat was so intense that it singed his own hair, and he had to quickly run back towards the decimated Quad building in order to survive the continuing rippling of blasts from car petrol tanks exploding in quick succession. He ran off towards the river and Exeter Bridge, and looking back saw that a huge conflagration was now enveloping all of the first two floors of the car park, the reception area and stairs up to first floor, and the whole of the Italian restaurant next door.

Hussein joined him and together they fled towards Exeter Bridge, with Hussein covering their flight with the now reloaded super-gun. It became a major incident, with 150 firemen converging on the Square with 25 tenders, all of the City police that could be spared, and a hundred from the Derbyshire County police force.

They reached Exeter Bridge, ran down the steps at the side, to where the small boat was moored out of sight of the road, and with an immense feeling of relief, set off up the river northwards, until they reached the Derby Rowing Club. They tied up the boat, jumped quickly out of their craft and walking into Handyside found their car. They made their way slowly out of the City, along a succession of urban streets fringed by terraced houses, keeping well away from the centre itself until finally, just before the University they reached the A38 dual carriageway and turned south towards the safety of Walton Priory.

Fifty One

Vladimir phoned Dreadnought on an untraceable mobile as they passed Burton-on-Trent on their left, not far from the Walton turnoff.

"It's been a great success sir. We've caused massive damage and significant loss of life at the Quad, severely damaged the Assembly Rooms and the car park next to it, and caused mayhem at the railway station with the bomb hoax. We have nearly reached the Priory. What do you want us to do there?"

"I want you to keep well away from it. It's been attacked and compromised. I have no details, but I believe it's in enemy hands now. Go on to London, and stay in the safe house near Marble Arch, until I contact you. If all goes well here at Kedleston, as I'm sure it will thanks to you two, I'll join you later to complete our takeover of the capital."

He ended the call and Clara asked, "Why are you doing all this. Is it revenge?"

"Well yes it's revenge on Bladon and all his cohorts, but it's much more than that. It's also about money. We will be very wealthy after selling the weapons to the Chinese. But it's mostly about taking control of the country. I was very close two years ago, but Bladon and the Prime Minister, Johnny Hanbury, stopped me. I want to use these attacks to shock them both, to destroy their credibility, and then use it as a springboard to taking control of the country and making it a benevolent dictatorship—well not that benevolent for most of the inhabitants. After the concussion effect of the attacks on Derby city centre, and the attack on Kedleston Hall, but most of all the death of the Queen, the country will be ripe for takeover and for a strong man to step in and oust Hanbury from power. I am that strong man. All I've got to do now is make sure that Fordingley ensures all the police around Kedleston are withdrawn and sent to the City, and then we are ready to put our plan into action."

"We will attack at 1.30pm," Dreadnought continued, "as I have just heard from a reliable source that the Hall and the grounds are now closed to the public, and that the Queen is arriving for lunch with the Curzon family in their personal quarters to the east of the main building, at 1 o'clock. I am going to use two Land Rovers for the attack which have been mocked up to resemble National Trust vehicles in their famous dark green livery. You and I will be in one with our most powerful gun, which we'll use on the Hall to destroy the private quarters to the east, and kill the Queen at the same time. Cameron and Aaron will be in the other as back up, but also to transport the rest of the weapons which we will sell to the Chinese in exchange for two billion pounds sterling."

"How much", whispered Clara in shock. "Two billion pounds. Wow that's a fortune."

"Yes," Dreadnought replied. "It's partly yours you know, and that's only the start. Wait until we have control of this country. We'll bleed it dry."

Clara had doubts about Dreadnought's plan. She did not think that the country would be quite so easily subjugated as Dreadnought seemed to think. However, the thought of all that money persuaded her to put her misgivings to one side.

At midday, a luxury coach turned into the parkland surrounding Kedleston Hall by way of the north gatehouse, crossed the bridge over the lake, drove to the gates to the Hall, and dropped off a party of about thirty industrialists and charity workers, who were welcomed inside the main Hall for cocktails and canapés before being ushered into the private quarters.

As ordered, Chief Superintendent Fordingley drove slowly through the western entrance gates into Kedleston Park at midday. He moved along the narrow road, with the sheep and Canada geese straddling the road and meadow, until he reached the Hall. He took a left turn, opened the ornate wrought-iron gates, and drove onto the circular gravelled sweep before the House, and stopped by the magnificent Palladian front of the Hall. He walked over to the Chief Inspector in charge of security at the Hall and saw to his relief that he knew him, and that he was from the north of the city, and hoped against hope that the news of his suspension hadn't reached him yet. He needn't have worried as Dreadnought had someone in place at Police Headquarters who had suppressed the news.

"Good day Smedley, you must have heard about the terrible events in the City Centre? Why are you still here?"

"Well sir, we've heard the reports over our radios, but we have strict instructions to remain here, to protect some VIP's."

"Yes quite, that's why I'm here, to countermand those orders. The Chief Constable has just phoned me, and the centre of Derby is in absolute uproar. It seems as though the whole of the Square in the Cathedral Quarter is in flames, and there are almost 100 injured and dead people lying around the Quad and Assembly Rooms. There's a full-scale bomb alert at the railway station, and I've just heard that some hooligans from the Normanton area of the City have taken advantage of the situation and are rioting, and making their way towards the new Intu Shopping Centre. You can leave me in charge of the Hall Smedley, and if I encounter any problems here I can always call for reinforcements. You must take all your men to help protect the city centre.

"Well I don't know about that Sir," said Smedley. "I understand that their are some pretty important visitors and they need protection. Some are here already but I've been told to expect someone very special."

"Don't you dare question my orders Smedley, or I will place you under immediate suspension. There is no need to worry about the situation here, I have got it completely covered."

Still unconvinced, but cowered by authority, Smedley

walked sullenly to his car in the driveway outside, and within five minutes he and his 30 men, and a further five from the firearm support unit, had driven rapidly back towards the Derby city centre. He could have checked with control but he didn't want to risk the wrath of Fordingly.

Meanwhile, Bladon was trying to allay Lexi's fears, as they stood by the cattle grid leading on to the car park. It gave them a panoramic view of the Hall, its grounds to the north, east and west, down to the lake, and on up to the road from Derby and the Golf Club.

"I'm expecting Dreadnought's attack to come from the north directly towards the front of the Hall, with at least one of his super-guns. I want to keep the area from the North entrance, near to Kedleston Golf Club right down to the lake and up to the Hall, free of any security forces, so as not to deter such an approach. I've taken extensive measures to try and protect the southern approach to the Hall and put several SAS units up in the woods overlooking the south wing of the Hall and also in the grounds to the rear of the property and also in the ha-ha. I know Lexi, it's that word again, but there is a steep drop from the rear boundary of the Hall, and I can keep a lot of heavily armed men there out of sight. The main bulk of the SAS forces however, are held in reserve in the woodland just beyond the National Trust office, out of sight and ready for action at any moment. They can access the Hall and the grounds very easily from there without being seen by hugging the high northern perimeter wall next to the outbuildings. Then they can go undetected straight into the gift shop and up into the Hall itself. I need to stay here, as I need to have a clear view of the whole of the area."

"What's troubling me," said Lexi, "is where Dreadnought will attack from, and whether we will have enough protection from his terrible weapons?"

"That's s very good point Lexi. Giancarlo and I have been pondering just that question, and we have both come up with the same conclusion. As you know we are both keen students of the Peninsular War, and in particular Wellington's battle strategy. His strategy was to seek battle at a place where he could take the high ground, and where the terrain sloped down to the enemy armies below. He always positioned the main body of his army on the reverse slope, away from the enemy, and not on the slope facing the enemy. This protected them from Napoleon's fabled artillery, and also created the element of surprise when the French attacked, and it had proved very successful in the early battles in Portugal. Then Wellington refined those tactics famously at Waterloo, and won a decisive victory when his men rushed over the reverse slope and swept what was left of Napoleon's army back down the hill."

"Sorry Lexi, this is no time to give you a history lesson, but it gave us an idea. You see that small elevation, that grass mound, between the car park and the road surrounded by trees? Well, that's where I'm going to put The Thirteen, on that reverse slope. From there we can't be seen from the road up to the Hall, or from the lake, or the road from the northern gatehouse. It's the perfect location amongst the trees, and we've strengthened it by placing logs and fence posts on the crest of the elevation, to look as if the estate workers are erecting a new fence, but it still allows us a clear view of the Hall and the grounds with no fear of discovery. We've positioned snipers there, and hidden them under the logs to try and take out Dreadnought's men. If they spot us though it will be very dangerous.

I've also left Willie, Terry and Will, with a rocket-propelled grenade launcher each, behind the rest of the men, which I hope will take out Dreadnought's weapons. As back up, we also have the two mini drones, which were so successful in Walton Priory. Dreadnought has no idea of their existence and they could prove very useful. Finally, we have two Apache helicopters waiting in the grounds behind the woods to the south; but I am doubtful about deploying them, knowing the immense power of Dreadnought's weapons."

Lexi knew that Bladon had made all the preparations that he could possibly think of, but she was still very unhappy and uncertain about the outcome. Reports were coming through of an atrocity in the city centre too.

"There's still the danger to Dame Helen and all of all those VIP's, and just as Adam and Faisal warned, it looks like much of Central Derby is under attack. It's all too much. Why are we doing this? Surely we should hand it all over to the PM, the Security Services, MI5, the SAS and the Army. Anyone but us. I'm scared and I'm out of my depth. It's much too big for us now surely. And what if we've guessed wrong, and the target isn't Kedleston?"

Bladon hesitated, understanding Lexi's deep misgivings, and finally responded.

"Well Lexi, of course I agree that it is too big for us, but it was on the last occasion that we faced overwhelming odds, when we attacked Dreadnought at Ilam Manor. Don't you remember? But our little band, The Thirteen, all know Dreadnought better than anyone else alive; and I think we can get into his mind and out-think him. We have done so far haven't we? Also, we may be amateurs now, but we are all ex-professionals, and elite ex-pros at that, and very, very, motivated. After all, what greater motivation is there, than to prevent someone killing you? Our lives, and all those we love are on the line here, not to mention this beloved country and all that it stands for. We know that whatever Dreadnought's plans are, they will ultimately mean total control and domination, and we in particular will be taken out very quickly. I think we are our Country's best chance of success, and besides that we're not on our own. The P.M.'s given us two squadrons of the best Special Forces on the planet. And we have the element of surprise, for Dreadnought will never expect to find us here. He will think his attack on Derby will have concentrated our minds and our resources over there."

"I think we're ready, but we've no certainty as to where precisely Dreadnought will attack, or when. We've put all our eggs in one basket here, and we must just hope and pray that we've called it right. One more thing Lexi. You do know what Dreadnought will want to do when he's finishing destroying the Hall don't you? He'll want to destroy our wonderful home,

Fifty One

and I don't know about you, but I've grown very fond of it."

"Me too," said Lexi. "You're right, we're not going to let him."

Looking up, Bladon noticed some activity around the front of the Hall and saw to his consternation that the Police were withdrawing from their positions in and around the Hall itself. Three panda cars and a Police Patrol Wagon slowly exited the gravel drive and headed down the road, crossed the bridge over the lake, and up through the trees to the northern gatehouse, and sped off towards Derby. Then in close pursuit followed a 4x4, with the armed response unit crammed inside. All of the Police, except for one car, had left their post, and headed off to Derby.

"Give me the glasses please Lexi."

He trained them on the uniformed policeman walking back to his car.

"Wait a minute," said Bladon. "I'd know that arrogant strut anywhere. Get down; it's Fordingley. He must have ordered his men out. But I thought he was supposed to be suspended.

"It looks to me," said Lexi, "that Dreadnought's tentacles can still reach even into Police Headquarters and delay his suspension."

Bladon turned to Sandy. "What do we do?"

"Well, it's too late to try and get them back in time to be any use. We'll just have to redeploy some of our SAS units to take over, but we mustn't alert Fordingley to that. It looks as though his job's done now and he's leaving. Let's wait until he's reported to Dreadnought, and he will think the Hall and all the VIPs are totally at his mercy and undefended."

"Great idea", said Bladon. "Willie, I want you to deploy 40 men from A Squadron to guard the Hall and perimeter, but do it quietly and don't show yourselves. I don't think Dreadnought is watching the Park at the moment, but assume he is, and keep concealed. They can go through the locked gate in the grounds at the back of the National Trust building, and go down the service road between the wall and the outhouses and get into the Hall through the shop.

Fifty Two

Just after midday, the Queen's official state car, created for her by Bentley on the occasion of her Golden Jubilee, left Chatsworth House, travelled along Estate roads and arrived in the little hamlet of Rowsley, where it joined the main A6 to Derby. It had a motorcycle escort in front, and the Monarch's special protection officers travelled behind in their black armoured Range Rover. No one who witnessed their progress realised that the regal personage in the Bentley sitting next to her lady-in-waiting was not the Queen. The state car had been brought to a side entrance of the stately home, and the lady who decorously entered the car was not the genuine Head of the royal family, but one only by way of cinema and theatre. In other words, Dame Helen Mirren now occupied the exalted position in the Bentley and not Queen Elizabeth.

The royal procession travelled at a leisurely pace through the county town of Matlock, on through the tourist attraction of Matlock Bath renowned for its popularity with hundreds of motor cyclists, and on to the little town of Cromford, passing on their left the imposing limestone cliffs rising from the river valley to the heights above. At Cromford, the Police outriders guided them to the right, and started to ascend a very steep hill crammed in between row upon row of terraced, quarry-workers cottages, and up to the beauty spot of Black Rocks at the top.

From here the road dropped sharply down into the market town of Wirksworth, a gloomy place of grey and grimy buildings. The Royal party passed swiftly through the town, and out into glorious open countryside, until they turned right and climbed up into the village of Idridgehay, and on to Turnditch and Windley.

They were beginning the approach to Kedleston and the motor cycle escort and the Range Rover imperceptibly closed up on the Bentley, as they entered the small village of Western Underwood. They passed through the village, and after negotiating three miles through a winding and undulating landscape with the Kedleston estate bordering the road on the right, they reached the north gatehouse and entrance into Kedleston Hall parkland. They meandered down the narrow road between ancient trees, crossed over the bridge designed by Robert Adam in the eighteenth century, and ascended the narrow single track road up to the Hall, through the majestic wrought iron gates, and parked outside the private quarters of the Curzon's, an old Norman family, for lunch at precisely 1.00pm.

The 'Queen's' party was ushered into the east wing of the Hall and taken to join the other VIP's and their hosts. Richard Curzon almost dropped the champagne flute he was holding when introduced to the 'Queen'. Dame Helen soon put him at his ease and accepted the role that Bladon had asked her to do, and using her natural authority explained the situation to all of his guests.

"Please, may I have your attention? I'm sorry for those of you who were expecting Her Majesty, and have got me instead, but we have a very serious security problem here today. Before I explain, I'm very sorry but I must insist that you give all of your mobile phones to the gentleman at the door. I will hand you over to him in a moment, but for our own safety, we must obey him without question, as otherwise lives will be at risk."

Dame Helen waited until all of the mobiles had been collected by the SAS major at the door, and then spoke again.

"I understand we have a major security alert, and I am told that a very dangerous and ruthless organisation have targeted not only Kedleston Hall, but also the Queen and the Curzon family, and all of you as well. I will hand you over to

Major Thomas, who is a high-ranking officer in the SAS, to explain the situation.

The major shut the door and spoke to the assembled gathering.

"Dame Helen, Lord Curzon, ladies and gentlemen, thank you for your attention. My name is Major Thomas, but please just call me Jerry. We believe that you are in very great danger from an immanent terrorist attack.

It is vital that the terrorists do not know that you have vacated this building. As far as they are concerned the Curzon family are hosting a special lunch for the Queen and special guests in their private quarters, and it is absolutely vital that they are not disabused of that fact.

Now, this is what I want you to do. Please follow the instructions of my soldiers to the letter. They are very heavily armed, but please do not be concerned, as they are only here to ensure your safety. Please walk quickly down the stairs to the rear doors in the east wing. Once outside the property, you'll be escorted by my men along the south of the main building of the Hall, and then along the hedges and trees that form the boundary of the church and churchyard, and you will then reach a series of long, single-story buildings, which we have made as secure as we can. They are not as comfortable as we would wish, but at least you will be safe from any attack that may be unleashed upon the Hall. We have elite forces nearby who are trying to stop the attack, but we are also preparing for the worst. Please do not be alarmed, as my men are very professional and very effective. If necessary we will escort you all to a place of safety in the woods above the southern boundary of the grounds, but I do not think that it will come to that. I have absolute trust in the man leading our forces."

Without further ado, they walked slowly and silently down to the rear exit and made their way to the barn-like buildings that had been prepared for them. The Major had also considerately arranged for the magnificent banquet to be brought down from the Hall, and even added a crate of champagne to keep their spirits up, quite literally! Major Jerry phoned Bladon and confirmed that all of the occupants of the private quarters had been transferred to the safe haven.

The Thirteen were all assembled and ready for action behind their prepared positions, and all knew their roles in the upcoming battle. Bladon, Wilf and Lexi, would be in overall tactical command, whilst John, Stefan, and Jeremy, had been issued with the L115A3 sniper rifle with which Jeremy had been so effective at Walton Priory. It was such an impressive weapon and had proved itself in combat in Helmand Province. The rifles were made by a small company based on the outskirts of Portsmouth, which had started out in a garage. A sniper in Afghanistan using the weapon, had killed six Taliban with a single shot by hitting the trigger of a suicide bomb quite recently. The near 1000 yard shot was at a Taliban machine gun position that was attacking an Afghan army patrol, and it took the sniper's bullet nearly 3 seconds to hit its target—a shot that he then repeated twice more. It was a phenomenal weapon in the right hands.

Giancarlo, now fully recovered after the attack on the Priory, was acting as liaison between the 'Thirteen' and Major Jerry, who was protecting the VIPs. Willie, Terry, and Will, were in control of the Rocket Propelled Grenade's, and Peter was in charge of communications with the Apache helicopter pilots. Phillip and Steve stood ready with their two attack drones.

Sandy, Wilf and Bladon, met one last time before going to action stations before the coming attack. Some SAS watchers were hidden near the western and northern entrances, to warn of Dreadnought's arrival, but there was still no word of any hostile movements.

"We've made all the preparations that we can possibly make," said Sandy. "But the elephant in the room is still Dreadnought's super-gun. I heard just this morning, that since we captured that gun up in the Peak District our boffins have spent hour after hour examining it, testing it, and firing it; and they have come to the conclusion that without the blueprints they can't find any way of stopping it. They have no answer to it.

They tell me what we already knew, that in a straight fight it can wipe out all our men, weapons, planes and missiles, and destroy Kedleston Hall in short order. What we do know about it, now that we've had a chance to examine it, is what we suspected, that its firing mechanism is initiated electronically. It has almost no recoil and no moving parts. Bullets or grenades can be fired at a rate of half a million per minute, a phenomenal rate, either from a single weapon or multiple barrels grouped together in pods. We are sure that Dreadnought will have made some multi-barrelled guns and they can direct withering fire at any enemy infantry, or tank advance, or even enable a warship to fend off a missile attack; they are that formidable. He can put an awful lot of lead into the air very quickly with these guns, and he can have lots of pods attached, and could then send out a cloud of gunfire in one or two seconds obliterating anything in the vicinity. They could certainly make a mess of our forces. The only reason we have had any success against them is by targeting the operators by stealth, or by close quarter fighting. Here in Kedleston we have the former, but not the latter, and I'm not sure whether it's going to be enough. I hope so.

Fifty Three

At 1.30 pm, the SAS watchers reported that two National Trust Land Rovers had entered the grounds through the northern gatehouse entrance, and were making for the bridge over the lake. As far as they could see through the dirty front windows, a man drove the first one with a woman passenger, all in the National Trust Ranger uniforms of dark green. The following vehicle also held two men, in the same uniforms, which seemed rather strange to Bladon. Why four Rangers in the same place at the same time, when they should have been taking a day off? What were they doing there? Bladon focused on the two vehicles with his high-powered glasses as they came up to the bridge, crossed over and carried on towards the Hall. They turned off the road almost immediately, onto the rolling grassland between the lake and the road and slowed to a halt. They positioned themselves just off the road, in front of the lake, with a clear view of the Hall, and stopped there. The first Land Rover was nearest to the lake and the other one pulled up adjacent to it, next to the road.

"That's odd," Bladon whispered to Lexi. "Those two Land Rovers should have been stood down by the Trust, and in any case what are they doing together next to the lake like that. What could possibly be interesting them there?"

As Bladon watched, he saw the man and woman from the first Land Rover erect a strange looking pulley device, and then manoeuvre a very large and strange looking weapon from the vehicle, and start to set it up on the grass facing the Hall. They then offloaded another large weapon that seemed to have some sort of attachment for fixing to a vehicle, or even a helicopter.

"Lexi, Wilf, Sandy," cried Bladon, "this looks like the start of Dreadnought's attack. Keep down everyone, as we don't want to be seen. It looks very much as if Dreadnought has just arrived and is unloading his weapons. I think we may have you at last Dreadnought! This is the perfect opportunity for our snipers, but they will only get the one chance."

Down by the lake, Dreadnought checked the weapons in the back of the Land Rover and shut the rear door. He and Clara concentrated on setting up the large, artillery type weapon, which they were confident would cause tremendous damage to the Hall. Cameron's Land Rover was there for backup and protection for Dreadnought, but they also had a substantial stock of weapons. Cameron and Aaron took a super-gun each, and jumping out, trained their formidable weapons on the Hall itself, thinking that any counter attack would come from that direction.

John, Stefan and Jeremy with their specialist sniper rifles, lay on the grass of the reverse slope, and relaxed their bodies and let the tension drain away. They all had their little idiosyncrasies before firing, and Stefan in particular had a set routine. He first adjusted his cheek piece, which allowed him to align his eye comfortably with the day scope; he carefully fine-tuned his adjustable Bi-Pod, which allowed him to support the rifle in just the right position. Next he adjusted his S & B 5-25x56 Day scope which magnified the subject up to 25 times allowing him to identify targets more easily. Then he carefully checked his suppressor was properly fixed, as this reduced the flash and noise signature, which in turn reduced the chance of detection, and thus increased his chances of survival. Finally he checked his magazine, which allowed him to fire 5 rapid rounds without affecting the alignment of the gun. They were all in order and he was ready for action.

"Both targets are green," Bladon whispered over the three headsets.

Stefan was the first to react and taking Cameron as his

Fifty Three

target brought him down with two shots. Jeremy targeted Aaron but although he hit him in the leg with his first shot, he reacted very quickly and ran for cover under the Land Rover, but John reacted quicker and killed him with his second shot.

"So far, so good," said Bladon to Wilf. "Two down and two to go."

But his elation was premature. Dreadnought had seen their firing positions, and ordered Clara to take out the hill. Clara, using one of the more powerful weapons, and using all her field craft, shimmied under Cameron's Land Rover, pointed her gun at the wooded hill, and completely destroyed it including all of the wooden defences and most of the trees. She was too late to stop Terry who came round from the side of the devastation, fired his RPG-26 Russian made anti-tank rocket launcher. The jack-knife fins on the rocket unfolded and flew straight towards the Land Rover smashing through it and continuing on into the lake, missing Dreadnought's vehicle by less than a metre. Cameron's Land Rover burst into flames milliseconds after Clara just managed to scramble away to the comparative safety of Dreadnought's Land Rover.

The small wooded hill that had been their refuge was now a scene of utter devastation. Of the snipers, only Stefan had survived unscathed due to his prompt action; but John was injured and Jeremy had been hit several times. The cover from the partially finished wooden fence had been blown away like matchsticks, and most of the trees were now no more than blackened stumps, smoking in the gentle breeze. Phillip and Steve were not in such forward positions as the snipers so they were unaffected by the attack, and were still ready to use the drones again, but many of The Thirteen were now shocked, bleeding, and temporarily out of action. Bladon, Wilf and Lexi, Phillip, Steve, and Stefan were now the only effective combatants.

Bladon risked a look through his glasses, and through the rising wisps of smoke from their wrecked place of safety, he saw that Dreadnought had still not assembled his big multi-barrelled gun, and therefore could still not unleash his attack against the Hall. As a final throw of the dice, Bladon ordered the two drones into action. This time however, Clara was alert, and as soon as the first one, piloted by Phillip, appeared over the remains of their hill position, she blew it out of the sky, before it could fire its missiles. Steve, seeing the demise of Phillip's drone, recalled his own to prevent that being shot down as well. Better to husband the scarce resources they had than risk a suicidal mission. Bladon agreed and ordered his forces not to risk another attack on Dreadnought and Clara, but just to watch and wait.

He suddenly turned and spoke to Lexi. "In the excitement of the firefight I had completely forgotten about the medallion the Professor gave us. But will it work?"

His thoughts were interrupted however as he saw that Clara had now rejoined Dreadnought and he had finally got the super-gun ready for firing and was aiming at the Hall. He waited for a moment to pick out his target correctly. He was not targeting the main part of the Hall, but the family quarters of the Curzon family to the east. He expected to find there various important personages, including the Queen, wining and dining, oblivious of any danger.

He had to demonstrate to the Chinese the gun's capabilities before they completed the deal, so he aimed the gun, fully expecting to kill and maim many people including the reigning monarch, and cause such shock in the country that it would precipitate the fall of the government, leaving him to usurp their power. He activated the fearsome weapon, and with a huge roar, it fired its bullets into the West Wing, which almost completely disintegrated, leaving smoking ruins.

"That's brilliant," shouted Dreadnought excitedly over the sounds of the dying building, "and I've also killed the Queen. Nothing can survive the power of our weapon Clara, we have won."

With that, he made a quick call from his mobile, and within two minutes a Chinese, Sikorsky S-76 chartered helicopter, appeared out of the northern sky, flew low over

Fifty Three

Kedleston Park Golf Club and landed next to the lake adjacent to Dreadnought.

As Clara kept watch for any movement from Bladon's forces, super-gun at the ready, the Chinese contingent of five men and a woman walked over to Dreadnought and congratulated him.

"OK, I guess that proves the gun works," said the leader of the delegation in a poor attempt at humour, as he looked approvingly towards the smoking ruins of the East Wing of the Hall. The Chinese, using the pulley, hauled the large gun into the their helicopter. They transferred the other guns from the Land Rover, and Dreadnought gave them the blueprints, whilst two Chinese technicians fixed the specially adapted gun to the helicopter. After checking that ammunition had been loaded for the helicopter-mounted gun, the leader of the Chinese wired the two billion pounds to Dreadnought's Bank from his laptop, in strict accordance with Dreadnought's precise instructions. A call to Dreadnought thirty seconds later from his Bank, confirmed that the monies had reached his account safely.

Meanwhile Bladon looked on impotently. He couldn't make any hostile move with Clara so vigilant and alert.

Dreadnought and Clara made their escape in the Land Rover, with Clara riding shotgun with one of the super-guns in case of one final desperate attempt from Bladon to stop them. They crossed over the bridge, powered up the tree lined road, by the northern gate house, and on to the road back to the Kedleston Hotel, still with a few of the weapons on the back seats, which they had kept back.

As they drove into the garage of the Hotel, and shut the door behind them, a huge explosion rippled through the air, and assailed their eardrums from the direction of Kedleston Hall.

Dreadnought turned to Clara.

"Don't worry Clara, that will be the Chinese finishing off the Hall. It's over now. We have finally prevailed, and also we are now extremely wealthy, and have comprehensively beaten Bladon. We are now ready to take over control of the country, and as part of our deal, the Chinese are going to destroy not only the rest of the Hall, but Bladon's house as well. Those dark days of defeat and failure are over and nobody can stop us."

The Chinese helicopter with the terrible gun attached, took off and flew away to the south of the Kedleston estate. Bladon realised that he had failed utterly, and that they were getting away with the weapons and the blueprints, to cause untold suffering in the future, but he could do nothing about it.

Sandy broke into his black thoughts. "What about the Apache helicopters, Bladon?"

"Yes of course." Bladon sprang back to life, and shouted to Peter to summon the two Apaches. They were soon airborne and immediately dispatched their Hellfire missiles to clinically remove the Chinese helicopter from the sky. However, to Bladon's horror, before either of the missiles could reach the Chinese helicopter, their newly attached super-gun blasted both missiles out of the sky.

Fifty Four

A distraught Bladon turned to Lexi, Wilf and Sandy.

"We can't stop them can we? It's over. It looks certain now that both the Chinese and Dreadnought will get clean away."

But as he looked up to the southern skies, he realised that it wasn't over. The helicopter had turned back towards them and the Hall, and he could see by the way they were positioning their craft, that they were preparing to destroy the rest of the Hall.

Bladon turned to Lexi and cradled her in his arms.

"I'm afraid there is nothing we can do. We have failed. Well, more specifically, I have failed, and failed big time. I think I'm so tough and always in control, but this is the biggest test I've ever had, and I've flunked it. I'm pathetic."

"Don't you ever say that darling," said Lexi. "You are the bravest, most resourceful, and most wonderful man I know. You don't have to defeat all of the world's evils on your own you know. We're in this together. Do you remember that dog attack in Cornwall? It was both of us pulling together that got us through that. And in our last terrible conflict with Dreadnought in the Peak District, he thought he'd won and killed us both, but we beat him together. We always act together."

Bladon was so proud of her.

He lifted his head and put aside his negative, defeated attitude.

"OK then. Let's concentrate. We only have a few seconds

before we are all blown away along with the rest of the House. Is there anything we can do?"

As he spoke it was almost as if a light came on in Lexi's eyes. She took the medallion out of her pocket and placed it in Bladon's hands. Inside was a small transmitter.

"We'd all forgotten about the transmitter that the Prof gave us in Italy." Lexi spoke excitedly. "Do you remember he developed it himself, without Dreadnought's knowledge? It may yet save the day if it works. It may not, but it's the only chance we've got. I seem to remember he said that the range was up to a thousand metres. That should put the helicopter within range. Shall we try?"

"Lexi. You're a genius. You may have saved the day again. Why don't you try it."

With that she took the transmitter and looked up. The Chinese were about to fire. They were just negotiating the gusty wind over the southern boundary of the Kedleston estate, and the gun was slowly, but inexorably, coming round to the optimum firing position. They had to allow for the wind, and any kick back from the massive force of bullets they were about to deploy. But they were nearly there.

Lexi activated the transmitter.

Nothing.

Ten seconds.

Still nothing.

And then just as the helicopter was about to open fire, and Sandy and Wilf had put their hands over their ears anticipating the impact on the building, there was an incandescent explosion of orange and red flames, and all the guns and ammunition inside the helicopter, and then the fuel tank burst into flame, and the stricken helicopter fell to the ground, killing all of the occupants, and destroying the weapons and the blueprints as well.

"What was that," said Sandy.

"Well, the Prof designed a fault into all of the guns during the manufacturing process. It's triggered by a tiny transmitter, which causes the weapons to combust on activation as long as it is within a 1000 metre range of the weapons. He told me that it was the only thing he could think of to stop Dreadnought, and even then it might not work. I didn't really think that it would work, if I'm honest."

"Well thank you Prof," Steve said. "He was a fine man, full of integrity and he didn't die in vain."

Relief flooded through what was left of the doughty Thirteen. But then reality.

"In our exultation, we're forgetting something", said Bladon.

"What's that", said Sandy, as uncertainty replaced relief on his face.

"It's not over. Dreadnought is still on the loose with some weapons, and presumably, lots of money in his bank account."

Sandy pulled out his phone and called his SAS watchers near the northern entrance to the Park and then reported back to Bladon.

"Dreadnought and a tough looking woman, exited the Hall grounds, turned right and headed back towards Derby. My lads discretely followed them and they are holed up in that derelict hotel just past the Golf Club. My men have sealed off the place; they are well concealed, and they've heard a helicopter engine warming up in a field next to the house. We must act before they get away with the remainder of the guns. They must be stopped, permanently if they won't surrender. We now have the upper hand with your little transmitter, but we must get to them before they leave and hope against hope that it works again.

Bladon, Lexi, Wilf, Sandy, Willie, Terry, Will, and Steve carrying the remaining drone, in two cars, turned right and drove slowly by the Golf Club. Just before they reached the derelict hotel on their left, they were directed right by two of their men down a farm track, for about a hundred metres until they reached the entrance to a small cottage which was set well back from the road in a large garden, screened from the road by tall conifers and hawthorn hedges. Inside the house, which had been commandeered by four SAS troopers, Bladon, Lexi and Sandy ran to the front bedroom, which had an unobstructed view over to the hotel and its large outbuildings and car park area.

To the left they saw a large field separated from a small paddock by a long and sprawling barn. On a large concrete hard standing stood a small helicopter, a Hughes MD 500, with a powerful engine. Its pilot had finished testing the engine, and it now stood in silence as a man and a woman scurried back and forth between the helicopter and the hotel building, carrying crates and loading them into the helicopter. Bladon peered through his glasses, and then called Steve to join them in the bedroom.

"Your men were right Sandy. That's Dreadnought and his number two, a very tough looking woman that we've seen before. They seem to be loading crates of what look like weapons, ready for a quick take off. We must be careful though, because they had obviously left the pilot behind during their attack on Kedleston Hall, and he is now pacing the perimeter of the hotel with one of those lethal weapons ready to use it at the first sign of an attack. I suggest Steve puts in the drone right now."

"Steve, if you can take out the pilot, they have nowhere to go, and you may get a chance to destroy the helicopter as well."

Steve opened the window carefully and launched his killer drone northwards, over the road and into the field to the west of the farmhouse. Carefully he manoeuvred the drone round the large hedge surrounding the hotel. Bladon spoke to him softly.

"Steve, be very careful that pilot doesn't spot you, because if he turns his weapon on this house, you could be in real trouble."

"OK Bladon, I understand. But you must get out of here to somewhere safer, because if he scores a direct hit on this bedroom, then we're all toast, including you and the transmitter. If I can take him and the helicopter out, then we're home and dry."

Bladon agreed, and he and Lexi left the cottage, and made their way to an old barn near the perimeter of the gardens, with views of the road and the roof of the hotel, but still well within 1000 metres range.

Dreadnought and Clara hurried back to the hotel kitchens, which were in a terribly derelict state, but were more than adequate for storing the weapons. Clara questioned the need for the pilot to guard the perimeter of the hotel.

"Why do we need Vasily to waste his time patrolling the grounds of the hotel boss? We could do with a hand loading up, and we'd be away from this place much quicker than with him just walking about outside looking macho. Your tame Superintendent sent all the police back to Derby, so it's going to take them a long time before they can react and get anyone up here, and when they do get here they won't be looking for us. They'll be more concerned searching the wreckage for the Queen and any survivors. Why don't we redeploy him to help us do the heavy lifting?"

"It's very tempting Clara. We've destroyed the Hall and killed the Queen and all her guests; also we've severely mauled Bladon and his friends, so yes I agree that there is probably no one pursuing us. In any case they don't know where we are. However, as you know, I am a very cautious man and I am not going to let my guard down until we're out of here and safely on the way to London. We must really..."

"Wait," said Clara interrupting him, "did you hear that."

"Hear what Clara?"

"It sounded like one of those drones that Bladon used. Listen carefully."

"Yes, you're right. Bring your gun quickly."

They ran to the western boundary of the hotel and saw Vasily the pilot taking a crafty drink from his hip flask, his attention elsewhere. They looked to where the noise was coming from, and saw overhead another mini-drone circling above Vasily and about to fire its missiles at him.

"Down Vasily now. Get down. Look to your right," shouted Dreadnought.

Whilst Dreadnought shouted his warning Clara had already brought up her super-gun, and blasted the drone out of the sky before it could deliver its lethal missile.

Clara took control.

"Boss, it's imperative you get out of here and back to London. They may have other drones or worse, so let me provide a diversion for you and take the van into Derby and try and draw them away from you."

"Thanks Clara. I agree, but do take care. I can't lose you now. Leave the rest of the weapons Vasily; we've got plenty on board already. Let's get out of here."

As they jumped aboard the helicopter he looked back just in time to see Clara's van roar out of the hotel, and speed towards Derby. Simultaneously Dreadnought's helicopter rose above the roof of the hotel, and circled the surrounding area.

Sandy reported to Bladon that an SAS unit near the gates had noticed Clara trying to escape in a van towards the City. One of the SAS troopers lifted an RPG to his shoulder, pulled the trigger, and the Ocado van exploded in orange flames, and slowed to a halt at the side of the road.

Looking up, Bladon realised that he and Lexi were in trouble. Dreadnought was not fleeing the scene in the helicopter as expected, but was searching with his binoculars for him and Lexi.

Bladon reached for the transmitter.

Their lives were in the hands of the Professor.

Dreadnought spotted them both cowering behind the barn.

He threw down the glasses, and reached for his assault gun.

Fifty Four

He swivelled it until his enemies were in his sights, and with such hatred closed his finger on the trigger.

At the same time Bladon clicked the transmitter switch for the second time that day, but this time it worked instantly and the helicopter exploded and dropped out of the sky.

"That's the second time that Dreadnought's been blown up in a helicopter, darling", said Lexi as he put his arm around her in utter relief and exhaustion.

"Yes, Lexi that's true. But this time he really has gone. He couldn't possibly survive that fireball. We are free of him. Free at last."

Epilogue

The Thirteen met two weeks later at Bladon and Lexi's house for a celebration dinner. They were all there, although some were bruised and battered and combat weary. There was John, Stefan, Jeremy, Giancarlo, Wilf, Andy, Patrick, Phillip, Steve, Willie, Terry, Faisal and Adam. Sandy had also personally collected the widows of Martyn and Greg.

In the lounge, overlooking the grounds of Kedleston Park, a gentle breeze wafted through the open windows and Bladon's mind drifted back to all that had happened just a short while ago, and where for a time they had stared utter failure in the face.

Sandy stood, and rather formally, reported that the Prime Minister and the Queen had expressed their tremendous gratitude for preventing what could have been a dreadful catastrophe. He explained that the renegade Inspector Fordingley had been formally arrested, taken to Paddington Green Police Station, and forcefully interrogated, with the threat, real or imagined, of a trip to Guantanamo Bay. He had cracked very quickly and given up all his police contacts in Derbyshire, and the Met. Hussein and Vladimir, who had caused such devastation in Derby City Centre, had also been captured and charged with murder.

The only disappointment was that Clara seemed to have disappeared. No body had been found in the burned out remains of the van near Kedleston Hotel; there was blood nearby, but no trace of a body. Video surveillance at Heathrow showed a rather blurred image of someone who looked like her boarding a plane to Paris, but whether it was her, and where her ultimate destination was, no one knew.

However they had at least verified the death of Dreadnought; no coming back from the dead this time! DNA and dental records taken from the remains of a body removed from the helicopter, confirmed that Dreadnought was now officially dead. As they relaxed in the lounge savouring the exhilaration of a job well done, and awaiting the call to dine, the atmosphere changed to one of menace, as to everyone's shock and horror, a drone whirred into the room. Willie jumped up and drew his pistol, but then through the speaker system in the lounge came a disembodied voice.

"I am pleased to announce that dinner is ready. Please follow your friendly drone to the dining room."

Sixteen very relieved friends joined a guilty looking Bladon and Lexi to behold a veritable feast set out on the long table in the large formal dining room. As soon as they were seated, the waiters, in black tie and tails, danced attention on the heroes now assembled. The maitre d' commenced carving from a large turkey and goose, and the glasses sparkled and tinkled in the light of the crystal chandeliers.

Finally, over coffee and liqueurs, the evening began to wind down to a happy and contented conclusion. There was however, still one more surprise ahead for the assembled company.

Sandy stood to his feet, called for order, and thanked Bladon and Lexi for such a delightful evening.

"I have a small surprise for you all. I hope you will forgive me. I have two very special guests who want to thank you for all you've done. May I firstly introduce the Queen," and without further introduction Dame Helen Mirren walked into the room in a regal white dress to gasps, and then tumultuous applause. When the excited chatter abated, Dame Helen read out a letter from Her Majesty thanking them for their valour and courage and for preventing a determined attempt to kill

Epilogue

her from succeeding. That wasn't all.

"May I introduce Prince Harry," she said, to further gasps from around the table, "who will show you his grandmother's gratitude in a more tangible form."

Without further ado, the very popular young royal entered the room, and explained his visit.

"Her majesty wishes to bestow on each of you, in recognition of your brave exploits on behalf of the defence of the realm, some tangible thanks for all your heroic acts. These awards are given in this way, not because you are valued less than other more conventional recipients; far from it, but because of the top-secret nature of your struggles against Dreadnought. I am afraid this recognition cannot be made public."

Without further ado, Prince Harry, in full dress military uniform, presented Bladon and Lexi with the George Cross, and the rest of The Thirteen with the George Medal, including posthumous awards to Martyn and Greg, proudly collected by their widows, Heather and Amy.

Later, when the celebrities and their friends had left, Bladon and Lexi relaxed on the patio, as the lights in the house cast a mellow tone into the darkness, until eventually Lexi broke their companionable silence.

"Is it really all over now, darling? What about Clara?"

"Don't worry about that. I don't think she'll trouble us ever again. It's over".

"I do hope so. Free at last."

Printed in Great Britain
by Amazon.co.uk, Ltd.,
Marston Gate.